The giant continued to pick at the bodies strewn about his feet, not yet seeing Rylee and Alex as they sprinted closer. Another volley of arrows came their way, and Alex let out another yelp, this one legitimate. A red-fletched arrow protruded from his shoulder, blood dripping from the feathers. Without breaking stride, Rylee reached down and yanked it out. Alex yipped and Liam growled at him. Right now they had to get past the damn giant; once they did that, Alex could whine all he wanted.

Pamela threw another couple of fireballs, which did two things. One, it took out another huge grouping of the creatures that by now were clearly visible—yet still unrecognizable—on the castle ramparts.

Two, her fireballs had drawn the attention of the giant.

Towering over them, he turned and gave out a gleeful cheer, clapping his hands together and stamping his feet as he saw them.

A garble of words poured from his mouth, along with stream of saliva as he bent at the waist and scooped Rylee and Alex up in one big, dirty hand.

Liam skidded to a stop, his heart pounding out of control. This was not happening, he couldn't lose her now.

"RYLEE!"

# PRAISE FOR SHANNON MAYER AND THE RYLEE ADAMSON SERIES

"If you love the early Anita Blake novels by Laurel K. Hamilton, you will fall head over heels for The Rylee Adamson Series. Rylee is a complex character with a tough, kick-ass exterior, a sassy temperament, and morals which she never deviates from. She's the ultimate heroine. Mayer's books rank right up there with Kim Harrison's, Patricia Brigg's, and Ilona Andrew's. Get ready for a whole new take on Urban Fantasy and Paranormal Romance and be ready to be glued to the pages!"

—*Just My Opinion Book Blog*

"Rylee is the perfect combination of loyal, intelligent, compassionate, and kick-ass. Many times, the heroines in urban fantasy novels tend to be so tough or snarky that they come off as unlikable. Rylee is a smart-ass for sure, but she isn't insulting. Well, I guess the she gets a little sassy with the bad guys, but then it's just hilarious."

—*Diary of a Bibliophile*

"I could not put it down. Not only that, but I immediately started the next book in the series, *Immune*."

—*Just Talking Books*

"*Priceless* was one of those reads that just starts off running and doesn't give too much time to breathe. . . . I'll just go ahead and add the rest of the books to my TBR list now."

—*Vampire Book Club*

"This book is so great and it blindsided me. I'm always looking for something to tide me over until the next Ilona Andrews or Patricia Briggs book comes out, but no matter how many recommendations I get nothing ever measures up. This was as close as I've gotten and I'm so freakin happy!"

—*Dynamite Review*

# BLIND
# SALVAGE

# Books by Shannon Mayer

**The Rylee Adamson Series**
*Priceless*
*Immune*
*Raising Innocence*
*Shadowed Threads*
*Blind Salvage*
*Tracker*
*Veiled Threat*
*Wounded*
*Rising Darkness*
*Blood of the Lost*

**Rylee Adamson Novellas**
*Elementally Priceless*
*Tracking Magic*
*Alex*
*Guardian*
*Stitched*

**The Venom Series**
*Venom and Vanilla*
*Fangs and Fennel*
*Hisses and Honey*

**The Elemental Series**
*Recurve*
*Breakwater*
*Firestorm*
*Windburn*
*Rootbound*

**Contemporary Romance**
*High Risk Love*
*Ninety-Eight*

**Paranormal Romantic Suspense**
*The Nevermore Trilogy:*
*Sundered*
*Bound*
*Dauntless*

**Urban Fantasy**
*A Celtic Legacy Trilogy:*
*Dark Waters*
*Dark Isle*
*Dark Fae*

# BLIND SALVAGE

### A RYLEE ADAMSON NOVEL
### BOOK 5

# SHANNON MAYER

TALOS

New York

Copyright © Shannon Mayer 2014

First Talos Press edition published 2017

Talos Press books may be purchased in bulk at special discounts
for sales promotion, corporate gifts, fund-raising, or educational purposes.
Special editions can also be created to specifications. For details, contact the
Special Sales Department, Talos Press, 307 West 36th Street, 11th Floor, New
York, NY 10018 or info@skyhorsepublishing.com.

Talos Press® is a registered trademark of Skyhorse Publishing, Inc.®,
a Delaware corporation.

Visit our website at www.talospress.com.

10 9 8 7 6 5 4 3 2 1

Library of Congress Cataloging-in-Publication Data

Names: Mayer, Shannon, 1979- author.
Title: Blind salvage / Shannon Mayer.
Description: First Talos Press edition. | New York : Talos Press, 2017. |
  Series: A Rylee Adamson novel ; book 5
Identifiers: LCCN 2016038949 | ISBN 9781940456997 (softcover : acid-free
  paper)
Subjects: LCSH: Missing children--Investigation--Fiction. | Paranormal
  romance stories. | BISAC: FICTION / Fantasy / Urban Life. | FICTION /
  Fantasy / Paranormal. | GSAFD: Fantasy fiction.
Classification: LCC PR9199.4.M3773 B58 2016 | DDC 813/.6--dc23 LC
record available at https://lccn.loc.gov/2016038949

Original illustrations by Damon Za www.damonza.com

Print ISBN: 978-1-940456-99-7

Printed in Canada

# ACKNOWLEDGEMENTS

Another book done, and again, so many people to thank. My writers group (Writing In Progress) has been a huge support during these last few months. They have helped buoy my spirits and have kept me going even on those days I was frustrated with how things were going. Thank you for helping me through those days.

Melissa Breau and N. L. 'Jinxie' Gervasio, you two ladies have come through as always, helping me fine-tune (and in some cases rip apart and re-write) this manuscript. I couldn't ask for better editors, and better people to work with. Mere thanks will never be enough to express my gratitude to you both.

I'd like to acknowledge all my 'non writing' friends for their willingness to put up with my discourses on marketing, writing, and pretty much anything to do with this business. I know that it is boring to you, and so I appreciate that you let me ramble from time to time.

To my proofreaders, thank you for taking the time to help me make sure the final edits were as clean as possible. You know who you are, and you rock!

Thank you to Lysa for all you do, but above it all for helping me keep perspective on this crazy journey. You are amazing and I am grateful to call you not only a team member, but friend.

This was a harder book for me to write, (I suspect because it was the fourth book in as many months) and I would not have completed it without the love and support from my husband. You truly keep my head above water, keep my floating in the right direction, and help me to see that the world won't come to an end if I don't get 10k words written each day. Thank you for who you are, and all you do for me.

# CAST OF CHARACTERS

**Rylee Adamson:** Tracker and Immune who has dedicated her life to finding lost children. Based near Bismarck, North Dakota.

**Liam O'Shea:** Previously an FBI agent. Now he is a werewolf/Guardian as well as lover to Rylee.

**Giselle:** Mentored Rylee and Milly; Giselle is a Reader but cannot use her abilities on Rylee due to Rylee's Immunity. She died in *Raising Innocence*.

**Millicent:** AKA Milly; witch who was best friend to Rylee. Now is actively working against Rylee for reasons not yet clear.

**India:** A spirit seeker whom Rylee Tracked in *Priceless*.

**Kyle Jacobs:** Rylee's personal teenage hacker—human.

**Doran:** Daywalker and Shaman who helps Rylee from time to time. Located near Roswell, New Mexico.

**Alex:** A werewolf trapped in between human and wolf. He is Rylee's unofficial sidekick and loyal companion. Submissive.

**Berget:** Rylee's little sister who went missing ten years prior to *Priceless*. In *Raising Innocence*, Rylee found out that Berget is still alive. In *Shadowed*

*Threads*, Rylee discovered Berget is the "Child Empress" and a vampire.

**Dox:** Large, pale blue-skinned ogre. Friend of Rylee. Owns "The Landing Pad" near Roswell, New Mexico.

**William Gossard:** AKA Will. Panther shape-shifter and officer with SOCA in London. Friend to Rylee.

**Deanna Gossard:** Druid, sister to William. Friend and help to Rylee.

**Louisa:** Tribal Shaman located near Roswell, New Mexico.

**Eve:** Harpy that is now under Rylee's tutelage, as per the Harpy rule of conduct.

**Faris:** Vampire and general pain in the ass to Rylee. He is in contention for the vampire "throne" against Rylee's little sister, Berget.

**Jack Feen:** Only other Tracker in existence. He lives in London and is dying.

**Agent Valley:** Senior in command in the Arcane Division of the FBI.

**Blaz:** Dragon who bonded (reluctantly) with Rylee in *Shadowed Threads*.

**Pamela:** Young, powerful witch whom Rylee saved in *Raising Innocence*. She is now one of Rylee's wards.

**Charlie:** Brownie who acts as Rylee's go-between when working with parents on all of her salvages. Based in Bismarck, North Dakota.

**Dr. Daniels:** AKA "Daniels". A child services worker and a druid Rylee met up with in *Raising Innocence*. Rylee and Daniels do not like one another.

# 1

I hated saying goodbye almost as much as I hated Monday mornings. And this day had both of those brilliant things mashed together.

"Rylee, you don't have to leave, you know that, right?" Will tried to capture my eyes with his. I avoided his seeking gaze and instead looked out across the pond, reliving recent memories as I stared. I could feel again the fear and adrenaline as the Beast ran me down, the crush of Eve's talons as she snatched me from his grasp in mid-air. The specter of death had hovered close lately. How many times had I dodged his grasping hands since arriving on this side of the ocean? Nothing had gone as planned, so much death and pain . . . so much loss.

I closed my eyes and memories far worse assaulted me, battered at me and forced me to feel them again. Berget's death rocketed through me, tearing what was left of my heart into pieces, and then the shock with her apparent re-birth as a vampire, her eyes pleading with me to side with her. To turn my back on Liam, Pamela, and Alex. To help her become the Empress in truth, so that she would have control of the vampire nation.

She forced me to make a decision between the family I dreamed of and the family who'd stood by me through thick and thin. And I'd chosen to turn my back on her; I'd left her behind.

Will's fingers brushed along the back of my neck snapping me back to the present. I stepped away from him and gave him a glare for good measure. He was lucky we were friends or I would have done a hell of a lot more than glare at him.

"No. I have to go. This isn't my home and I don't belong here." I looked around me. My bag of weapons was at my feet, full of all sorts of goodies. Alex splashed at the edge of the pond, near Deanna and Pamela. We were as ready to go as we ever would be.

Deanna hugged Pamela and whispered something in the young witch's ear. While Deanna had petitioned me to let Pamela stay with her and train to become a druid, Pamela chose to come with me. Unlike her predecessor, Deanna had let it go at that. Good thing, too. I would have hated to kill her when she'd helped me get Liam back. Her predecessor though—I would have gladly removed Daniels's stupid head from the rest of her, but this time around that hadn't been my job. Nor had I been given the chance.

Even before we made it back from Venice, Daniels had gone 'missing', and Deanna was back in charge of the druids. I had to give it to the Beast, he didn't waste any time making good on his word to clean house with Daniels. One less lunatic in the world was a good thing. Particularly when the lunatic had a serious hate on for yours truly.

Will surprised me again, pulling me out of my thoughts, as he tugged me into his arms. Hugging me tight to his chest, his arms clamped around my upper body as if he would hold me there forever, his heart beating hard against mine. He spoke softly into my ear, his breath tickling my skin, warm and gentle.

"You will always have a place here, Rylee. I need you to know that. No matter what came, you would be safe here, with me." He held on too long and I squirmed, more than feeling the overtones of what he wanted, of what I couldn't reciprocate. Maybe, *maybe* if Liam hadn't come back to me this moment would be a different story. But Liam had come back, so there was no guessing about this, about Will, for me. Besides, if he thought he could keep me safe in a world where death and disaster were my constant companions, he didn't know me as well as he thought he did.

A low growl came from the left of us, and Will let me go. Kinda. He still hung onto my forearms as he glared over at Liam, letting out a low rumbling kittycat growl of his own. I jerked my arms out of Will's hands, but it didn't help. The testosterone and tension in the air grew heavy, broken up only by sheer luck. Alex bolted in between us, slammed into me and then Will, like a freaking ping pong game gone awry, and then knocked us both to our knees.

"Home, home, hooooooooooooome!" His howl quivered in the air, dissipating the two alphas' staring match. His timing was perfect, and I let out a quiet sigh of relief. I didn't want to play referee between the two alphas. I had enough on my hands just trying to keep us all alive.

In the two days since Liam had been back, this was the third time the two alpha shifters had started to lock horns. And it was the third time Alex had interrupted them, essentially keeping them from each others' throats. Sensitive as the submissive werewolf was, I wondered if he picked up on the combative vibes, didn't like them, and had realized he had the ability to stop the fights before they even occurred. But was he really that intuitive? As if to confirm my thoughts, he rolled his eyes up to mine as I stood. One long slow wink and he put his index claw to his muzzle.

Smiling, I reached down and scratched him behind his ears. "Alex, you are the best."

His tongue lolled out, flipping spit as he nodded vigorously. "Alex knows that."

With a laugh, I stepped away from Will, putting Liam between us, and headed to the car, acting like nothing had happened. One thing I'd learned with supernaturals, you just moved on. No need to point out what could have been, unless you were spoiling for a fight. Particularly with alphas.

A part of me wished Eve was still here, that I could hop on her back and fly the hell away from all of this. But Eve had already left, choosing to hopscotch across Iceland and down the east coast of Canada before banking to the west to North Dakota. The trip would take her a few days, maybe a week depending on her wings, and she'd probably get home not long after us. She knew to take it slow, but even with that, I worried. She was young and wanted to prove herself. I knew what that did to people. The need to prove oneself could make you stupid and encourage stupid decisions. I, of all people, should know that better than most.

Will cleared his throat, maybe started to say something, but was cut off.

I turned around in time to see Liam lift his hand, his light golden eyes narrowing. "Enough. She isn't yours and she isn't staying here. Let it go, cat, before this gets ugly."

Wow. I swallowed hard, a part of me bucking under his assertion that I was his, as in belonging to him, as in not my own person. I took a deep breath, opened my mouth, and then shut it with a click. Maybe I'd matured, probably not, but whatever the case, I let that bucking part of me settle down, calmed it with the simple truth: Liam was right, but it went both ways. I was his, and he was mine through and through.

Will needed to understand that. He drew himself up, his brown eyes bleeding to the kitty-cat green that preceded a shift to his panther form, and irises contracting as the feline in him rose up.

"Why don't you let her decide that for herself? Damn wolves, you think you rule the whole bloody world."

Liam tensed, fists clenching. At his feet, Alex let out a whimper. Looked like it was my turn to break things up.

Yippy.

"Seriously?" I put my hands on my hips. "Grow up, Will. Untwist your balls from the knot they're in and chill the hell out."

Pamela joined us, her face clearly showing her confusion, as she glanced from Will to me to Liam. "What's wrong?"

"Nothing. Say goodbye to Will. We're leaving." I pointed at him and she shyly stepped close to him to give him a hug, her face pinking up, lashes lowered over her bright blue eyes.

He spoke to Pamela, but his eyes never left mine, the intensity in them undeniable, even though there was no return of emotion on my part.

"Stay clear of wolves, they will pull you apart."

Damn, he was going to push this with every second we had left here. Liam flexed his muscles and growled under his breath, and I had no doubt we were as close to a fight between the two of them as we'd ever been.

We needed to leave, now, or there was going to be a mangled body that had once belonged to a friend. Someone would get hurt badly, or worse, killed. And I knew it wouldn't be Liam dying, not with the Guardian blood flowing through him. No matter how much Alex might interfere, the two men were going to come to blows very soon. And I really didn't want to stitch either of them up. Will was a friend and an ally, but I would always stand with Liam.

Always.

I flicked a hand beckoning to Alex who scampered to my side. He whispered out the corner of his mouth, "Boss is maddy mad."

"Yeah, but he'll chill out once we get home." Gods, I hoped that would be the case.

A quiver ran along my shoulders, a solid feeling of being watched rolling through me. I turned to see Jack standing in the doorway, watching us leave. He hadn't spoken to me since Liam had shifted back, and Milly had stolen the violet book of prophecies. He didn't come down to see us off, or even wave good-bye. Not that I cared, at least that's what I told myself. The old bastard had lied and manipulated me with the best of them. Not something I tolerated well on my good days. But a part of me felt sorry for him, and I fought the urge to go and tell him he could come with us, that he didn't have to die alone. In that, Jack was right. I had to start putting my foot down. No more charity cases, no more wards to take care of. I had enough trouble keeping those I cared about alive as it was.

The sound of tires on gravel brought my head around. Our ride was already here. Who the hell was it now?

A black, sleek sedan rolled to a stop, blocking off the driveway. Liam's former boss—and my onetime boss—Agent Valley pulled his short stubby body out of the car with some effort.

"Adamson," he said, straightening his suit coat over his portly frame (which didn't really help). "Why is it that I had to learn through the rumor mill that you'd found Agent O'Shea?"

I pursed my lips. "Sorry, my secretary must have lost that memo. Alex, why didn't you tell Agent Valley we'd found Liam?"

Alex did an exaggerated point at himself his lips twisting comically. "Rylee said no tells."

"Right, that's why." I lifted an eyebrow at Agent Valley.

Liam moved up beside me. He had shaved off the beard, but had left his hair long. Black as the night sky, it brushed the top of his shoulders, very definitely not FBI agent styled; there would be no more short cropped brush cut for him. I liked it.

"Agent O'Shea. Good to see you." Agent Valley held out his hand and Liam took it.

"Just Liam now, sir."

Agent Valley blinked several times. "What does 'just Liam now' mean, exactly?"

Liam took a slow breath, but never looked away from his boss. "I'm not coming back to the office. Things have changed."

Frowning, Agent Valley shook his head. "No, I won't accept that. You are one of our best agents, O'Shea. My understanding is you are a . . . werewolf now. Is that correct? We can find ways to work around this disability. I have no doubt of that."

Liam stiffened, his whole body seeming to freeze up.

I stepped in between them, stuck my face in Agent Valley's, about as pissed off as I'd ever been. But I did manage to control myself; damn, I didn't even pull a blade on him. Go me.

"Take your disability and shove it up your ass, Agent Valley. We're leaving."

Alex and Pamela made their way to the cab without being told and slid into the back seat. I scooped up my bag of weapons and followed them. Liam, though, stood there unmoving. Shit, the last thing I needed was for him to be unsure about this. We'd talked about it already, and Liam had agreed that the FBI put too many stipulations on its agents that worked with the supernatural. There was no way either of us could truly work for the FBI and still get the job done.

They just didn't understand what it took to get a job done, and they weren't willing to bend.

Not to mention, Agent Valley had tried to throw me under the bus when I'd worked with him last. Not cool, not cool at all. And it wasn't something I was about to forget.

Liam reached out and shook Agent Valley's hand. "Thank you, sir. But we'll both pass."

Agent Valley, King of Dramatic reveals, waited until Liam was at the cab, his hand on the door.

"Of course, if that's your decision, then I can respect that. But tell me just one thing. What do you know about a demon named Orion?"

# 2

My back stiffened and I clenched my jaw shut to keep from giving anything away. I turned ever so slightly and caught Liam's eyes as they widened a fraction before he, too, caught himself.

"Nothing, sir," Liam said, his voice even and smooth. Perfectly believable, I thought. Yet Agent Valley didn't look convinced. Not a bit. His eyes narrowed and he clasped his hands in front of his belly.

"You're telling me you don't know anything about a demon named Orion? Or some prophecy that goes like this: *the heart of the mountains he will prick, and the land will know Orion's fury for being condemned to the seventh Veil. He shall cleanse the land with fire for his coming.*" Agent Valley's eyebrows shot up over his muddy brown eyes. Liam shook his head and I mimicked him, as did Pamela and Alex. All together now, kiddos, and maybe Agent Valley would believe us. Though how he had this information intrigued me, it wasn't enough to make me ask.

Will and Deanna withdrew. Though they didn't know the particulars, they did know that I'd stuffed the black-skinned demon book into my weapons bag, which happened to speak a great deal about Orion.

Not that Jack knew I'd taken it—no, we'd left a dummy book in its place.

I shrugged, going for casual. "Nope, not a single thing." Nor did I want to know what Agent Valley had going on with his intelligence gathering. Humans were notorious for reading into things that weren't there and missing the things that did exist. Nor did I want to guess at the prophecy he'd quoted to us. I'd been reading the black-skinned demon book of prophecies and there was nothing good in them. Not all of them were about Orion, but a lot of them were, enough to seriously worry me. Mostly, they were about how he would help the demon nation be reborn to the world, how he would kill the 'Tracker', and defile her corpse in a variety of ways.

Yeah, not exactly bedtime reading material.

Giselle had always told me prophecies were not to be ignored. But honestly, they were all so freaking contradictory, particularly when it came to comparing the demon's prophecies to any other supernaturals. Black and white. So how could they both come to pass? That's right, they couldn't. I had to believe that. Giselle's teachings, her words, floated in my head.

*Different branches of possibilities. You know that. Don't delude yourself, either side of a prophecy can come true dependent on people's decisions.*

Yeah, I did know it. I just didn't want to think about any of the demon prophecies as being even remotely possible. Or of people being stupid enough to help the dark branches of prophecy along.

I slid into my seat beside Pamela in the back of the cab and shut the door. Or tried to. Agent Valley stuck his hand out and caught the door before I could shut it completely.

"Adamson, this is serious. The rumors that are flying—they make our little zombie problem from last month look like a picnic on a fine summer's day. We don't even know what the seventh Veil is—worse, we have nothing on this Orion fellow. We need your help."

I shrugged, did my best not to let him see my mind working. "Not my issue. I'm going home. And for the record, I don't know what the seventh Veil is either." And that was the truth; whatever the Veil fully encompassed, I didn't know.

Liam slid into the passenger seat next to the cabbie.

Agent Valley took his hand off the door. "We think someone is trying to bring Orion through, to our side, and with everything I've heard about how very bad this demon is, I would think you wouldn't want that."

How the hell did he know all this? He'd gone from all but begging me to help him and his Arcane Arts division, to now knowing shit about the supernatural that we didn't? The only answer was that he'd found someone to help him, someone who knew the supernatural. Maybe a Reader like Giselle; that was my guess. Not that it mattered. If he got the information he wanted and didn't need us, all the better.

I glared at him. "Guilt trips aside, who the hell *would* want a demon on our side of the Veil, you moron? Find somebody else to do your dirty work. I find kids; I don't go after demons. I don't have what it takes to be some fucking superwoman."

Liam gave the cabbie a nod and the driver turned over the key.

Nothing, the engine didn't even sputter once. Fuck me sideways, it looked like Monday had struck again. I looked over Pamela's head at Liam. "Too many of us."

He gave a quick nod, and then opened the door. "Alex and I will meet you there."

In other words, he would shift, and the two boys would run all the way to the point out in the bush where the cabbie would drop us off.

Pamela slid closer to me. "Will we have to wait for them?"

I snorted. "Not likely, they'll probably beat us there, going as the crow flies."

Liam and Alex disappeared around the side of the house. Agent Valley followed them, close on their heels. Shit. Liam would have to just deal with his boss without me.

"Ma'am, are you ready to go now?"

"Yes."

I slammed the door shut and leaned back in my seat. The cabbie had no problem with the engine this time, and he maneuvered around Agent Valley's black sedan.

Not a word was said, not one word. But my gut was rolling. Without a doubt, this news about Orion was bad . . . very, very bad. But I was being honest with Agent Valley. Demons were not my forte. Just look at what had happened when I'd tangled with the last one—a minor demon, on the scale of things. I'd almost died, and in the process, had nearly caused an apocalyptic winter. I was nobody's hero.

Liam strode toward the back of the house, Alex tight on his heels.

"Running, Boss?" Alex panted eagerly, his ears flicking up and down several times.

"Yes." Liam didn't want to get in any sort of a discussion with the more submissive werewolf. While Liam liked him well enough, *his* wolf wanted very badly to remind Alex that he was still a submissive. Not that Alex stepped out of line very often, but there were little things.

Like Alex eating before him and Rylee were done. Or knocking into their legs, or pissing on the shrubbery around Jack's mansion as if it was *his* territory. And the wolf in him was already on edge from dealing with Will and his pussycat attitude. Will's desire for Rylee was obvious, both in his actions and his scent, and it sent Liam's wolf into a rage he could barely contain. All of that together set the wolf in him off something fierce and made him want to pin the goofy werewolf to the ground and force him to submit. The logical side of his brain knew that was ridiculous; Alex was zero threat to his leadership or his relationship with Rylee. But the other side . . . .

"Liam. We aren't done yet." Agent Valley called to him, bringing Liam's feet to a standstill. Even with the wolf in him, there were too many years of obeying his superiors to just turn it off completely. Besides, he owed Agent Valley a moment of his time, if nothing else.

Even his wolf understood that.

"Agent Valley, there isn't anything I can do to help change her mind, so don't bother asking." Liam placed his hands on his hips, his back still to his former boss.

Agent Valley caught up to him, out of breath, his face flushed pink even with the cool mist that floated down on them. Liam took a breath in, scenting the air around them. Agent Valley didn't smell like he'd been hanging out with humans. There was something else clinging to him, a faint hint of rot, though . . . .

"O'Shea, I don't think anyone could change her mind once she's set on a course; Adamson is stubborn as a rock. That's what my mother would say." Agent Valley walked along beside him.

"Then what is it you want?"

Alex angled his head so he could stare up at Agent Valley with one big golden eye. "Yeah. What you want with Boss?"

Valley startled, a shiver visibly running through him. "He never ceases to give me the heebie jeebies." Then, seeming to catch what he'd implied, he lifted his hands. "I'm sorry, no offense meant. I'm still getting used to the idea of the supernatural even existing. Never mind going for a walk with one of them."

Liam grunted, but didn't excuse his former boss. He was one of those supernaturals now. And though it felt as natural to him as breathing, and he wondered how he had existed without knowing the supernatural before, he did understand what Valley was saying. It took some getting used to. Hell, he'd been far more freaked out the first time he'd met Alex.

"How are you handling the transition?" Agent Valley tucked his hands into his coat pockets.

Liam would never tell Valley the truth. Since he'd been freed from Milly and then freed from the control of his own wolf, there was a good deal of peace in him. For the first time in his life he knew where each step took him.

Rylee. Always Rylee.

And being a werewolf meant that no matter where she went, or what she was up against, he would be there to protect her.

"The transition has been fine. Easy."

"I thought when you'd run off, back home, that you'd lost it altogether. There are numerous cases where that has happened."

Alex gave a low growl. "Fatty stupid head. Boss is strong."

Agent Valley glared down at Alex, who glared right back up at the agent. Liam had to bite his tongue to keep from smiling. Instead, he cleared his throat.

"Agent Valley, I have to go." He didn't want to say he had to shift forms in order to catch up to Rylee and Pamela. "So if you have something of importance to share with me, I suggest you do it now."

His former boss drew his eyes away from Alex and refocused on Liam.

"If you don't want to work for us directly, that's fine. But as a former FBI agent, I'd ask you to keep us informed of the goings-on that you observe."

Liam's eyebrows shot upward. "Goings-on?" He damn well knew where this was headed and he didn't like it. They were in the backyard now, and Jack watched them from an upper window. He probably thought that they couldn't see him, but the flutter of the curtains as the old Tracker stepped up to the window caught Liam's eye.

Agent Valley flapped his coat with his hands still in his pockets. "We need to be kept up to speed on what is happening in the supernatural world. I have only one other contact, and between you and me, that makes me nervous. I can't be certain the information is correct when it is only from one source. You are our best bet for additional information, as Rylee seems to be at the center of so much; hell, she's nearly always in the thick of things. Will you help us?"

Liam crossed his arms over his chest. Rylee would be beyond livid if she found out he was secretly feeding information to the FBI and Agent Valley. Loyalty, though, was something Liam understood all too well. As loyal as he was to Rylee, he had a loyalty to those he'd once worked for too. And a part of him recognized that Valley was right. The Arcane Arts division of the FBI needed help and information badly.

He took a deep breath, the decisions weighing in his mind. He stuck his hand out, and Agent Valley shook it.

"Good man. I'll expect you will have something for us on a regular basis, say once a week?"

Laughing, Liam shook his head. "You'll get what you get and nothing more. Everything I can send you will be via snail mail. Electronics aren't all that favorable around me anymore."

Agent Valley frowned. "That will take too long; we'll be behind the eight ball right off the start line."

"That's all I can offer." He waited, knowing Valley would take him up on it. Liam also knew that, in a pinch, the AA division could be useful for Rylee; might even have information that she could use in her salvages. That was how he justified it; how he soothed the niggling thoughts that he was making the wrong decision.

"Fine. We'll try it."

Maybe it was some perverse pleasure he took in making his old boss uncomfortable, but he didn't look away from him as he shifted. The wolf in him clamored up, eager to break free of the bonds of the human flesh that held him.

Agent Valley's eyes widened and his face drained of color. "Mother of God have mercy," he whispered as he stumbled backward.

Alex looked from Liam to Agent Valley and snorted. "Pussy."

In the back of the cab, Pamela hummed a song under her breath, her toes tapping the floor. She was obviously restless, and though my body was still, I wasn't much better. I pushed Agent Valley and his request for help with Orion aside in favor of other things. My mind swirled back to my conversation with Doran, just before he left for the states. A conversation I hadn't even shared with Liam.

*"Rylee, I need to speak with you."* Doran put a hand to my elbow, quickly dropping it when I glared at him.

*He wasn't cowed by me, but I'd saved his ass by breaking the bond between him and Berget, and he wasn't likely to forget that. That gained me some leverage that I would use whenever I had to.*

*He owed me, and I would use that to benefit the salvages I would go after. We knew where we stood with each other, which was as it should be.*

*He led the way to the rooftop, the night sky clear of clouds for what had to be the first time since I'd been in London. The bite of the wind reminded me of home, and a longing to be away from this place shot through me. I knew that it had less to do with sleeping in my own bed than it did with all that had happened here. All that I'd had to fight through and the secrets that had been uncovered, even the questions that had yet to be answered.*

*Eve slept deeply off to one side, her head tucked under her wing, feathers ruffling in the breeze. At least if Doran acted up, I had back up. Not that I was worried, not really. More than once Doran had had the chance to kill me, or at least the chances had presented themselves on a number of occasions.*

*I kept my voice low, so as not to disturb the Harpy. She didn't do well being startled awake. "You want to tell me what this is about?"*

*"I think you need to understand what happened with the vampires, how Berget became what she is. I can give you everything I know. Which is a lot in some ways, and not near enough in others." His green eyes were serious, something Doran didn't do often. It made him look more mature, far less the punk rock boy he presented to the world, and more the powerhouse Shaman I knew*

he was. There was no teasing light in him, no double entendre to piss me off. This shift in him was almost as worrisome as his lack of control when he first showed up in London.

I turned my back to him and set my hands on my hips. I wanted to know, I needed to understand. But I had a feeling that knowing wasn't going to make me feel any better about Berget and this current situation. I blew out a sharp breath between my teeth and turned back to Doran. "Tell me."

He dove right in. "You understand that Berget was initially taken because of her blood, that she was one of those our kind can't resist?" He lifted an eyebrow at me.

I nodded. "Louisa told me that, the first time I visited her."

Doran clasped his hands in front of him and pursed his lips. "She was taken to be a gift to the Emperor and the Empress. A blood gift to secure the favor of Faris's old master. That is why he was sent to steal her away."

I grit my teeth. I was angry with Faris, but even angrier with myself that I'd let myself trust him, let myself believe that a vampire could be trusted. He was the start of all my troubles, the one who'd stolen Berget away and had set me on the path I'd walked since then. Regardless of who had ordered it, in my mind this all fell squarely on him.

"Are you telling me it wasn't his fault?" Eyes narrowed, I glared at Doran.

He shrugged, unperturbed. "Most of those that are Fanged do not have the luxury of doing what we want. Depending on who holds the reins of power we can be used as they see fit."

*I could blame Faris for his lies, that was straight forward. But maybe I couldn't blame him for taking Berget. I shook myself and pushed away that thought. No, I'd seen Faris there, seen the light of hunger in his eyes. He'd been hoping for a taste of her too.*

Doran's eyes slid to half-mast as he spoke. "When they got her back to Venice for the Emperor and Empress, it was apparent that the Empress was taken with her youthful beauty and sweet disposition."

Six years old. Berget had been only six when she was taken. My guts rolled with disgust. "What do you mean by 'taken'?"

The Daywalker shook his head. "Not like that." He took a breath and shook his head again before he went on. "Vampires can't procreate; they can't have children unless they steal them. It was immediate, the bond the Empress had with Berget. I knew the Empress; she was my master before Berget. It was more than a bond of mother and child. It was almost like the Empress saw a future for Berget. Which wouldn't surprise me since the Empress was a Reader long before she was a vampire. In the end, she chose to keep and raise Berget rather than . . . ." His eyes opened and he stared into mine, the air between us chilling. "It would have been better if they'd killed her, if there had been nothing more than a meal in your sister's future."

I clenched my fists so hard my nails dug into the palms of my hands, the minor pain welcome and easier to focus on. It didn't matter that I knew Doran was right. I just hated to hear him say it, hated that the truth sucked so badly.

"Keep going."

"They kept her secluded, let her feed off them. That is the start of Becoming."

The first memory Faris had shown me, I'd seen tiny bite marks all over the Empress's body. Now I knew them for what they were. Berget's bite marks. Nausea rolled up, hot and acrid as it coated the back of my tongue. I clamped my mouth shut, clenching my teeth until they ached. Doran waited for me, letting me absorb his words at my own pace.

My heart rate slowed back down and I waved him to go on, afraid that if I opened my mouth, I'd spew chunks all over the roof.

"I cannot tell you the ritual of how a vampire is created, but" —he unclasped his hands to set them on his hips— "you will have to trust me that what I'm telling you is the truth, as far as I am able to share it with you. Becoming a vampire, it takes time. There is no instant creation—a one night blood exchange—as some would have you believe. Berget, the Berget you knew, became buried under the blood she was taking, of what she was becoming. Glimpses of her showed from time to time. A child full of love and compassion. I had hope that things would be better with her as a leader. But then . . . ." He shook his head. "I was there, when Faris killed her parents—"

I snorted and he lifted a hand to stall me.

"They were the only parents she recalled at that point. They'd made sure of it. And she saw Faris and his three brothers take on her parents. His brothers were killed, but he survived, barely, and finished the job, taking the Empress's head and heart. Berget saw it all. She was fourteen at the time."

*I managed to speak around gut churning nausea. "That doesn't explain everything. She knows me still. It's not like her memories are all gone."*

Doran stepped closer to me, almost as if he would give me a hug. I didn't step back, and he didn't encircle me with his arms.

"When the Empress and Emperor died, they spilled their auras to her, giving her their abilities, their powers, the bonds they held over those that called them master, as well as their memories. She did not lose her own memories, but they are faint with the past staining them, and those older memories coating them. She is a child carrying the power of two ancient vampires and all that they know. She does not have the strength of mind to handle this, very few would. She is going mad. Slowly, but very surely."

"And I suppose you want me to do something about it? Kill her and end her reign of madness?" Fuck, everyone thought I could be this supposed demon slayer or whatever the hell the prophecies were spouting. Why not be a slayer of psychotic vampires too? The thing was, a large part of me did want to save her, to bring back the little sister I so wanted to believe was buried inside. What if she could be separated from those memories and all that power? Could she possibly be brought back to some semblance of the Berget who was my sister?

He dipped his head so that we were cheek to cheek. Intimate, yet I wasn't getting that 'take me baby' vibe from him. "No, this is information. Information you need so that if the chance comes, you don't hold back. She is not your sister. What is left of her soul is . . . not gone, but missing. All that is left is what they were. If there is a *way to free her, I do not know it."* His breath was cool against my skin as he breathed each word into me.

*"Tyrants, that's what lives inside her. Mad, power-hungry tyrants who want to rule the world, both the humans and the supernaturals. That cannot happen."*

I closed my eyes, grief spilling up through me. You'd think that after all these years of hurting, of saying goodbye to her over and over in my head, that this moment would be easier. Yet it wasn't. Because for a few brief weeks, I'd thought I'd be able to have my little sister back. That I could heal up some of the gaping wounds in my soul I'd pasted over with brash words and a hard exterior. It just wasn't to be and the wounds haunting me cracked and bled with a pain I didn't know how to stem as Doran's words sunk in. The hope I'd clung to faded to a feeble whisper as it died inside of me.

His hands skimmed up my arms, fingers light against my damp bare skin. *"I'm sorry, Rylee. I truly am."*

I just stood there, eyes closed, waiting for more. His hands slid off my arms as the distant rumble of thunder rolled toward us, bringing another storm.

Even with my eyes closed, I could tell we were getting close to our drop off. The road got rough, bumps and drops jarring me from any semblance of rest. My brain wouldn't let go of what Doran had told me. He hadn't answered all the questions I had, but I wasn't ready to ask them yet either, so that was fine by me. Like what he knew of the Blood that both Berget and Faris wanted me to find for them to secure their leadership.

"Why didn't we just have Will take us? He has a car that would fit us all." Pamela's voice pulled me out of my reverie.

I turned to her, an eyebrow arching up. "Really? You have to ask that?"

She blushed. Yeah, she just wanted one more glimpse of Will. "You don't think they'd really fight, do you?"

The upside was she didn't know *why* Will and Liam didn't like each other. And I certainly wasn't going to tell her that the man she had a crush on had a bit of a thing for me. No, that wouldn't go over well with a teenage witch whose hormones were, on a good day, all over the map. So I fudged it.

"Alphas can rarely be in the same room together. It's just the way they're hardwired. They will end up fighting if they stay in close proximity. Just one more reason for us to go home."

"Will could control himself; it's Liam that can't," she said, her nose turning up with a snobbery that only came to her when she spoke about Will.

I snorted. Nothing Will ever did would be bad in her eyes. Nor would she see that he was pushing hard to get Liam to step away from me. Again, I wasn't going to explain that part to her. "Right, whatever."

The cabbie pulled off to the side of the road, where we'd asked to be dropped. Pretty much in the middle of nowhere. From here, the directions were straight forward. Follow the dirt path to the rundown castle at the end of the road. Easy peasy.

We stepped out of the car, grabbed our bags, and paid our fare. The cabbie turned his car around, and then headed back down the poorly kept road to the main thoroughfare. As the cab disappeared over a hump in the road, a rustle from the bushes turned us both around.

"Tell me you brought clothes." Liam said, standing strategically behind a bush so that he didn't flash Pamela. I reached into my bag and tossed him a shirt and pair of jeans, and the last pair of shoes I had in his size. With all his shifting, we were going through clothes like crazy.

He dressed and stepped out from around the bush, Alex right behind him. Tongue lolling out, he had a big grin on his misshapen face. I had no doubt that the run had been a blast for him.

"Have fun?"

"Yuppy doody. Boss is good boss."

With that, we headed out. Liam led, Alex tucked in behind him, then Pamela, and then me.

The heavy brush on either side of us would make for a perfect ambush, which was not something I was interested in dealing with. Without a break in my stride, I pulled a sword from my back, and adjusted the bag of weapons so I would have an easy swing at anyone, or anything, that might pop out to say 'hello.'

With my luck, the chances were high we'd run into at least one nasty ugly.

Pamela glanced back at me, saw the sword, and lifted her hands to prep a spell. I didn't stop her. The more ready we were, the less likely we were to get our asses tromped by something. No need for the Monday blues to kick us into next week if we could avoid it.

Alex trailed behind Liam like a well-trained dog, never once straying out in front of his alpha. Liam's steps slowed and he turned his head to look into the bushes, as we slid down a small slope into a depression in the ground. Along the edges of the path the trees were bent, large branches snapped like twigs, and sap ran freely from the wounds. Whatever had caused the damage, it had been recent and on the far end of the 'big-ass' scale.

"Something rather large has come this way." Liam reached out and touched his fingers to the jagged edge of a tree, then closed his eyes and drew in a deep breath as he scented the air.

I tightened my grip on my sword and slowly lowered the bag of weapons. "Yeah, I was thinking the same thing. Wait, how the hell can you smell 'large'?"

"I don't know. A lot of whatever came through here. Look around. That's how I can tell."

I pulled my other sword from my back and rolled it in my hand. "Alex, can you smell what it is?"

The werewolf stuck his nose to the ground and moved in an ever-widening circle, finally stopping about ten feet out in front of us, his eyes round with fear, as he whispered. "Big bugger."

Obviously, he'd picked up on the local lingo. "What kind of big bugger?"

He mouthed the word, and I groaned. No. Fucking. Way.

Liam spun slowly. "Did he say what I think he said?"

I nodded. "Yup. He did."

"Yuppy doody," Alex said softly. "There be giants."

Crouching over my bag, I opened it with a yank on the zipper and quickly geared up. Was it fun to run with all my weapons on? No, but running with my weapons on was a hell of a lot easier than running with a bulky bag. I handed out the few weapons I couldn't strap onto my body. A short sword for Pamela, and Liam took the crossbow. Yes, I could have strapped it on, but if I needed speed, it would get in the way and Liam could handle the extra bulk better than I could. Finally, I pulled out the burlap-covered black demon book. Cold seeped through it and into my fingers. Liam took it from me and shoved it under his shirt, tucking it into this belt. "I'll take it."

I gave him a tight smile. The thing gave me the willies, but there was no way we could leave it behind.

Pamela's fingers tightened on the handle of the short sword. "Are we going to have to fight a giant?"

"Hopefully not. They aren't real bright and love to be destructive. They would make Blaz look neat and tidy."

There was a twinge in the back of my head as Blaz, even as far away as he was, perked up as I said his name. I ignored him.

She swallowed hard. Liam shifted his shoulders, glanced at Pam, and then away into the forest. Yeah, he wasn't real comfortable with the young witch yet, but we didn't have time for worrying about who liked who the best at the moment.

Liam stared around us, touching the broken branches closest to him. "Why didn't we feel the giant walking?"

Pamela answered for me. "I read that they move on the other side of the Veil, that only when they move on this side of the Veil can they be felt moving around, and then the humans think it's just thunder." She looked to me for confirmation. I nodded.

"She's right. And they tend to be lazy, sleeping for days, sometimes weeks at a time. But when they wake up . . . ."

I stood and put both swords back into their sheaths. Liam frowned. "What about when they wake up?"

I gave him a tight smile. "Hungry. Like sharks on the prowl, they'll eat anything, friend or foe, alive, dead, rotting. Whatever. If it's even remotely edible, they'll scoop it up and eat it. Then they crash again."

"Well, that's just fantastic," he grumbled. "Should we be expecting more than one?"

Pamela shook her head. "There are less than six giants left in the world. Only one resides here in Great Britain, and from what I read, he spends most of his times in the wilds. It would be quite unusual for him to come this far south, actually."

"How do you know all this?" Liam glanced down at the young witch, making eye contact with her for a split second. That was an improvement for him.

She gave him a tentative smile. "I like to read, and once Jack's library was opened up for us, I read everything I could about our world."

Smart girl.

We left the empty bag behind and started out again along the path. The depressions we had noticed before were clearly visible for what they were now—giant footsteps.

"Rylee, do you think the giant is here for us?" Pamela's eyes flicked up to mine, then back to the ground at her feet.

I couldn't lie to her. "Probably. Though how the hell anyone knew we were coming this route, I don't know."

I had made sure that only Deanna and Will understood why we were choosing to use the castle as our means of travel. It hadn't been our first choice. Liam, Pamela, and I had gone to an airport and boarded; Alex was put underneath in the cargo hold. We'd sat in the plane for three hours before everyone was forced to disembark.

Apparently, the engines wouldn't start, and the humans couldn't figure out why—as soon as all the passengers were off, the engines miraculously revved to life. Supernaturals causing grief again and the humans were none the wiser. Though it had been a pain in the ass for us.

I'd suggested going to Agent Valley, to use his specially rigged jet that blocked whatever vibrations supernaturals gave off, but Liam had wanted to avoid his old boss. He wouldn't say why, even when I pressed him. My suspicions were that he didn't want to get roped into working for the AA division. Which, with Agent Valley showing up when he did, was exactly what would have been required of us in exchange for using the FBI's plane.

That had left only one option.

In order to get us all home together, this was the only route we had left to us. Even if I knew how to jump the Veil like that asshole Faris, Liam couldn't cross the Veil like that. It had to be a physical crossing, like the way he'd come with Milly. A pain in the ass, but it was what we had to deal with unless we wanted to take a boat across the Atlantic in the dead of winter. Not something I was interested in, thank you very much.

The path wound through the forest, and as we walked, a light drizzle started. Alex grumbled up ahead about the 'fucking wet', Liam chuckled softly, and even Pamela laughed.

Me, not so much. All I could think about was why the hell this giant showed up here. Now.

Right in our way. And how the hell we were going to get by it?

I had a sudden, terrible feeling that someone didn't want us going home. Unfortunately, I didn't think it would be Will popping out to stop us from leaving. Not this time.

# 3

The castle stood on an outcropping of rock that overlooked the channel, but calling it a castle was a bit of stretch. A pile of crumbled rocks, which maybe at some point had been a castle, were strewn about for at least a quarter mile. Maybe a thousand years ago it had been a fortress, a stronghold on the edge of the island. But not anymore.

"Holy shit," Liam whispered.

I pulled up my second sight and sucked in a gasp of air. A castle it was, indeed. But it wasn't the castle that made me suck air, no, the castle, turrets, and thick stone walls weren't the issue. The issue was the giant sprawled out in front of it sleeping on his side facing us. His body stretched the entire front entrance to the castle, blocking it effectively. Tanned a deep brown, the giant looked just like a man, only on a gargantuan scale. Ruddy brown hair topped his head and dusted the parts of his body that were visible—which was a lot of him since he seemed to be wearing nothing but a loincloth that happened to be hanging to the side, giving us a full view of his—

"Nasty," Pamela said softly. I had to agree, there was far too much visible in the way of what the loincloth was supposed to be hiding.

On the top edges of the castle, along the battlements, movement caught my eye. I squinted, but couldn't tell what I was seeing. "Liam, can you see what's moving around up there?"

He stared long and hard, as did Alex. Liam spoke first. "Humanoid, but bigger. If I can see even that much at this distance, they've got to be competing with Dox for size."

Shit, ogres and Trolls were comparable in size. The last dealings we'd had with Trolls had been nothing short of a clusterfuck, though we'd come out on top. Sort of. And ogres? Well, unless they were blue like Dox—which I was doubting—we were in serious trouble. Ogres, like so many supernaturals, were territorial and freaking touchy about what they deemed as 'theirs'. Not to mention, they loved to fight and took any reason, good or bad, to start one. Neither option left us in a good spot.

"I just don't understand, why is the giant here?" Pamela stared out across the rocky ground, and her question was spoken softly. Almost like she wasn't aware she asked out loud.

"I think someone doesn't want us going home, or at the very least, they want to split us up." I turned a slow circle to check behind us. There were a few possible culprits. Faris was at the top of the list, Milly was close behind, and much as I hated to admit it, Berget was on that damn list too. So much for trusting family.

Did it matter which one of them was trying to stall us or split us up? No, not really. We just had to deal with the shit they tossed our way. But if I had to put money on anyone, it was Faris. Milly seemed to be out of commission since her pregnancy was progressing, and Berget . . . well, maybe I just didn't want to believe it was her. Faris though, he had some serious motivation. He needed me to solidify his throne, and I'd turned him down. Berget needed the same thing from me, but she already held the throne. As long as Faris didn't prove her claim false, she was sitting pretty.

Vampires were not known for going easy on people that had pissed them off.

And I'd definitely pissed Faris off.

To be sure, I Tracked the three possible culprits. I couldn't feel Berget or Milly, which told me they were both still on the mainland, across the water.

Faris though, he wasn't far at all. From the direction his threads pulled at me, he was at Jack's place; I Tracked Jack. Faris was right on top of him.

Every instinct in me jammed up my throat and tried to force me to turn around. I wanted to protect the old Tracker, even though he'd been a total dick. Damn him, and damn my innate tendencies. No, Deanna and Will were with Jack, I would have to let them deal with the vampire. Though how the hell he'd managed to get so close to Jack during the day was beyond me.

Liam moved silently to my side, and thoughts of Jack had to be pushed to the back burner. "We have to plan this. We can't just run in like you usually do."

My spine stiffened and, irritated, I glared up at him. "What's your plan then, *Boss*?"

His jaw tightened for a split second, then relaxed. "Whatever is up on top of the battlements will alert the giant when we're seen. We need to take them out first if possible, and then we can slip around the big bastard and into the castle."

"You don't know that they—whatever they are—will alert him." I crossed my arms. He'd been a supernatural for less than two months, for him to think—

He shrugged. "It's what I would do. Why put myself in danger if I had a giant to do my dirty work for me?"

Damn it. Time to swallow my pride.

Liam was right.

"Pamela." I reached out and touched her shoulder, drawing her back to us. "What kinds of spells have you got that might be able to help us here?"

She sucked in her bottom lip and frowned in thought. "I could start a fire. Or cause an earthquake."

I was already shaking my head. "No, something quiet and stealthy. We need to get by that giant without him ever waking up if we can."

She lifted her hands, palms up. "Everything I've learned is destructive and rather loud. And I don't think I could pin him" —she pointed to the sleeping giant— "down, he's too big."

I glanced out again toward the castle. Where we stood, we were still hidden by the trees. But the minute we stepped toward the castle, we would be in the wide open, exposed to everything across the open field.

There was no way to make this easier. The front gate was the entrance through the Veil; there was no other entrance from here. We had no choice, we had to go in that way or we would have no shot at getting home. Fuck, this was not going to be easy.

"I think we're going to have to just make a run for it."

Liam snorted. "What happened to having a plan?"

"This is a plan, not a great one, but do you see any other way? Cause if you do, let's hear it."

The three of them were silent. That's what I thought. No, it *wasn't* a great plan. Shit, I knew that. But what other choice did we have?

I fingered the handle of my sword. It looked to be about a mile between us and the castle. I knew that I could run it in under ten minutes, and both Liam and Alex could outstrip my time with ease.

Pamela, though, was not as fast as us.

"I'll pack her," Liam said, surprising me. No, *really* surprising me. Not because he knew what I was thinking, but because of his willingness to let Pamela so close to him.

I didn't question him though, just nodded.

Pamela chewed on her lower lip, and Liam turned his back to her so she could climb on. This was about to get interesting.

The little witch hadn't even climbed on his back and he was already sweating. Maybe he just needed to prove to himself that he could handle being around a witch. No, he needed to prove it to Rylee so that he could work with Pamela. Even though she was young, she was a part of Rylee's team. A part of their pack.

Going to one knee, he crooked his finger at Pamela. Her blue eyes were full of distrust, but she drew close and put herself behind him. Her fear lay heavy on the air, sweet and cloying, and he drew it deep into his lungs, the wolf in him waking up.

*Bite her. Break her neck. Taste her blood.*

She hopped onto his back and he stood, grasping her legs with his hands, tight, but not crushingly so. Every scrap of control he had was going into not throwing the kid from his back and ripping her apart. Breathing slow and even, he focused on Rylee.

She watched them, her tri-colored eyes taking it all in. He gave her a small nod. There was no doubt that she could read him and see just how difficult this was for him. He could see her thoughts before she spoke them, but she could do the same to him.

With a sharp movement, she turned her back on them. In a way, it was a compliment. Rylee trusted him to take care of Pamela. Trusted him to control himself and his wolf.

"Here we go. Alex and I will lead. Liam, you and Pamela stick close on our heels. Pamela don't use any spells unless we're in serious trouble. Got it?" Rylee pointed at each of them as she spoke.

He could feel Pamela bob her head. "Yes, I've got it."

Rylee took the point position, Alex tight against her legs.

Liam adjusted his weight, tightening his hands on Pamela's jean-clad legs. "Ready?" He asked over his shoulder.

"Yes."

Much as he hated to admit Rylee was right, there was no other way. The castle was on open ground, without a single twig or rock to hide behind. They were just going to have to run like hell and hope that they could at least make it past the giant.

Rylee broke from cover at full speed, Alex all but glued to her side. With a few long strides, Liam had caught up to Rylee and Alex. Pamela's fingers gripped his shoulders. "They've seen us already."

Damn, this was about to get ugly. He lifted his eyes to the battlements.

The creatures roaming the castle howled and cheered, as they pointed at the foursome. Worse, the creatures pelted the sleeping giant with large rocks, bringing him to life.

The giant gave a low rumble and rolled from his side to his belly, shaking the earth. Rylee pushed harder, picked up speed, but he knew it wouldn't be enough. Alex let out a yelp as the first arrow hit the ground right in front of him, far too close for comfort.

"Pamela," Rylee called out and Pamela took her hands from Liam's shoulders.

His spine itched as she called up a spell, and the wolf in him rolled upward, struggling to take control. A snarl escaped his lips and the first tingle of a shift crawled along his spine.

*Let me out.*

His breath came in a hard gasp as he fought the wolf for control.

A fireball flew from Pamela's fingers and slammed into the first row of creatures along the top of the castle walkway. Bodies exploded, some landing on the giant who was only just now getting to his knees. The bodies that rained down on him didn't seem to faze him. No, he reached down and grabbed half of a body from the ground and put it in his mouth, broken teeth digging into the still-twitching creature. The sound of his chewing was audible, even a half mile away, the snap of bones echoing across the open expanse of

ground. The wolf in him retreated. If they were going
to survive this, they would have to work together.

With Pamela.

The giant continued to pick at the bodies strewn
about his feet, not yet seeing Rylee and Alex as they
sprinted closer. Another volley of arrows came their
way, and Alex let out another yelp, this one legitimate.
A red-fletched arrow protruded from his shoulder,
blood dripping from the feathers. Without breaking
stride, Rylee reached down and yanked it out. Alex
yipped and Liam growled at him. Right now they had
to get past the damn giant; once they did that, Alex
could whine all he wanted.

Pamela threw another couple of fireballs, which did
two things. One, it took out another huge grouping
of the creatures that by now were clearly visible—yet
still unrecognizable—on the castle ramparts.

Two, her fireballs had drawn the attention of the
giant.

Towering over them, he turned and gave out a gleeful cheer, clapping his hands together and stamping
his feet as he saw them.

A garble of words poured from his mouth, along
with a stream of saliva as he bent at the waist and
scooped Rylee and Alex up in one big, dirty hand.

Liam skidded to a stop, his heart pounding out of control. This was not happening, he couldn't lose her now.

"RYLEE!"

Liam screamed my name as the giant's hand closed
around us. Ignoring Liam was hard, but I had to. I

had to focus. Before the log-sized fingers curled tight on me, I yanked my swords free and slashed upward with them, cutting through the giant's fingers. Two fell off; two others were left hanging by tendons and ligaments, blood spurting out around us.

Squealing like a two-story stuck pig, the giant dropped us. Falling, I realized—belatedly—that we were a hell of a lot higher up than I'd thought. I hit the ground with a solid thud, and the crack of my ribs filled my ears as I slammed into a barely protruding rock. *That* was going to leave a mark. Alex rolled across the ground beside me, snarling up at the giant.

"Stinky nasty bugger. No touching Ryleeeeeeeee!"

Hands jerked me to my feet. "Rylee?" Liam was trying to help; I know he was. But I couldn't breathe, and pain shot through my middle, a band of red-hot knives jabbing into me with each tiny bit of movement. I forced myself to shove him away, to stand on my own. If he knew how badly I was hurt, he'd try to carry me too.

"Go. We have to go," I managed to gasp out.

Far too slowly for my taste, Liam led now, Alex limped along beside me, and somewhere in the next ten steps I found the ability to breathe again. Broken ribs were a bitch at any time, but when trying to outrun a massively hungry, fingerless, and peeved giant—well, let's just say I could have done without.

The slam of the giant's foot into the ground scooted us forward faster yet, and my ribs protested yet again, stealing my ability to breathe. We were just twenty feet from the open arch of the castle entrance way. Pamela pushed herself off Liam's back and turned to face the giant. The look on her face was one I was beginning to know all too well.

Eyes narrowed, chin tipped up, she lifted her hands and flung them toward the giant. Two fireballs erupted from her fingertips, hitting the giant in the chest.

Damn, I wish I'd thought about that . . . nope, never mind. The giant patted the fire out, almost calmly, and then snarled at us. His jagged teeth had hunks of flesh and armor clinging to them, and from between them protruded a thick, long tongue that he used to clean his own face with in single lick.

"Fuck, that is nasty," I spit out, along with a gob of blood. "Move it, Pam. Your fireballs are just pissing him off. Just get inside. I don't think he can follow."

"What? Why not?"

"Giants aren't real smart and as soon as we're out of sight, we're out of mind."

Gods, I hoped that my memory was right. Grabbing her by the arm, I ran as fast as my labored breathing would allow into what I hoped would be the safety of the castle.

Right, I'd forgotten for a moment about the creatures we'd not been able to identify, a part of me hoping Pamela had taken them all out.

The creatures that had been firing on us were not Trolls or ogres.

They were gods-be-damned big-ass red caps. I did a fast count. There were at least twenty red caps. Two arms, two legs, built like a man, but their faces looked as if they had been smashed with a shovel, flat with just slits for noses and no lips to cover their blocky square teeth. Each of them was close to seven feet tall, carried a wicked iron pike, had heavy iron boots, and then there was their namesake. On each of their heads was a cap made of some sort of viscera, blood from the organ poured down the sides of their heads, and stained their skin a rusty brown.

"We can't outrun them," I said, as I slowed to a stop.

Liam grabbed my arm. "Yes, we can—"

"No, we can't," I snapped. "They can't be outrun, not on their own turf, at least."

The red caps started pounding the butt of their pikes into the ground at their feet, each thump bringing them a step closer. They had ringed us. From what I knew of them, which wasn't a lot, we were in for a fight. Trained warriors who bathed themselves in the blood of their victims. Yeah, not really how I wanted to start my week. Freaking stupid Mondays.

"Pamela, to my back." Thank the gods I'd been training her. She responded without question, pressing her back into mine. Alex tucked his butt in next to mine.

Liam didn't question, just slid his back against ours.

"Head shots, people," I said, my words calmer than I felt. Twenty red caps was no small feat to take on at the best of times.

As if in response, as I steadied my stance, something shifted inside of me, and one of my ribs pressed against my right lung. Shit, this was about to get tough.

Their pikes still thumping into the ground, the red caps were twenty feet away in all their blood-and-viscera glory. This close they looked like Dox on steroids, all muscle and small beady black eyes, bloodstained skin, with armor stretched taut over their bodies. My guts churned; injured, I was going to be more of a liability than a help in this particular situation. As if to drive the point home, pain rippled sharp and intense through my chest.

Four red caps engaged us, and I spun my swords out, crisscrossing them to catch the downward blow of a pike. The red cap forced me to my knees, the stone biting through my jeans. Alex leapt forward, snagging the red cap's belt and yanking him off balance.

The red cap spun toward Alex, giving me his back. Thinking I was the weaker of the two of us. Perfect. He snapped his pike back in order to drive it into Alex's side, but I beat him to the punch.

I drove my sword through the base of his neck, then yanked the blade to the left, beheading the big fucker before he could complete his swing.

"Good job, Alex."

Alex blew a raspberry at the red cap. "Bloody stupid messy bugger."

Yeah, he'd definitely picked up the local lingo.

A roar came from outside. The giant was still stomping around, and pissed as all get out. He gave me an idea. A bad idea maybe, but it might be the only chance we had.

"Pamela, knock out that arch."

She spun, clapped her hands together and then flung them apart. The arch over the entryway blasted apart with the force of her spell, and as the dust settled, a loud, booming laugh floated down to us.

Garbling his language, whatever it was, the giant stomped into the courtyard, scooping up the closest red cap and jammed him, pike and all, into his mouth.

I blinked several times. That had been the hand that I'd cut off his fingers. And while they were maybe a bit on the short side, they'd grown back. Son of a bitch, I didn't know giants had *that* ability.

The red caps were torn, half of them engaging the giant, the other half standing in our way. Better odds than we had before. Liam fired the crossbow, the bolt taking the closest red cap in his right eye. With a scream, the red cap went down to his knees, and then fell forward onto his face. Liam was already reloading the crossbow before the red cap hit the ground.

"Pamela, out front," I said. "I'll keep an eye on the big bastard."

Trusting my crew, I let them take the lead. Which meant I had to let them guard my back while I watched the giant take out the red caps one by one. Their fighting style was guerrilla, striking hard and then darting out of the giant's way, inflicting blows, but not any real damage that I could see. The giant's skin was thick, and the red caps weapons weren't spelled to cut deep like my swords.

Unfortunately for them, the giant caught on faster than I had thought he could, and in a matter of minutes, he'd eaten four more of them, armor and all.

"Rylee, we have a problem," Liam said calmly, like he was telling me about the upcoming weather.

I turned away from the giant and his snacks. Ahead of us another legion of red caps trotted into the castle courtyard. Three rows of ten—maybe that wasn't a legion, I didn't really know for sure. But another thirty red caps? Shit.

A body went flying by us and I ducked, rather belatedly. I turned to the giant, who had demolished the last of the red caps and was now eyeing us up. I saluted him with my sword, another idea forming.

"You remember this?" I called up to him.

Apparently he did, as he flexed his hand with his newly regrown fingers. He roared and I did the only thing I could think of. I ran toward him.

# 4

Okay, so maybe—again—it wasn't the best idea I'd ever had. "Stick with me," I gasped out, and again, Liam and Pamela moved with me. I wasn't worried about Alex; he wouldn't stray from my side with a battle like this going on. He panted, alternating between whimpers and swearing at the red caps, but he didn't get in the way.

Through the giant's legs I ran, skidding through the blasted rock and vaulting over a downed block. My feet hit the ground on the other side and the rib that had been knocking on my lung slid through it. Sharp, piercing pain rocketed through me, and I clutched my chest, still managing to get around the broken entryway, before flattening myself against the outside wall of the castle. Now the giant stood between us and the red caps, giving us time to regroup.

Pamela and Liam plastered themselves next to me.

Liam smiled over at me. "Out of sight, out of mind. Too bad it isn't always that easy."

I couldn't smile back, just slid to the ground, blood bubbling up to coat my tongue. I swallowed the coppery flavor back, knowing that if they saw it, they would panic. And while it was bad, I would survive; it just hurt like a son of a bitch to breathe. Or move. Or blink.

"Rylee bleeding." Alex sniffled, the little rat fink.

"I'm fine." Okay, that's what I said, but the blood in my mouth made it a rather garbled 'I'm fine.'

The sounds of death and destruction rolled out of the castle around us. The giant was cleaning house, as I'd hoped.

"Rylee, open your eyes." Liam called to me, and I wondered when I had closed them.

I took a slow, shallow breath. "Ribs should only be outside of lungs."

His hands hovered over me. "Shit."

"I can carry her, if you can clear the way," Pamela said, and I started to protest that I could walk. And while my legs weren't injured, with each breath, the rib pushed further in and it felt like it was aiming for my heart, the traitorous little bastard.

It didn't matter how tough of a supernatural you were, heart shots tended to be deal breakers, and I was no exception to that rule.

"Alex helps."

"Yes, Alex, you guard Pamela against anything that shows up," Liam said, and my eyelids fluttered. Gods, this hurt. The pain and lack of oxygen was beyond mind-numbing.

"Pamela, you take Rylee to the dungeons. Just keep heading down."

I wanted to protest, point out that the exit in the dungeons would take us to New Mexico, not North Dakota. Why would we be going to New Mexico?

"I can't lift her!" Pamela cried, and I did open my eyes then. This was one of those rare times that my Immunity was a real bitch, and peeling it back over my whole body, well, I didn't think I could do that. Liam's arms went around me, and I had to bite back a whimper as he lifted me up, doing his best not to jostle my body.

"Rylee." Liam brought his face close to mine so I could clearly see his pale gold eyes. "We have to turn back; we need to get you help."

"We do that, and then whoever is doing this will have time to plan something new to stop us. We don't have a choice, we can't go back."

He let out a breath, his nostrils flaring. I thought he would argue, would try and force me to do what he thought was best.

"Then that means you're up to bat, Pamela," Liam said, his voice deadly serious.

"I can do this." There was movement to my left, and then her hand curled around mine, giving it a quick squeeze.

He grunted. "You have to, or Rylee is going to die, and a good chance we will follow her shortly down that dark walk."

Hell, I wasn't in that bad of shape, was I? No, a punctured lung wasn't that bad.

Liam's arms tightened around me, and we started forward. With each step he took, the rib shimmied forward. Maybe only a breath forward, but still, it was working its way closer to my heart. Awesome.

A whoosh of something, and then there was a chorus of high-pitched screaming. My eyes were closed, and I drifted in and out of consciousness, the pain making me black out.

I saw Berget, somewhere in my in-and-out state, my mind playing tricks on me, no doubt. The Berget I remembered, yet not. She was older, but she wasn't the bitch vampire I'd met in Venice. No, this was the girl I had called my sister. Blonde hair, blue eyes, a sweetness that she'd had in all of her early years. She reached for me, her hand brushing mine, fingertips resting on my pulse.

"Rylee, you'll save me. I know you will. Don't give up. Please." Her fingers stroked down the length of my cheek.

"You're gone."

"No, I'm not. There is a way to untangle this monster that I've become."

I didn't want to hope for this, not again. Each time I believed her salvageable, her life was snatched away from me.

Maybe she sensed that. She leaned close and put her lip to my ear. "You will find the way to release me from the bonds they placed on my heart, soul, and body. I believe in you. You are my hero still."

I turned my face from her, unable to say anything. And then we were below ground, and Liam lowered me to sit against a wall. "Stay here, and don't move."

Right, that was not high on my priority list.

Alex curled up beside me. "Pamie hurt."

My eyes shot open and I Tracked her, felt her threads above me, and though they were strong, she *was* hurt and her last emotion before she blacked out was a fear so strong it could still be felt along her threads. With the last of my strength, I pushed myself to my feet, using the wall as a brace, and I started up the stairs. Two steps up, and Liam was rushing down, Pamela in his arms.

Blood, lots and lots of blood. Liam was covered in it, but I knew through the thread I Tracked Pamela with that she was the one hurt, not him.

I tried to speak, but that required a deeper breath. So I had to settle for snapping my fingers at Alex. He moved to my side and I buried my hands into his thick coat. Damn it all to hell and back, how was I going to walk when each step sent waves of pain and darkness my way?

Liam blocked my way. "Wait here, I'll take her through, and then I'll come back for you."

I shook my head, swayed on my feet, and managed to whisper. "That's what they want. Can't split up."

So in the most painstakingly slow parade, we inched through the dungeon. No red caps showed up, so I assumed that Pamela had taken care of them all. The girl was one hell of a witch.

I used the wall and Alex to brace myself, pain darkening my vision twice before we reached the exit through to New Mexico. At the last second, I remembered that the exit had been blocked, and I cursed under my breath.

*Gods help us, let it be open now.*

With the last of my strength, and with the gods apparently looking out for us, I stumbled through, crossing the Veil into the icy blast of the New Mexico winter. There the morning had only just started; a hint of the night still clung to the edges of the land.

Though, the fact that we had come out in a cave probably wasn't helping any with the light. Stumbling forward, I didn't see him until he grabbed me. Hands, big, blue gentle hands caught me, shocking the hell out of me.

"Dox."

"Hey, Rylee. Heard you were coming my way and might be in some trouble."

Distantly, I knew that there was no way Dox could have known where we were going to come out, or that we'd need help. So how had he found us? Who had told him?

"Don't try to talk, Rylee," Dox said, his face coming into view as he carefully scooped me into his arms. "We need to get you two out of here."

Liam and Dox carried Pamela and me out to Dox's oversized, bright red pickup truck. The back seat was big enough for a twin bed and had leather seats that matched the exterior paint, which would at least make for an easy cleanup. Pamela came around as Liam laid her on the seat. She sat up fast, her eyes wide and hands up in prep for a spell, aiming straight for Liam. I reached over and grabbed her hands, my wayward rib wriggling closer to my heart.

"Stop," I gasped out, blood trickling down the edge of my mouth. Crap, if she let loose on Liam, there was no guarantee I could convince him not to take her out.

There was a split second where I wasn't sure she heard me, and then she lowered her hands. "Sorry, I thought we were still in the castle." She turned to look at me. A large gash over her right eye seemed to be the cause of all the blood. Dox leaned in and pressed a wad of cloth against her wound.

He introduced himself to her, and when he stepped out to get into the driver's side, her eyes widened even more.

"I've never met an ogre."

I didn't answer her, just focused on sitting still. Liam slid into the passenger side of the truck and the engine choked, then died.

Just brilliant. What else could go wrong?

"Alex and I will run, we'll meet you there," Liam said, and before I could protest, he'd stepped out of the truck and slammed the door. Dox turned the key in the ignition and the engine rolled over without a hiccup.

Dox didn't take us back to his place, but to Louisa's. He pulled in as the sun climbed the rest of the way up over the edge of the horizon. Her house, built in a classic southwest style, hadn't changed since we'd last been there. Dox parked the truck, and then slid out, reaching for Pamela first. She turned her head to me, and I gave her a nod. If I couldn't trust her with Dox, I couldn't trust her with anyone.

Louisa met Dox on the front porch and ran her hand over Pamela's head, then pointed into the house. Without waiting for the ogre to come and get me, she instead climbed into the backseat of the truck beside me.

Her hair was cropped short, still growing back after her time spent with a Daywalker who'd used her as bait for me.

"Rylee, do you want to call in your favor to me?"

"Heal us both," I said, the rib digging in hard. I wanted to cough, fought the urge and held my breath against it.

She put her hands to my ribcage, clucking her tongue as her fingers prodded at me. "The girl I can heal; you are going to need more help than I can give. I will need to call in another Shaman."

"Do it." They all owed me a favor, so if I had to cash in two favors to save both our lives, I would do it.

Would I heal on my own, without her help? Possibly. But with my rib so far out of place, I wasn't 100 percent sure. Even supernaturals healed wrong if the bones were broken too badly, or too displaced. Made for some seriously ugly and misshaped bodies.

She left me there, her beaded necklace and bracelets jangling with each step as she walked away. I leaned my head back. Right there, in that position, I didn't hurt too badly. The pain still hummed under my skin, but with my eyes closed, I could believe that I was suffering from nothing more than a bad fall.

A whisper of wolf musk curled into the truck and then Liam was there, staring up at me. He didn't shift back into human form, which worried me. I reached out to him.

"Liam."

He whined and licked my fingers, shaking his head afterward. Louisa came out, and shooed him away as if he were a wayward mutt, and then she stilled, her eyes widening as she took him in. "I'd heard a rumor that a great wolf had been born. But I didn't truly believe it."

"Later," I whispered.

She pointed at me. "You stay there. We aren't moving you again; the rib is too close to your heart. But you knew that, didn't you?" Her shrewd eyes snared mine, and I couldn't look away. I also couldn't get enough breath to answer her so I just nodded.

"And you continued on anyway?" Her hands were working fast now, a sharp knife in one as she cut away my shirt.

I wanted to slap her hands away, but even if I could have lifted my arms, I knew she was helping me.

She peeled off my shirt and cut through my sports bra to reveal not only my shattered rib cage, which had some really interesting points pushing up against my skin from the inside, but the black snowflake that had been permanently etched into my breast bone.

"Well, if you can survive a Hoarfrost demon, you can survive this," she said. The cool air ghosted across my skin and an involuntary shiver grabbed me. Locking my jaw, I could only just stop myself from arching my back against the pain. Louisa shouted for Dox, and the rib shifted, slicing through what was left of my lung—and my world went black.

He was inside the Shaman's house, shifting, when Louisa shouted for Dox. The fear in her voice reverberated through him. With a growl, he forced his body to hurry. Panting, the last of the shift ripped through him and he stood, grabbed a blanket off the couch and tied it around his body as he ran out the door.

Dox blocked his way on one side, and Louisa blocked his way on the other. Intellectually, he knew that there was nothing he could do to help, but his instincts were to push them aside, bare his teeth, and chase them away from Rylee. To protect her at all costs. From there, he could smell her blood, and it sent him to the edge of his control.

"What can I do?"

"Go get some hot water going on the stove. And stay in the house. There are extra clothes in the guest room." Louisa's eyes flicked up to his, briefly, and he saw the command in them. His spine stiffened, and a growl slipped past his lips.

Dox smoothed things over. "Another Shaman is coming, you need to get some clothes on and have that hot water ready for her."

Frustration coursed through him. Yet again, there was nothing he could do, not really. He knew a make-work job when he was handed one. Shit, Alex could have gotten the water hot—where the hell was the submissive werewolf anyway?

Liam jogged into the house, grabbed some sweatpants and a shirt from the guest room, and yanked them on. He had to stop shifting while still wearing his clothes.

There were two pots of water already on the stove, and all he had to do was turn the heat on. Two clicks later, there was nothing else he could do but wait. And pace.

Not until he'd passed the couch twice did his eyes really flick over it, showing him what his nose already knew if he'd been paying attention. Pamela watched him warily, covered to her chin with a blanket the same color as the couch. Alex was curled up on her feet, his big eyes brimming with tears.

"Rylee die?"

Liam let out a growl. "No. They're going to save her." He had to believe it. There was no room for doubt in his head or he'd lose it completely, the wolf in him already making it hard to stay calm. Surely, they wouldn't be brought back together just so he could watch her die. He closed his eyes, fought the panic that gripped him, forced it down as he would the wolf in him. Opening his eyes, he stared at the witch in surprise.

Pamela held a hand out to him. He clenched his jaw and ignored her offer of comfort. He wouldn't hurt her, would help her survive, would even carry her if he had to, but he didn't have to be her friend. The wolf in him agreed. Pamela was a part of their pack, but on the outskirts as far as he was concerned. She could never be fully trusted, not like he'd like to. Again, he paced the living room, his bare feet slapping against the floor with each step he took. The whole place smelled like a hospital: astringents, bandages, sterilization. There was almost no smell of a home that was lived in.

The witch sat up, struggled to get her legs out from under Alex's weight. "The Shaman knew we were coming. There were bandages and everything already laid out for me and when they put me on the couch...."

Liam paused in his pacing long enough to stare down at her. "What happened?"

She bit her lower lip. "They already knew that it was Rylee that had been hurt. The Shaman muttered under breath, 'That's what you get for tangling with a giant'. I think she didn't know I could hear her."

He rocked back on his heels. "How the hell did they know?"

The sound of footsteps brought him around to see a grim-faced Dox.

"Crystal, the other Shaman, is here helping Louisa."

Pamela beat Liam to the question burning through his mind. "Is Rylee going to be okay?"

Dox gave a slow nod. "I think so. They're shifting the rib back in place. Once it's there, then she should heal up."

"How are they shifting it back in place?" Liam asked, a cold pulse of dread thrumming through him.

Dox swallowed hard, the glint of his lip ring catching the light. "They had to cut her open. I left before—"

Without another thought Liam bolted for the door, but Dox caught him around the waist and threw him backward.

Snarling, Liam charged forward again, but he hadn't taken two steps, and then he couldn't move at all. Not even his head. A spell held him fast, took away his freedom. Just like before. Sweat and fear slid through him, which only enraged his wolf.

"I'm sorry, Liam. You have to stay here," Pamela said, but all he heard was Milly's voice, her taunting words, and the feel of the collar around his neck.

No, Pamela would never be trusted. And if she wasn't careful, that lack of trust would bring them head to head.

And just like the other witches he'd dealt with, she'd lose.

# 5

The thing with being unconscious is that your mind can play tricks on you. Nasty ones, as usually is my case.

I could have sworn that there were hands *inside* of me, moving bits and pieces around. I didn't feel pain, just pressure and soft voices, then the sound of my skin popping, as a needle and thread sewed me up in layers. But how could that all be when we were in London, at Jack's place . . . no, there had been a giant and red caps. The memories slid through me as the last stitch tightened, pulling my wound together. I lay there on my back in the back seat of Dox's truck, my body slick with sweat and blood, the smell of whatever herbs and poultices the Shamans had used were heavy in the air and gave me a pleasant, tingling numbness all over.

"Good afternoon, Rylee." Louisa stood hunched over in the backseat of the truck and stared down at me.

I took a shallow breath, noting that the pain had lessened to the point where I could at least breathe without wincing. "I don't know about the good part."

She smiled and put her hand above my ribs. "Any day you wake up on this side of the Veil is a good day,

Tracker. We were able to put you back together, and your ribs are already healing."

"Point taken." I itched to sit up, but when I tried to move she tsked at me.

"Give yourself a few hours before you attempt anything even remotely strenuous. I'm going to send you home with Dox. You can recuperate there. Before heading home to Bismarck."

I didn't bother to argue with her, what was the point? As a Shaman, she was used to being listened to. But I did have questions, and I needed them answered. Even if I was half-baked on herbs.

My words came out in a slurry jumble. "Louisa, how did you know we were coming through? How did Dox know when we would bust across? Was it you who opened up the block on the Veil?"

She tapped her finger against her lips several times before answering me. "Both Dox and I received a phone call an hour before you came through, saying that you would need help and that you would be gravely injured. I don't know who it was, but there was truth in the words I could feel through my bones. So I listened and prepared for your injuries. If I'd have known that they were as bad as they turned out to be, I would have had Crystal come sooner. And yes, I opened the block on the entrance to the Veil, but that was some time ago."

I frowned. This didn't make any sense. Who could have known? The only person who *might* have had an inkling that injuries would be involved would be someone who'd known that the giant and the red caps were there. Like someone who'd set the whole damn fiasco up. But that would be ridiculous. Unless whoever set it up had a henchman who wasn't kosher with the plan to take us out. "Was it a man or a woman?"

"While they tried to disguise their voice, I do believe it was a woman. Now, rest, for whomever it was that made the call surely saved your life."

Well, shit. To owe someone your life was one thing, but to not even know who it was? That was just damn weird.

I thanked Crystal, who blushed and stammered while she covered my upper body with a blanket and then backed out of the truck. The youngest of the Shamans in the area, she had a lot to learn about keeping her emotions off her face. Pamela wobbled down the porch and pulled herself into the truck, but she wouldn't make eye contact with me. In her arms, she held clothes that were far too large for her.

Dox followed her out and slid into the driver's seat. "Alright, ladies. Let's go. The wolf boys will meet us back at my place."

Pamela was silent on the drive to Dox's, though he made every effort to engage her. Finally, I'd had enough of her quiet brooding, the itching feeling in my belly having nothing to do with the fast healing stitches there.

"Pamela, what happened? Why are you being so quiet?"

I watched with amusement as her spine stiffened, and her shoulders tightened up. She was so easy to read, not unlike Crystal; Pamela had yet to learn how to hide her emotions.

"What are you talking about?"

Dox cleared his throat. "I can answer that for you. Liam wanted to rush out and help Louisa with you. I couldn't let him, so we got in a little tangle; nothing I couldn't handle mind you."

Pamela let out soft breath. "And I wrapped him up in a spell so they wouldn't fight."

I groaned and closed my eyes. Shit, the last thing we needed was Liam to get worked up about Pamela. His time with Milly had not left him particularly forgiving when it came to witches. To say the least.

"Unless he's going to kill you, you don't touch him with a spell. Got it?"

She stared straight ahead. "Yes, ma'am."

A few minutes later, we were pulling into The Landing Pad, Dox's bar and hotel. I sat up, slowly, to see that Liam and Alex were already there. Alex was panting hard, his overly long tongue hanging out, and as soon as the truck door opened, I could hear him complaining.

"Too fast, Boss. Feets hurt like hell." He shoved one of his paws under Liam's nose, as if to make his point, and Liam bit him. Not hard, but enough to make Alex back down. The submissive werewolf slunk over to the truck, his eyebrows drawn sharply over his golden eyes. "Damn bossy Boss."

Dox opened the doors and held his hand out to me. "Louisa said you were okay to walk once we got here, just nothing else."

Good, at least I had that going for me. I put my hand in his and he helped me down out of the truck. Nothing hurt yet, but that didn't mean it wouldn't soon enough. I clutched one arm around my middle to brace my ribs.

Sure, I would heal fast, probably be 100 percent in two or three days. That didn't mean during that time things wouldn't hurt, or that I couldn't re-injure myself.

Dox helped me into one of the spare motel rooms set off the side of the Landing Pad, and Liam slipped inside, still in wolf form.

"Dox, would you look after Pamela and Alex for a bit?" I lowered myself onto the bed and kicked off my boots.

"No problem. They get in my hair and I'll just feed them some ogre beer." He winked at me, and then closed the door behind him as he left. Thank the gods for loyal friends I could trust.

Liam shifted as soon as the door was shut. Closing in on midday, and all I wanted to do was sleep, but first I had to hear his side of the story.

"What happened at the castle?" I peered up at him as he slid my jeans down over my hips. My shirt was cut up the middle so that was easy enough for him to slide off, and in any other circumstance, my blood would have been pounding at the care he was taking with me, his fingers brushing lightly against my skin here and there. As it was, I was just grateful to have someone looking out for me for once.

"The red caps surrounded us, and Pamela said she was right behind me. I got you down the stairs, realized she wasn't with us, and went back for her."

He pulled back the covers and helped me into bed, then crawled in with me, pressing his body along the length of mine, laying his arm across my hip to avoid my ribs. Heat from his body wrapped around me, burrowing under my skin, and with it came a sense of calm.

He tucked his mouth close to my ear. "She had killed all but two of them, and they had her pinned down, unconscious. I killed them, then brought her down to you."

I breathed in his smell, fought the drowsiness that pulled at me. "And at Louisa's place?"

A rumbling growl escaped him. Maybe Pamela and Crystal weren't the only ones who needed to learn some control. This was not good; I needed them to be able to work together.

"She wrapped me up so I couldn't move."

I waited for him to say more, and when he didn't, I didn't dig. There was no point. If he could move past the incident at the house, it wouldn't matter what had happened. We were a family, and I had to believe that above all else, Liam and Pamela would hold to that.

Now if I could just figure out who had wanted to keep us in London, and who had saved our asses on this side of the Veil. Then I could relax. Or at least know whose ass to kick, and whose to—no, not kiss. Thank, who to thank.

Liam's breathing evened out in a matter of minutes, a tactic I'd never really learned. As drowsy as I was, there was too much going on inside of my head, and too many questions left unanswered for me to just ignore them.

Of course, when Giselle materialized on the rickety chair across from me, I suspected I was asleep, but I wasn't 100 percent sure.

"Rylee, you are sinking fast. You know that, don't you?" She leaned back in the chair, looking as solid as if she were really there. There were subtle differences though. Her hair was no longer white, but had darkened to the dirty blonde I remembered from pictures long before I'd met her. More than that, her eyes were clear of the madness she'd suffered from for so long. She laced her fingers, tucking them under her chin. "You cannot run from what you are."

"Are you a ghost, or am I sleeping?" I asked softly, not wanting to wake Liam.

Giselle smiled. "You are awake. I heard your call for me, when your heart broke. But I couldn't cross the water. It is a barrier to much of the supernatural."

I wanted to get up, to reach out to her, but I knew that as a ghost, she would be immaterial. A tear slipped from my eye, and I scrubbed it away. Probably just a result of the herbs Louisa stuffed into me. "I thought you'd abandoned me."

Her smile faded at the edges. "I will do my best to stay with you, as long as I can. But each time I come to you, I am pulled a little further through the Veil. I have a duty on my side of the Veil. One that I cannot ignore."

"Then you thought I needed something, that it was worth it to let me see you?"

She nodded. "I am forbidden from telling you all I've learned since I crossed over. But I can tell you that what your eyes see, and your ears hear, they can be deceived. Those that you love, they can always be saved." Giselle grimaced and clucked her tongue. "I cannot say more than that."

"Do you know who saved us? Or who set us up?"

Leaning forward, she locked her eyes onto mine. "They are the same person."

Well, I'll be screwed sideways into next week.

Her eyes softened with sorrow. "I must go now, Rylee. Do not fight your destiny so hard. You are meant to stand between our world and the darkness that would swallow it. This moment, these dark days are what I trained you for, though the madness carried much of my understanding of the prophecies away. Believe in yourself, you are strong enough to carry this burden. And when the time comes, I will be there." Her voice faded along with her body, but I continued to stare at the spot where she'd sat.

Dead, she was more lucid than she'd ever been in life. Yet, her words still swirled like a deadly, mind-numbing fog in my head. She'd trained me to stand between the world and the darkness? Had she known the prophecies all along? Had I been just a tool to her? No, I couldn't believe that. But why hadn't she told me? Chills swept through my body, and I rolled so that I could bury my face against Liam's chest. At least with Liam I knew he loved me for nothing more than who I was; he didn't want to use me, or make me face demons; he didn't want to put me in the line of fire.

No, Liam was the one place I would always be safe. And with that thought, I finally drifted off to sleep.

We woke hours later. Darkness had fallen, and the clock on the side table blinked a lazy one in the morning. Liam was already awake, his breathing faster and less regular than when he slept. I sat up, grimaced at the twinge across my ribs, then traced my fingers along the stitches that went from the bottom of my sternum almost to my belly button. Good thing Crystal had small hands or I had no doubt that line would be even bigger.

Liam swung his legs over the edge of the bed. "You hungry?"

I smiled in the darkness, wondered if he could see my lips curve upward. He hadn't asked if I was okay, or how I was feeling. Damn, each time I thought he might not know me as well as I thought, he showed me how wrong I was. Good man.

"Yeah, let's get something to eat."

At some point while we'd slept, Dox must have brought in clothes. My jeans had been washed and dried, and there was a fresh button-down shirt for me. Jeans and a long-sleeved shirt for Liam. Even as a werewolf, the early December weather was cold for him.

"You never even twitched when he came in," Liam said as he stepped into his jeans.

I frowned. That wasn't like me. Then again, I *was* safe with Liam; maybe that was it. I buttoned up the shirt and slid the jeans on, then looked around for my weapons.

"Dox has them."

"Am I that easy to read?" I pulled on my leather coat. As much as I'd missed this clean cold snow while in London, now that I was home, I was back to hating it. And while it wasn't raining or snowing at the moment, the New Mexico winter was in full swing.

He opened the door and gave me a cocky grin. "For me, yes. Anyone else, probably not."

With a snort, I headed out, pleased to note that while my ribs ached, they were indeed already healing well. More than halfway healed from what I could feel with each step I took.

We headed to the bar that thumped with loud music and had strobe lights on the roof, as if to call down some alien space ships as per its name.

"What can we expect?" Liam moved to my side, but didn't take my hand. No, we weren't really the hand-holding type of couple. More the kick your ass if you look at us wrong type of couple. The thought made me smile.

"I don't know. I've never been to The Landing Pad when it was open and full of patrons."

"You can't get jostled."

We stopped outside the door. I put my hands on my hips. "Your point is what?"

He mimicked me. "Let me go in and get Dox, or at least make sure that I can clear a path."

Irritation flared along every synapse I had. A small part of me knew that he was just doing his job as 'the guy' and as 'the alpha', but it bothered me. I was no shrinking violet to be handled with fucking kid gloves.

Before he could say anything else, I turned and kicked the door open. Patrons scattered away from the door and a path opened up straight to the bar.

I raised an eyebrow at a seriously frowning Liam. "Thanks, but I think I've got it." Okay, so it was brassy and maybe stupid, as my ribs reminded me with a sharp twinge that they weren't fully healed. But I just couldn't let him take care of me in public like I did in private. I just didn't have it in me to be *that* girl.

Growling under his breath, he followed me in. No one even stepped close to us. The crowd there was mostly humans, but I caught sight of a few supernaturals trying to blend in. A leprechaun in the far corner chatting up a pretty red-headed girl, a water nymph sitting on a table surrounded by men . . . and Doran, his arm slung over the shoulders of Crystal, the young Shaman who'd helped save my life. His eyes tracked me as he whispered in her ear. I just shook my head and moved to the bar.

Dox gave me a big grin and shouted over the music. "Your girl is a natural bartender!" He pointed to the far end of the bar where, to my shock, Pamela was slinging drinks. And I mean slinging them. Spinning the glasses across the bar, she flipped them into the air at the same time as she grabbed a bottle of booze from under the table. I squinted, watched the half pause of the bottle and the glass in midair. The patrons cheered as she poured drinks with a flare that most bartenders took years to learn, if they ever managed at all.

"Well, I suppose that's one way to practice being subtle with her spells," I said softly.

Liam didn't laugh, didn't answer; he just closed the distance between us. "Dox, you got any food in this joint?"

Dox raised his eyebrows, silver rings glinting in the light. "Don't go insulting me, Agent. You remember what happened last time? No, never mind, you wouldn't remember much of that."

I laughed, grimaced as my stomach muscles clenched, and slid onto a barstool. Liam sat beside me, but turned sideways so he could keep an eye on me, no doubt. I stifled the urge to tell him to chill. Alpha, I had to remember he was an alpha to the core and every urge he had to protect was in overdrive because I was hurt. Still, I struggled not to tell him to back off.

Dox slid a stack of chicken wings and carrot sticks in front of us. I dug in, sucking the meat off the bones as fast as Liam did. My belly grumbled . . . no, that wasn't my belly. I looked down to see Alex staring up at me, pointing with one claw to his mouth. He mouthed "hungry please" at me, and scooted closer. I grabbed a chicken wing, intending to give it to him, when Liam's hand covered mine stopping me.

"He eats after us."

Shock filtered through me, and I turned to stare at Liam. "What did you say?"

Liam didn't even twitch, his eyes not giving me any indication that he was joking. "He can eat after us."

Okay, so shit, I knew this was going to happen, maybe not this exactly, but something where the alpha in him would show up and start a pissing contest. But did it have to be right now with me and Alex?

Liam let go of my hand and I flipped the chicken wing to Alex. Submissive, he might be, but I would be damned if I treated him like a second-class citizen. Liam snarled and stood. I followed him and put myself between him and Alex.

"This isn't a pack. Not like your wolf wants it to be. I won't have you treating Alex like shit."

Liam closed the distance between us so that we were nose to nose. Taking me right back to our early days with him as my nemesis instead of my lover and mate.

"I don't treat him like shit. I treat him like the submissive he is." Liam's whole body quivered with suppressed emotion. I was putting my money on 'pissed'.

"Not around me you won't." I stepped back, and Alex wrapped his paws around my calves.

"Sorry Boss, Alex waits." He pushed the chicken wing across the floor to Liam's feet.

Well shit. I hadn't expected Alex to side with Liam on this. Before I could say anything else, Dox rapped his knuckles on the bar. "Rylee, you've got a phone call. You can take it in my office."

"Who the hell knows we're here?" I snapped. The bar patrons closest to us backed away. Yeah, I was being a bitch, but I didn't like seeing Alex get treated like he wasn't good enough. Especially not by Liam.

Both werewolves followed me, Alex at my heels and Liam moving up to my side. Not that anyone was standing in my way.

I strode through the bar and down the short hallway to Dox's office, all the while doing my best to ignore the growing ache in my ribcage. The office was neat and tidy, though everything was sized up for his larger-than-life build. His desk and chair were made of some sort of high polished dark wood that was almost black except for the soft swirls of caramel here and there. I slid around the desk and sat down in the chair, my feet dangling, barely brushing the floor.

"We need to talk about Alex," Liam said, leaning across the desk, his hands flat on it. Alex peeked up over the edge of the desk, then moved to mimic Liam.

"Yuppy doody, Alex is good wolf."

I didn't answer, but instead picked up the old school phone lying on the desk.

"Who is this?"

"Me. Who the hell do yous thinks it was going to be?"

I let out a sigh of relief. Of course, Charlie knew to call Dox's place if he couldn't reach me. As my middle man with the parents of lost children, the brownie needed to be able to get a hold of me, or at least get a message to me via one of my friends.

"What's up?"

"Yous going to be at the big blue ox's place for a bits?"

"Yes, at least another day."

"Good. I be sending a parent to yous. I've done me best to puts them off, but now that yous be back, yous can deal with them."

I closed my eyes and leaned back in the chair. "What are the particulars of the salvage?"

"Nope, I can't tell yous. They said that yous need to be hearing it straights from the father." His voice sobered. "And I'd be making sure that yous and me do rights by them. I think they be holding your bird hostage."

My jaw dropped, and I scooted forward in my chair. Liam leaned over the desk, eyebrows furrowing. Right, of course he could hear everything.

I licked my lips. "Eve? They have Eve?" She must have flown straight across again, instead of hopscotching like she'd said she would. Damn it, she just had to prove herself, no matter the cost.

Charlie let out a sigh. "Yes, theys don't be calling it hostage per se. Buts they does be saying they will be 'caring' for her until yous bring their kidlet backs to them."

Damn it all to hell and back. "Charlie, are they threatening her?"

He clicked his tongue several times. "I think they would kill her if yous don't be bringing the kidlet back to them. I'll do what I can, but all I can do is stay with your bird. Right now she's in your barn, so easy enough for me to keeps me eyes on hers."

Much as I appreciated what he was willing to do, Charlie staying with her wouldn't work, not on Eve. "Charlie, give me second. I have to think this through."

I put the phone down on the desk and relayed what Charlie had told me to Liam; though he didn't need me to, I needed to say it to clear it in my own head. I couldn't believe that someone would hold Eve ransom, or that they'd be able to for that matter.

Liam went directly into agent mode, which was what I needed. "Blackmail? Have you run into it before?"

"No." I shook my head. "I have to say this is a first."

"And Charlie can't tell you anything about the kid or the parents?"

Charlie squawked through the phone. "Nots if yous want your bird kept off the rotisserie. My instructions were clearer than a midsummer's night sky. No telling yous nothing."

Liam and I stared at each other. We had no choice but to go along, or Eve was done. And if they—whoever they were—could take out Eve so easily, I wasn't so sure that we weren't in for a wild fucking ride of a salvage.

"Send Pamela and Alex back to keep her calm; you can't go if the parents are coming this way, and you can't save Eve *and* the kid if you go to Eve," Liam said, his voice calm, casual as if it was the logical solution.

"You're just trying to get rid of Pamela," I countered, irritation flaring in my guts. "You have to learn to deal with her; she's a part of this family, pack, whatever you want to call it, as much as you or I am."

He ground his teeth, and when he answered me, he did so without acknowledging my words. "This time around, you need her to help, but not at your side. She can keep Eve calm, and if necessary, she can probably get Eve out of there if the shit hits the fan."

Damn, he was right, that was the sticky part. Not that I couldn't let someone else be right, but that he was neatly avoiding Pamela, without actually having to avoid her.

I picked the phone up, but my eyes never left Liam's. "Charlie, I'm going to send Pamela and Alex to you. Tell Eve that they are coming, that should help. Tell her that I will find this kid, where he is—"

"It be a girl, I can tell yous that much."

"Fine, I'll find this kid wherever she is and bring her home."

"Okays. Be quick about it, Rylee." He hung up the phone, the line going dead in my ear.

# 6

Pamela was eager to go 'save' Eve. Maybe a little too eager.

"Are you sure you want me to just go and sit with her? I can get her away from them, I know I can."

Before she'd even finished speaking I was shaking my head. "No, I don't know what these people have, but if they can hang onto a Harpy, they aren't to be messed with. Just keep her calm. That's your job." Only an hour since the phone call from Charlie. An hour and things were already ramping up. We waited outside The Landing Pad in the cold, winter night for Pamela and Alex's ride. Dox had shut the bar down early, and had put the word out through the locals that we were expecting some hostiles. Shit, not even home twenty-four hours and life had tossed a twist at us I could never have seen coming.

A cold nose shoved into my hand. "Alex's job?"

"You keep Pamela safe. That's your job. Protect her."

Alex sat back on his haunches and saluted me, albeit a bit sloppily. "Gots it."

All but bouncing, Pamela stood in front of me, eyes bright, ready to face another challenge. There was no regret in her over killing the red caps, as there shouldn't be. A part of me was pleased, she would suffer a lot less in our world doing what had to be done and not getting her panties twisted up with guilt. Yet, another part of me was sad. To be so young, and hardening up so quickly—I wasn't sure that was a good thing. I'd been two years older than she was when Giselle had found me. And even then I'd hardened plenty fast enough.

"You have Terese's phone number?" I handed Pamela the bowie knife I'd started with, the one she'd carried in London. She tucked the knife in the sheath that would hold the blade in place over her lower back.

"Yes, I'll call her as soon as I get there. Are you sure she'll help?" Pamela had reason to be wary. The only other witch she'd met had been Milly, and both times Milly had not treated Pamela well. If one can say that having a death spell thrown at you was just poor treatment.

I nodded. As soon as I'd gotten off the phone with Charlie, I'd called Terese. Told her that I was sending Pamela to my place and that it might be prudent for Terese to go and spend some time with her. Of course, it didn't hurt that I was sending Terese a young witch that would rival Milly's abilities one day.

Pamela's eyes suddenly narrowed. "Are you just sending her to check up on me? I'm not a child. I'm almost fifteen, you know."

"No." I bit back a smile; the kid was too damn smart sometimes. "She has to check on every witch that comes into her territory. Not to mention you'll be training with her once things settle down."

Liam snorted. "Like that's ever going to happen in your life."

A big, pale green Cadillac pulled into the parking lot of The Landing Pad. In order to get Pamela and Alex back to North Dakota as fast as possible, I'd had two choices. Try to cross the Veil by going back into the castle and hoping like hell that there was no one waiting for us in ambush.

Or cash in one of my favors with another of the Shamans. I went with option number two. No need to see who was waiting for us back at the castle.

Crystal leaned out the door of the Cadillac. I handed her a cell phone. "If something goes sideways, I'll call and you bring them back here to Dox, got it?"

The young Shaman's eyes were somber. "You think there might be problems?"

Liam snorted softly, but I ignored him and leaned in close so Pamela couldn't hear me. "You are taking them out of the firing range here. I don't want them to be around this psycho parent that's going to show up. If I call, it's because I think it's a trap on the other end. If it's safe, you won't hear from me, and you can take them all the way to Eve and drop them there. Got it?"

She gave me a tight smile. "I can't stay with them. Louisa needs me back here." I said nothing else, just stepped back. She understood what I was trying to do. Keep Pamela and Alex safe, while not showing them my hand. Keeping Eve safe was important too, but if this parent was the psycho I was counting on . . . I Tracked Eve, felt a current of fear, but no pain, and no terror. More worried than anything. That was a good sign. Maybe this salvage wouldn't be the mess I had already assumed it would come to.

Crystal waved out the window to Alex and Pamela. "You two ready?" Even though she'd helped saved my life, I managed to talk her into throwing in a ride for Pamela and Alex too, since she'd been helping Louisa, and I hadn't directly asked her for help. Bonus. Didn't hurt that she was young, and new to her profession as Shaman, making her easier to persuade.

Pamela gave me a hug, Alex followed suit, and then they were running toward the long, slightly anemic-looking car.

"Like kids off to summer camp," I said, crossing my arms to block the snap of cold wind. Crystal backed the caddie out, and Pamela and Alex waved to us. Shit, it felt like we were sending babies off into danger to save another baby. I had to force myself not to run out and stop the car, to call them back. In my head, I knew Eve needed them, and that I needed to be here to deal with the psycho father Charlie sent our way. Motherfucker was going to get a piece of my mind, and maybe even a piece of my sword before this was all said and done. Splitting my team up was not something I wanted to do. It just felt wrong. Yet there was really no other choice for me at this point. Liam was right; we had to do things this way, at least this time.

Liam moved up beside me, his chest so close to my back I could feel the heat radiate off him, but he didn't touch me. "Summer camp in the dead of winter, with werewolves, witches, and Harpies. Sounds like fun to me."

I didn't fire anything back, just watched the caddie disappear into the frosty cold night. With no one around, Liam slipped his arm over my shoulders, and I turned and slid mine around his waist.

"They'll be fine," he said, squeezing me gently to his side. I pushed away from him, the moment of solidarity gone in an instant.

"Don't say shit like that, you don't know they'll be fine. That's not how it works in our world. People die all the time. This isn't a movie where the good guys always miraculously pull through."

He growled, low and under his breath. "What, do you want me to say that they're going to get themselves killed?"

My feet stilled, the loose gravel underfoot shifting even though I'd stopped moving. "You know what, just don't say anything. Can you manage that?"

The main door to the bar slammed, and Dox took a single step toward us, then froze. "I thought you two were getting along now."

"We are," we said at the same time. I drew in a sharp lungful of cold air, the bite of it along the back of my throat cooling my anger a little.

"I'm just being a bitch," I grumbled.

Dox laughed. "You worry like a mother hen. It's kinda cute."

I punched him on the arm as I passed and headed into the bar. "I'm not fucking cute."

Liam followed me in, and as he passed Dox, said, "Mother hen?"

Dox shrugged. "Well, I didn't want to go with the more obvious mother bear. No need to encourage her bad behavior."

The two men laughed together and I kept my back to them so they couldn't see the smile that crept across my lips. No need to encourage them ganging up on me.

I stepped up to the bar and slumped onto one of the stools.

Doran emerged from the shadows and slid into the seat beside me. "Good to see you've kept your humor intact."

I lifted an eyebrow at him. "Dox, I thought you said you cleared this place out?"

The ogre grunted as he stepped behind the bar. "Daywalkers, they're like every other species of vermin. You think you got them all, but you always miss one."

Doran pressed a hand to his heart, batting his eyes. "You wound me. But even if you had tried, I would have stayed. I have a message for you, Rylee." His green eyes darted away from mine, unable to make contact. Crap, we'd done this dance before. Everything in me tensed. It seemed that lately, Doran was my messenger boy, and none of the news he had for me was good. I didn't like it.

"She sent you something for me?" She being my little sister-turned-psycho-vampire, Berget. I was just guessing that she was the one with the message for me. Who else would Doran have contact with? Louisa and the other shamans would just contact me through Dox. They wouldn't use Doran. I really didn't want any messages from Berget. Like as in pretty please leave me the hell alone.

"I did not see her, but yes, she sent one of her messengers to me. She wants to make peace between you and her." He did make eye contact with me then, and in them I could see the fear that I would take her up on her offer. Not likely after everything he'd told me.

I snorted, let the interior tumbling of my emotions continue while I did my best to keep my face smooth. "You mean after she tried to have us killed, and didn't succeed, she wants to make nice? Play in the sandbox together like one big happy messed up family?"

Doran shrugged and slid closer. I put a hand on his chest, keeping him at arm's length, my eyes flicking to Liam. Doran was a touchy-feely kind of guy. Though I didn't actually care, Liam would. "That's close enough, thanks."

"She wants to hire you to Track for her. The money is considerable; you probably would never have to work again. Could go pro bono for every other salvage for the rest of your life."

I drummed my fingers along the wooden bar, not really contemplating. I already knew my answer. "Would you do it for her, if you could?"

His eyes were as serious as I'd ever seen them. "Not even for the redemption of my soul would I do this for her. It will solidify her as the Empress if you do what she wants, and that is something the world cannot have." He paused and gave me a wink. "In my humble opinion."

"Humble. Yeah." I took the glass of orange juice Dox slid across to me and took a sip before saying anything else. "What is it that she wants me to Track, do you know?"

He shook his head. "No, I don't know. I was to give you the message that she wishes peace and wants to hire you. That's it."

Dox snorted. "Like always, not much help, are you?"

Doran turned to him. "Tell me, how is it that you came to be here, in this ogre-less place, anyway? Did you leave to see the world? No, wait, that's right, you were kicked out, banished by your own kind because of how weak you are—"

Dox smacked the flat of his hand on the bar, startling the hell out of me and stopping Doran mid-sentence. His eyes narrowed and a faint purple flush ran up his neck and over face. "Shut your mouth before I remind you why even Daywalkers don't piss off ogres."

Well, well. This was a side of Dox I'd never seen. Not in all the years I'd known him had he been anything but pleasant. I'd never seem him pull any of the 'ogre-ish' tantrums I'd heard about his kind.

His eyes flicked to mine and he let out a big breath, the additional color fading from his blue skin. "Sorry."

Fatigue washed through me, and as much as I wanted to wait up for the assholes that had a missing kid and thought blackmailing me was a good idea, I also knew I needed to sleep if my body was going to be even close to healed for this salvage.

"Doran, tell the messenger no. I won't do it. I won't help her."

He nodded and let out a sigh of relief. "She won't give up. She will try to force your hand."

"I know."

Berget was a spoiled child and she wanted what she wanted. No doubt her next message would be less polite. Seriously, even knowing that all families are messed up to some degree, this—having a psycho, power hungry vampire for a sister—was going a bit far. Even for me.

"Dox, you'll let us know if anyone shows up?" I knew his schedule was wonky, awake all night, and then sleeping through the better part of the day, so I could trust that he would be awake to receive this parent when they showed up.

He rapped his big knuckles on the bar twice. "You bet, Rylee."

I slid off the stool, but Doran stopped me, his hand shooting out to grab my elbow. "Do you have your obsidian blade, the one I sent for you?"

Frowning, it took me a second to remember that he had indeed sent me an obsidian blade via Eve on her last trip home from New Mexico. "No. Why? Is it something special?"

His eyebrows quirked up to his hairline. "You just need to keep it with you."

Warmth circled around me as Liam moved to stand behind me. "Why does she need it?"

Doran let out an exasperated sigh. "Listen, getting a read on Rylee is impossible, you know that, right?"

Neither of us moved, and Doran seemed to take that for encouragement.

"So when I have a niggling suspicion that you need something, *Tracker*, I follow through. I don't know why you need the damn blade with all the other ones you have. Just that you need it. Maybe not now, maybe not tomorrow, but at some point, you will need it."

I shook my head; there was nothing I could do about it. The blade was at home in North Dakota. "I'll get it when we're home next. For right now, I'm going to bed."

As we walked across the parking lot, Liam took my hand. "We still need to talk about Alex."

I stopped walking. "Seriously, now?"

He glared at me, his jaw working for a moment before he answered. "No, that discussion can wait until after the salvage. But this can't be ignored."

"Fine, after the salvage, once we're home, we can talk about Alex." Yeah, not like I was going to for one second let Liam pull the alpha card. Just because he *was* an alpha, it didn't mean he had to act like one all the time. Okay, shit, I *knew* that was naïve on my part. Maybe I'd just dealt with too many asshole alphas and there was a large part of me that was worried Liam would take that route.

Our room was cool and the sheets downright frosty, but with Liam wrapped around me, I warmed up fast. And that was the beautiful part of him and me. Only moments before we'd been glaring at each other, and he wasn't happy with me. But there was no way we'd let that get between us. Not after everything we'd fought through.

Again, Liam passed out before me, but I wasn't far behind.

This time there was no Berget, no Giselle. Nothing but a blissful, deep sleep that was interrupted by a loud banging on our door.

"Rylee, you'd better get your ass out here," Dox called, his voice only slightly muffled by the thick door.

I groaned and rolled over in bed, reaching for a pillow to cover my head before I remembered the night before.

Eve. The missing kid. The psycho father showing up.

As I flipped off the covers, my skin danced with goose bumps, the cold air waking me faster than anything else could have. I slid into my clothes, my ribs feeling like they were about 98 percent. Good, I wanted to be able to run this asshat through if he gave me even a tiny bit of grief.

Liam was dressed, and he handed me my swords as I slid the straps of my shoulder holsters on. I took the swords from him and slid them home, then strapped on my whip so that it hung low on my hip.

"Ready?" He asked.

"Yeah, let's get this over with and get this psycho's kid home."

Liam led the way, and I slammed the door behind me. Dox waited for us, his eyes wide.

"The father is in the courtyard, behind the bar."

"Is it that bad?"

He just shook his head. "Not what I was expecting, that's all. And don't ask me to tell you, you wouldn't believe me if I did."

"Well, that's just awesome," I muttered. This was one of those times that I wanted to remind people how much I hated surprises. They never turned out well in my world.

Never.

Liam put his hand out, blocking me. "A plan would be good here." Damn, he was like a broken record lately.

My fist clenched involuntarily and I forced myself to relax. "I'm just going to talk to them. No fighting today."

"Unless they piss you off."

"Yeah, I thought that was obvious."

Of course, if I'd known what was waiting for me in the courtyard, I wouldn't have been worried about getting pissed off. I would have been more worried about *me* being run through.

# 7

"Is that what I think it is?" Liam breathed out beside me.

There was no way to answer that without sounding like a condescending bitch. *It's a freaking unicorn, what do you think it is?* Just doesn't have a polite ring to it. And there it was, a gods-be-damned unicorn, standing in the middle of Dox's courtyard. Silent and motionless, if I hadn't known better I would have thought I was looking at a statue. Except that when the wind blew hard, the stallion's jet-black mane and tail flew out around him. How did I know it was a stallion? Because I'd met him once before, on the first salvage Liam had ever done with me.

Like a waking dream, staring at him reminded me again that there *were* beautiful and good creatures on this side of the supernatural, they were just few and far between.

A single, golden horn jut from the middle of his forehead, but otherwise, he was a solid, glistening black from his hooves to the tips of his ears. Leader of the Tamoskin Crush, he had struck me as fair and wise. Not the psycho I was waiting on. Unless he was here for something else? Only one way to find out.

"Wait here for me." I slid out of my weapons, laying them one at a time on the bar.

Liam put a hand over mind. "What are you doing? You don't know that he won't attack you."

"If I can't even trust a unicorn, then this world has a hell of a lot more problems than a few missing kids."

Liam slid his hand from mine slowly, reluctance in his every move. "Be sure about this, Rylee."

Swallowing hard, I nodded. "I am."

He stepped back and I opened the door to the courtyard. If the stallion was here because of a missing child, all I could wonder was how the hell the kid had been stolen. A unicorn crush was harmless until threatened, and then you'd better hope that they didn't mistake you for an enemy. There were not many supernatural creatures that could stand and survive the single-horned equines when they worked together.

I closed the distance between us, leaving about ten feet of space.

Just in case.

*Tracker, there is no time for pleasantries. A foal has been stolen, the first born to us in fifty years.* His words rang through my mind, not unlike Blaz's voice, but with a distinctly different feel. Like a bell being rung as opposed to the distant rumble of thunder that was Blaz's voice.

"I can vouch for Eve, you need to let her go." I put my hands on my hips and spread my feet slightly apart. "She hasn't even been on this continent for the last few weeks, and even flying straight across she would have just arrived home. No time to go foal-napping."

He shook his head, mane flicking in the frosty air. I smelled lavender and springtime, even though neither was possible.

*The crush has spoken; she will be held until the child is returned. Though we are not happy with her presence, you are showing her the way to her roots, to the Harpies of old that we danced with on moonless nights. No, I do not believe your Evening Star did this.*

He pawed at the tiled courtyard with an iron-hard hoof and tossed his head again, mane flying about. His hide shivered, as if touched with flies. But I knew there were no flies, not in this weather. And what was this about Eve? She was my Evening Star? This was one of those times I just pushed it all away. Supernaturals loved their 'Confucius says' shit. You just had to learn to ignore it, or you'd end up never able to do anything, so afraid that you might take a step wrong.

"You want me to Track your foal?"

*Yes. Track her, and bring her home.* Sorrow, heavy and thick like fog in the morning, laced his words.

I removed my hands from my hips, slid them into my pockets. "This is your daughter that's gone missing?"

*Yes. She was stolen away from us, six nights ago. There were no footprints, no sign of another passing this way. Harpies were our first thought. Except for a single mark in the snow, there was nothing.* Again he tossed his head, eyes flashing. *But there are no Harpies in this area except for your Eve. If you do not find my daughter quickly, it will be all I can do to keep the crush from ending her life, regardless that I know it was not her. Our children, they do not come along often and are treasured by all.*

Crap, I would have to move fast. If I didn't find the foal, Eve was toast. "So we're assuming something that flies took your daughter? What did the mark in the snow look like? Presumably something large enough to pick up a . . . how old is she?"

*She is nigh on six months old, a suckling filly, yet. Unable to fend for herself, her horn is a bare nub on her forehead, dull and useless.* He gave a long, low snort. *The mark resembled that of a talon or claw, digging through the crusted snow.*

I tapped a toe on the bare red tiles. Already the urge to go after the foal had begun to eat at me. Like a sickness I had no cure for, Tracking was something I couldn't run away from, didn't want to. Unlike other things.

"I need a picture of her, and her name."

*Her name is Calliope. She will be our mystic when she is of age.*

Without any warning, an image flashed in my mind, the 'picture' I would need to Track the foal. Gangly long legs, petite head and ears, miniature nubbin of a golden horn. Her body was white as new snow, but her mane and tail were jet black, and she had black socks up to her knees on all four legs. A black star sat at the base of her horn. She was stunningly colored, and I knew without asking that she would be a prize mare in the tribe as she grew, regardless of her apparent status as an up-and-coming mystic.

I closed my eyes and Tracked her, tied myself into her threads. Her life force beat strong through me, humming lightly with an energy very different than the human children I Tracked. For lack of a better term, her threads vibrated, dancing and jumping about as if they were a true electrical pulse.

"Her name suits her. Is there anything else I should know?"

*If I had more information, I would give it. Bring her home, Tracker, and you will have our loyalty past the day that you die.*

"Well. Thanks." I frowned. "She may not be alive, when I bring her to you, you need to know that. And that cannot affect the outcome of Eve's life."

*Just bring her home, and all will be as it was.* There was no threat, no 'or else.' Just those words echoing inside my skull, and then he spun on his haunches, the tile below his feet cracking, springing up around him in large shards that hovered in the air for a split second, and then crashed to the ground.

I watched him gallop away, his black coat disappearing into the darkness that was left of the morning.

A hand touched my shoulder, and Liam leaned his head close. The scent of distant winter mountains, pine trees and a faint hint of musk swirled around me. I reached up and touched his hand where it curled around my shoulder.

His eyes searched my face. "How bad is it?"

I stared at the place where the stallion had stood, the possibilities swirling through my mind.

"Maybe not as bad as I thought. A simple salvage, and Eve will be safe." I glanced over my shoulder at him. He frowned.

"Is it ever a simple salvage?"

I let out a sigh. "Unfortunately for me, no."

We went back inside and I grabbed my weapons, quickly putting them back on. "Dox, I need a favor."

The ogre twisted up his lips. "Depends on what you want."

"Your truck."

He grimaced, and I raised my hands, palms up. "What the hell, I've never wrecked a vehicle." I didn't count flipping my Jeep when I was under the influence of the Hoarfrost demon. In my mind, that wasn't my fault.

He continued to grimace, but I could see through it, he was just making it look like this was hard. The thing about Dox was, he always came through. He was one of my better friends.

"Where are you going to take my baby?" He propped himself with his hip against the bar.

I Tracked Calliope, her vibrating threads a pleasant hum inside my skull, soothing away the last of the ache in my body. Now that was an interesting development. I shook it off and focused on the *where* of her.

"Pacific Northwest."

Dox paled, as in his blue skin faded to a dull grey in a matter of heartbeats. That couldn't be good.

"That's ogre country. You don't want to be going there, Rylee. There's a reason you don't find other supernaturals round about there." He waved his hands—the size of frying pans—back and forth. "That is a seriously bad idea."

I grunted. I'd never Tracked into that area before. The outskirts of it, yes, but never into the Pacific Northwest itself.

"Doesn't matter, Dox. If that's where the foal is, that's where I'm going."

He licked his lips, but the fear on him was obvious. So much so that he wouldn't even meet my eyes. Shit, that did not bode well for us. Doran had said he'd been kicked out for being weak . . . damn, I wasn't sure I could push him on this.

I stepped back. "Don't worry about it. I'll rent a truck." Liam leaned over the bar, shook Dox's hand. "Thanks for your help. Next time we're here, I'd like to have another go at your beer. See if it still kicks my ass."

The ogre watched us go, but didn't stop us.

"I thought he'd offer some advice at least," Liam grumbled as we grabbed the last of my weapons and gear from our room.

I counted my weapons and the few pre-made spells I'd had Deanna make for me before we left. "Doesn't matter, if he was kicked out at a young age, he won't be much help. My training with Giselle covered ogres. I probably know more than he does."

Liam tried to phone a car rental company and promptly handed me the receiver. All I got was static and then, as Liam stepped away, the static faded and I could hear the ringing line. Shit, it looked like he was going to be the problem when it came to technology now. Next to him, I was almost normal. Almost.

While I spoke to the agent, all I could think about was that Dox didn't think this—going into the Pacific Northwest—was a good idea, and he'd seen me in some of my worst situations and never batted an eyelash. Hell, he'd just seen me get an impromptu surgery in the back of his truck without so much as a 'hey that's not very sanitary, you know.'

I hung up the phone. "They'll have a truck here in an hour."

Liam flopped onto the bed. His hand drifted to the spot just below his heart, where his gun used to sit. I knew what it was to be without a weapon when you were so used to it.

"You want something to fill that spot?"

His eyes flicked to his hand. "You got a gun that would work?"

I raised my eyebrows at him. "Really, you want a gun?"

He shrugged, but his face sobered. Yeah, I remembered his last partner too, and the wayward bullet from Liam's gun that had taken his life. No need to repeat that scenario.

"Maybe not. What else have you got?"

I dug into the new bag Dox had provided us with, now stuffed with all my weapons. Along with the black demon book.

I grabbed the tome, my heart icing over. "Hang onto that thought, I'll be right back."

Jogging out of the room, I slipped into the bar. Dox leaned against the bar, his eyes closed as if deep in thought. I cleared my throat.

"Dox, can you stick this in your safe?"

He reached for it, and took the burlap sack, his fingers barely touching it before his eyes flew open. "Do I want to know what it is? I can feel it through this. Something very dark and very ugly."

"No." I shook my head. "You don't want to know what it is. Just lock it up."

Without any more questions, Dox disappeared down the hall, holding the covered book just with his fingertips. I knew he had a safe, I just didn't know where it was. Which was fine by me. I didn't have time to read that thing yet, but my gut feeling was that I would need it, and soon. I left him there and headed back to the room. Dox seemed torn up by the fact that we were headed into ogre territory. I probably should have been more worried, but I wasn't.

Back in our room, I leaned over the bag again, I handed Liam two short blades, each one about twelve inches long, bright pristine steel with smooth caramel-colored wooden handles. "You can set these up with a slight adjustment on your shoulder holster. They fit nice under a jacket and can be used in close quarters, and in a pinch, they can be thrown."

He took the bright blades from me, rolled the handles between his fingers. "These are a start."

I helped adjust a shoulder holster for him, fitting it with the sheaths that would keep the blades from cutting into him.

"Are they spelled like yours?"

"Yes. All my blades are spelled, so watch your fingers."

He slid a jacket over the swords and holster, and he looked about as normal as any person out for a walk in the blistering cold could look.

I flopped onto the bed and threw my arm over my eyes. Half an hour and the rental truck would be here.

"What do you know about ogres, besides Dox?" Liam sat down beside me, the bed sagging under his weight.

"Volatile, territorial, prone to fighting and fucking. Sometimes both at the same time. Other than that, I don't know. They keep their customs and tribes very close to the chest." I flipped my arm off my face. "Hell, I hadn't even known there were that many colors until those damn books of Jack's."

"Bigger than Dox?" Liam fingered the blades he'd just strapped on.

"Yeah, I think he's pretty small for an ogre."

He sat up with a swiftness my eyes struggled to follow. "Seven feet is *small?*"

"For an ogre, yes."

I Tracked Calliope. The tingling of her emotions spoke of her fear, but she wasn't hurt. A good start. My mind flickered over the possibilities of what kind of creature could have snagged her. Something from the air, something with talons. Dragons and Harpies were the two obvious choices. A dragon was unlikely; they resided in Europe and Asia for the most part, rarely coming across the water to North America. At least from what I understood.

A Harpy, taking Eve out of the equation, was a good possibility, as there was a running animosity between Harpies and unicorns. But they—Harpies—were territorial too, and I doubted they would go so far out of their own area, even to snatch a foal belonging to their rivals.

"What is going on in that head of yours?" Liam brushed his fingers across my forehead.

I caught his fingers in mine. "Why would anyone want a unicorn foal?"

His jaw flexed and his pale golden eyes grew thoughtful. "They haven't contacted the crush for ransom, so it isn't a power trip."

"Breeding rights, maybe?" She was surely a pretty enough little thing. I leaned across the bed and picked up the pale yellow rotary phone, dialing a number without thinking.

The phone rang four times before a groggy voice came on the line. "You know what time it is here? I need my beauty sleep. I just got back from Europe."

"Kyle, get your ass out of bed and on the computer."

There was a resounding thump and it sounded like the phone was dropped, then the shuffle of blankets before he came back on. "Shit, Rylee. Sorry, I'm going, just give me half a second."

"Tell him to put some clothes on," Liam said.

I put a hand over the receiver. "How do you know he's naked?"

"I can't hear the rustle of clothes."

Shit, I didn't realize Liam's hearing was *that* good. "Kyle, throw some shorts on."

Another rustle and then the sound of bare feet slapping on cheap linoleum floors.

"How did you know I was home?"

I snorted. "Agent Valley told me he sent you home after you nearly crapped your pants when the Beast made his appearance at the police station."

He cleared his throat and Liam leaned forward. Static, loud and crunchy, filled my ears. I pushed him back. "Too close." I mouthed at him. Technology and supernaturals never did go hand-in-hand, but with Liam it seemed even worse. Like the combination of werewolf and Guardian made him extra difficult around technology.

"Kyle, have you got all the Arcane Arts files?" I was banking on this actually.

"Um. Yeah. But I'm not supposed—"

"See what we've got on unicorns in the Pacific Northwest." My gut twisted just saying the words. Never in all my years knowing what the supernatural was had I shared so easily with a mere human. Not even with Liam.

The click of fingers on a keyboard. "No, nothing in the Pacific Northwest. Wow, but would you look at—"

"No, don't look at anything else or you'll be nothing more than a smear of shit on the wall if Valley catches you."

"Wait, I thought you were working with him?" Kyle's voice rose in pitch until it was a mere squeak.

"No, I'm not. But your ass belongs to me, not him."

His swallow was audible. "Right. Anything else?"

"Can you look up sub-species? Like, if I ask for anything with wings?"

Liam nodded in approval, and then stood and went to the door, opening it. As Kyle searched for me, I turned to see Dox standing in the doorway, a glower on his face, the silver piercings in his lip, eyebrow, and ears standing out even more in the morning light.

Two things happened at once. With a grumble Dox, tossed me his truck keys. "I can't damn well let you go on your own. But you have to listen to me, when we get there. You have to trust me when it comes to my own kind."

I gave him a sharp nod and Kyle spoke softly in my ear.

"Rylee, you aren't going to believe this."

Contrary to what Kyle thought, I knew that I would believe it. And knowing how the world was when it came to me and mine, whatever 'it' was wouldn't be good.

I was right; it wasn't good, not by a long fucking shot.

# 8

I hung up the phone, plans already whirling through my mind. As difficult as it might be, there were going to be no surprises this time around. Just a simple, straightforward salvage. Before I could tell Dox and Liam what Kyle had shared, the phone rang. I scooped it up, thinking the kid had forgotten something.

"What did you forget?"

A low chuckle whispered through the line and I recognized Doran's charming tones. "Rylee, I need you to swing by my place before you leave on this blind salvage of yours."

"Doran? What are you talking about? The salvage is on this side of the Veil, I don't need extra help."

He laughed again, any reluctance he'd shown earlier in the bar completely gone, and more than a hint of his old confidence rolling through the phone line. "Rylee, you need to come see me, because I just found out something rather interesting about you, something you are going to want to know."

"Yeah, like what?"

The bastard hung up on me. Damn him, he knew me too well for my liking. I hung up the phone and turned to see Dox and Liam waiting on me. Liam spoke first.

"You think he's bluffing?"

I shook my head. "No, I don't. We'll go to him, but we'll make it quick."

Dox let me drive, since I was the one Tracking and could make adjustments as we went. That, and he didn't look to be doing all that well. Much as he'd agreed to come with us and to act as a guide and help, I was pretty sure he'd rather be anywhere else. I glanced over at him, took in the pale tones of his blue skin, not the bright vibrant blue that I was used to at all. Yeah, something was going on with him for sure and I couldn't help but think about what Doran had said. That Dox had been kicked out for being weak. If that was the case, Dox might be more of a liability than an asset.

Dox stared out the window and scrubbed a hand over his head. "What took the foal, do you know?"

"Kyle said that the only thing with wings big enough to carry the foal, and actually identified as using the Pacific Northwest would be a Roc." I took the turn onto Shawnee Road.

The ogre sucked in a sharp breath and turned his face to me, eyes wide with alarm. "Seriously? Please tell me you're joking."

I shook my head. Nope, I was not joking, though I wished I was.

Liam lounged in the back seat, as if he didn't have a care in the world. Of course, he still didn't have the full understanding of the supernatural to scare the shit out of him. He leaned forward, placing a hand on each of our seats.

"So what is a rock?"

Dox beat me to it. "Spelled R-O-C. Giant bird—"

"Like a Harpy?"

"No, bigger." I slid my hands over the heated steering wheel, pleased that the truck had started with the three of us in here. Though it had been questionable, the engine managed to turn over. I hadn't been looking forward to getting into ogre country on my own, or even with just Dox at my side. No way was I leaving Liam behind. Not this time. Not with a Roc and ogre country coming up.

"How big?"

I took a breath, but let Dox tell him. The ogre needed something to do other than fret about his people, who we would invariably run into.

"Dragon size, but without any real intelligence, which makes them easy targets for those who want to control them." Dox leaned back in his seat and closed his eyes. "They don't resemble a bird other than the fact that they have wings, which is what a lot of the old legends show them as. They're more like one of those flying dinosaurs the humans dig up."

Liam's eyes slid to half-mast. "Pterodactyls. Giant leathery wings?"

"Yeah. And they're mean bastards. They like to play with their food like a cat. But why the hell there would be a Roc in those mountain ranges bordering ogre territory? It doesn't make sense to me."

I checked my mirrors and changed lanes, scooting the truck around a tiny blue VW Bug. "Why not?"

Dox scratched at his chin. "They love heat, lots and lots of heat. Like a snake. I don't remember any

Roc's there when I still lived—" He cleared his throat. "Anyway, if there *is* a Roc hanging around, it can't be good. Someone has to be holding the reins in order for one to fly this far north. They're native to South America, if I remember correctly."

Liam snorted. "And that's all Kyle could find when it came to possible suspects?"

"The only thing in that area that has the strength to pick up a six-month-old unicorn foal and get away with it, *and* has the Pacific Northwest as a home territory, even if that is only a temporary home territory." I tapped my fingers lightly on the wheel. The fact that the AA division had even that much info on a creature that was not in its home territory . . . I wasn't sure how I felt about that. Either the AA division was getting better at finding supernaturals or they had someone helping them. I was betting on option number two. Not that it pertained to me and this particular case, but it was a good piece of info to tuck away. For later.

I Tracked the young foal as we drove to Doran's place. Still alive, her vibrant threads soothed the darkness that had begun to cling to me. The fears that were being dredged up, the uncertainties, and all that fate had been throwing at me lately. A vacation, that's what I needed after this. Maybe Liam and I could get away somewhere, use the Veil to make a jump somewhere warm and cozy. I snorted softly to myself. Yeah, I could hope for that all I wanted, but I had a sinking feeling that 'trials and tribulations' was going to be my middle name for a while.

Calliope's threads hummed through me, stronger now, spreading peace over my worries. A peace that previously I'd only ever found in Liam's arms.

Holding her threads lightly, I Tracked Pamela, and then Alex, and then Eve. Pamela and Alex were in high spirits, laughter dancing along the threads of their lives. I smiled and Liam caught the reflection of it in the rearview mirror. No words were needed. He gave me a wink and smiled back. I didn't let him see my face as I Tracked Eve. She was terrified, fear coursing through her threads strong enough to bring tears to my eyes. At least she wasn't hurt. Gods, let Pamela and Alex get there fast. For all that Eve was a Harpy, and deadly dangerous, she was still just a child. A juvenile at best.

Liam surprised me out of my Tracking.

"Tell me about the Veil."

I blinked several times, gathering my thoughts before I answered. We were still a ways from Doran, so I had time to try and explain this to him. "Well, it divides the world. Supernatural on one side, world the humans see on the other."

"Yeah, I've got that, but why don't all supernaturals reside there then? Why not just stay out of the humans' way?"

Funny how quickly he put himself separate from the humans. Good too, because he no longer was one of them. I'd seen people fight what they'd become and it had killed them in the end.

Again, Dox beat me to it, twisting in his seat so he could look Liam in the eye. "The Veil is a safeguard, somewhere we can go if we need to, but with so few entrances and so little room, it isn't feasible that all creatures live there. That was why it was created, at least from what I understand."

I shifted gears. "And it was never meant to be a place to live. Just a help. That's what Giselle told us. The problem comes when those who would fuck with the rest of it use it as a tool to hide the shit they do."

Liam took that in, his lips quirking to one side. "And what about the levels of the Veil? How many are there?"

Now that was a question I wasn't sure how to answer. I settled for brutal honesty. "I know that there are at least three because Jack talked about a Tracker named Brin getting dropped into the third level, where apparently a ghost took him. But I don't know how many Veils there are." I thought about what Agent Valley had said. "If what your ex-boss said has any bearing, then there are possibly seven. But I'm not sure how accurate a human's understanding of a prophecy would be."

Dox sucked in a sharp breath. "Shit. I didn't know that."

I glanced at him. "I don't think it's common knowledge. Giselle never spoke of more than the one Veil to us. And anything that slipped out of her mouth about deeper Veils I just chalked up to her madness."

We pulled up to the curb across from Doran's place and I waved a hand at the empty lot with the scrub brush and garbage floating through it. To the humans, it was nothing but a run down piece of property without even a house. A lone cactus grew on it, looking extremely forlorn. Pitiful. "Perfect example of using the Veil to hide yourself."

"So he's on the other side of the Veil?" Liam frowned out the window, his eyes narrowed.

I shook my head. "No. Not exactly. More like it's a mirror reflection of the Veil he's using to cover himself up. His home isn't truly on the other side of the Veil, and it isn't an entrance. Just a ruse to keep the humans at bay. It works pretty well too, by the looks of things."

Liam gave a slow nod. "Like being able to see the doorways that are hidden that lead through the Veil. They aren't on the other side, just a reflection? Is that how creatures that are as big as Blaz and this Roc go undetected, by using the Veil to hide?"

"You got it, wolf boy." I slid out of the truck, and the sharp winter wind bit at my face. Before I'd crossed the street, Liam had caught up with me. But Dox . . . I turned around. The ogre sat in the truck, staring straight ahead.

"What's with him?" Liam grumbled.

"I don't know. I suppose we'll find out soon enough. Hell, we've got a long enough drive, we'll need something to talk about." Oh, boy, not looking forward to that. If Dox was all wound up about going into ogre territory, I should probably have been shitting my pants. Dox was the most mellow, laid-back guy I'd known, human or supernatural. For him to be high-strung was making my skin itch.

"He'll tell us when he's ready," I said softly.

A laugh wrapped around us. "Don't count on it, Rylee."

Liam took a step and put himself just in front of me, a low growl escaping his lips, vibrating through him and into me. Yeah, the whole alpha thing was really going to have to be addressed soon or we were going to have problems. He had to let me do my job, regardless of how he felt about protecting me.

I did not need to add 'talk with Liam about not being such a pushy alpha' to my list of things to do. I stepped sideways so I could see Doran. And then I understood why Liam was pissed and I felt like a shit for thinking he was overreacting.

Doran wore an ankle-length wolf pelt that was fully intact, the wolf's head sitting on top of his. Grey fur dusted with red highlights here and there; it was a beautiful coat, but no doubt he wore it for a reason. As in he wanted to piss off Liam. And it was working.

"What the hell, Doran?" I shook my head at him. "You ask me to come here, and then you pull this shit?"

He grinned widely at me, flashing his fangs. "Whatever do you mean? It's cold out; I thought I'd wear something toasty and warm. You of all people should know how warm it is to be wrapped up with a wolf." He gave me a long slow wink and blew a kiss at Liam.

*Yeah, welcome back, Doran.* Whatever help he'd been, whatever changes I'd thought I'd seen in him, this was the Doran I'd first met. The shit disturber.

Liam vibrated beside me. "You blood-sucking piece of shit. You might have helped in the past, but we don't need your scrawny ass."

Liam grabbed my arm and started to drag me back toward the jeep. I knew what Doran was up to, and

I shouldn't have been surprised that it was working. Liam just wasn't used to this sort of manipulation. To be fair, the Daywalker had a talent for sure, and he could get me riled up with the best of them. "Liam, let me go."

He kept dragging me. Damn Doran for this, for forcing this issue. I pried Liam's fingers off my arm and jerked away from him. "I said, let me go!"

Eyes narrowing, Liam glared at me. Yeah, here we go, revert to past tendencies in three, two, one.

I lifted my hands in the air in mock surrender. "Go sit with Dox, I'll deal with Doran because apparently you are going to get sucked into his stupid games."

His face twisted up in a snarl. "Are you . . . dismissing me?"

Short and sweet. "Yes." I turned my back on him and walked toward an openly gloating Doran.

Watching her walk away from him . . . damn, it took everything he had not to grab her and throw her into the truck. Doran wasn't a physical threat to Rylee. No, that wasn't the problem.

What bothered his wolf was that Doran *liked* Rylee. The smell the Daywalker gave off wasn't quite lust, but close. Like a strong affection that could be more than what it was. And it reminded him of Faris. Which pissed him off and made controlling his wolf very, very hard.

It took everything he had to turn his back on them and stand there, breathing in the sharp cold air, clearing his nose of the scent of the Daywalker. He glanced over his shoulder once and caught Doran smiling at him, his eyes glittering with mirth. He turned away again. Shit, he hated that his rational mind claimed one thing, and . . . their footsteps crunched on the dirt as they walked away from him. With a growl he couldn't stop escaping his lips, he forced himself to walk normally to the truck, open the door without wrenching it off its hinges, and slide in the back seat.

"She'll be okay," Dox said. The ogre turned in his seat to look at him. Liam's jaw twitched, but he managed to keep his response civil. Which was more difficult than it sounded.

"I know." He slumped into his seat and passed a hand over his face. Never in his life had he felt so protective of someone. Sure, he'd always wanted to be the guy that people could depend on, but not like this.

"You've got to find a way to relax," Dox said, his seat creaking as he shifted his weight. "Or you're going to push her away. She's too damn strong to be with someone who can't let her be who, and what, she is. And she is one tough woman, used to taking care of herself."

That was exactly what he was afraid of. Rylee helped ground him and his wolf. Losing her was the last thing he wanted. He needed a distraction though, or he'd be back out of the truck and beating the shit out of Doran for how he smelled. Which was beyond ridiculous.

"Dox, why did you really leave your home?"

The ogre tipped his head back in his seat. "A lot of reasons."

"You know she's going to ask you about it on the way there. She won't let up until she gets what she wants." If nothing else, Liam knew that to be as certain as the sun rising each day. Rylee would never give up once she headed down a course of action. She didn't have it in her.

Dox turned so he could make eye contact with him. "She can try."

Oh, he had a feeling this was going to be another one of those epic Rylee road trips.

Just brilliant.

"I knew you'd pick me over the wolf." Doran reached for me and I pulled a sword from my back in a single fluid move. With a practiced ease, I swung it forward so that the tip rested in the hollow of his throat.

"Don't try to set us up against one another, Doran. You will always come second."

He smiled past me, and I knew, could feel him making eye contact with Liam. "Then why are you sending him to the truck like a naughty little boy?"

"Because I know you, and I know your games. Liam doesn't. Not yet."

Doran's eyes sparkled with laughter. "Oh, Rylee. You make me smile." His lips drooped. "But today, maybe neither of us will be smiling by the time this is all said and done."

Spinning on his heel, he strode toward the empty lot, disappearing when he stepped past the realtor's sign.

I glanced over my shoulder, but Liam had his back to me, hands on his hips, a visible tremor running across his upper body. Saying he was not happy would be a ridiculous understatement, but how did I get him to understand that there were times he needed to listen and times that I would need him to lead, and that today just wasn't one of those days? Not easy, not with the wolf in him clamoring to be a true alpha.

I followed Doran, stepping across the shimmer of the Veil's reflection into the unseen.

His house was a two-story adobe structure, multiple fountains, herb garden, and in general, quite nice. Swanky even, if I was recalling my first impression of the place right. The koi weren't swimming in the fountains, too cold was my guess; another gust of wind whipped my hair out around my face, obscuring my vision for a split second. Through the auburn strands I saw Doran slip the wolf cloak from his shoulders, revealing a much more demure outfit of trousers tucked into knee high leather boots and a loose fitting white shirt that was open at the throat. Very pirate of him.

Doran snapped his fingers over the fire pit and flames curled up toward his hand. Orange and red, there was a flicker of blue, and then a shimmer of all the colors in the rainbow before the fire went back to a normal setting of orange and yellow.

"Have a seat." He indicated to a bench carved out of what looked like the shoulder blade of some ginormous-ass animal.

"What is it?"

He glanced over, green eyes tracing the seat as if just seeing it for the first time, but his words had nothing to do with the seat. "Rylee, there has been a development with my ability to Read you. I can see flickers of what is coming your way."

I sat on the bench and rested my hands on my knees. "How is this even possible?" To say that I doubted him would be an understatement. Though I was beginning to trust him, I knew he had his own agenda. Anything even remotely vampiric always did. As an Immune, magic couldn't touch me, and those who could Read couldn't see anything about me, not my future, not my past, nothing.

He shrugged and then shook his head. "I think it has to do with taking your blood. Faris was able to give you some of his powers, from what you've said, and it looks like your blood gives me a glimpse into what is coming your way. If I'd known that was a possibility, I would have tried to Read you sooner."

I didn't say anything right away, the crackle of the flames the only sound. The scent of sage drifted over to me as the wind shifted. Glimpses of my future— only Giselle had done that for me in the past, reading my palms. Tracing what was coming on my skin like a road map. I'd never had anyone *Read* me before.

"And you think I need to know what you're seeing?"

His eyes softened. "Yes. This has happened for a reason. But, understand that what I can see doesn't really make sense. I'm not getting the full picture, just glimpses here and there. I think it's because it has been some time since I took blood from you."

I rubbed my hands on my legs, thinking fast. The thing was, any sort of heads up of what I might face would be of help. "Tell me what you see. It might not make sense to you, but it could to me."

He nodded and strode around the fire pit, the flames seeming to reach out to him as he passed. Crouching down right in front of me, he rested the backs of his hands on my knees and beckoned with his fingers. I put my palms against his, a whisper of electricity passing between us, as if I'd plugged directly into a wall socket. Not unpleasant, but not real comfortable either. The tips of his fingers pressed up against the pulse in my wrists, but he didn't grab me.

His eyes slid shut and his head dropped forward almost between my knees. "Your life will not be without trials. Ever. What is left for you is battle after battle. This will never change." A shiver ran through his body and seemed to course up through mine, sending gooseflesh up and along my arms. Fan-freaking-tastic. Just what I wanted to hear.

"The darkness is rising around you, surrounding you. But you have all you need to face it. You are going to lose people you love in these battles. There is no way around this."

I wanted to jerk my hands out of his, but held still. "I thought this was about me?"

He didn't answer my question. His fingers brushed along my pulse. "I see lights in the darkness, and fire. Your past and your present will collide with what is coming."

I stared at the top of his head, the black tips of his hair spiked in its punk-rocker style. And I wanted to believe that he was just making this shit up. But I felt the truth of it in my bones, as I did whenever Giselle had read my palms.

"Will I find this child in time?"

His fingers wrapped around my wrist and he slowly lifted his head, eyes meeting mine. They were filled with a sadness I could barely breathe past, and again he didn't answer my question but spoke words I could barely believe.

"You will love another."

I snapped my hands out of his and scrambled away. "Fuck off, that isn't funny, Doran."

He rocked on his heels as I skittered across the bench and got to my feet. My heart was out of control pounding. I didn't love anyone else, couldn't love anyone else. Liam was it for me and I knew that in my heart and soul. So why did Doran's words freak me out so badly? Will's eyes flickered across my mind and I pushed the image away. Nope, that so wasn't happening.

I shivered, cold to the bone as if the Hoarfrost demon and I had gone a second round.

"Rylee, I can't see who or what. Only that there will be someone else. Maybe not the great love that Liam is. But someone else." He shrugged, the strain of reading me visible in the tight lines around his eyes and lips.

I didn't want to hear anymore. "Anything pertinent to this salvage?"

He flashed me a grin, the other side of him showing back up. "You will have fun with the ogres. Don't let Dox tell you he knows what he's about when it comes to his own kind. He doesn't. Follow your instincts; you're more like an ogre in some ways than Dox." With a wink and a flourishing bow, he pointed to the road.

"Just like that, we're done?"

He stood back up, a decidedly wicked gleam flickering through his eyes. "I am more than happy to have you stay the night, Rylee. But I have a rule. Everyone who stays has to be naked and covered in coconut oil. To be fair and all."

"I mean about the salvage, you called it a blind salvage, but the foal isn't on the other side of the Veil." Gods, he had a one-track mind. Typical man, typical bloodsucker.

He pursed his lips. "You still owe me a kiss. Maybe I should trade it in for the answer?"

Really, a one-freaking-track mind. "Seriously? You don't want to save that for a more humiliating time?"

He threw back his head, laughing uproariously. With what looked like great difficulty, he pulled himself together. "You're right, I'll save it. Maybe for when Liam is on the brink of snapping."

Fuck, and he would do it too. Back to the point at hand, though. "Blind salvage—spill your guts."

He walked toward me, stopping only when we were a bare inch apart. Just like on the rooftop. He was only a little taller than me, so he couldn't pull off looking down his nose at me like Liam did.

"This salvage is not what you think it is. That's what I can feel. You think you see the truth of it, but you don't. There are forces I can't divine, forces that are blocking me from seeing what they wish to hide.

But the glimpses I've caught make me think that you could be tangling with a demon again. A Unicorn foal would be a perfect sacrifice . . . ."

His lip ring glinted in the firelight as he spoke and I found myself staring at it as I absorbed his words.

Doran lowered his voice. "Perhaps you would like me to cash in my kiss now?"

My eyes snapped up to his, my mind about as far from *that* as it had ever been. "I'll pass."

"Too bad."

"Goodbye, Doran."

I stepped back from him and spun on my heel. Jogging down the driveway, I passed through the mirrored reflection that kept his home hidden from human view and back onto the human plain. Demons, damn, lately it seemed to be always coming back to those nasty fuckers. Hoarfrost demon, then the prophecies about Orion, and now this. If this salvage was because a demon had snatched the foal, there wouldn't be a lot of time to get her back alive.

With a sacrifice, there would be some sort of time period that would have to be perfect. If I could figure that out, I would know how much time we had to succeed in getting Calliope away. I wouldn't think about the other alternative.

I jogged around to my side of the truck and slid in, rubbing my hands together. Whatever conversation the two men were having ended the second I opened the door.

I turned the key over in the ignition. "Don't let me keep you two hens from gossiping."

Dox chuckled, but it was strained. Forced. I lifted my eyes to Liam's in the rearview mirror, but there was no hint there, either. What the hell had they been talking about? Curiosity flowed through me. I couldn't help it.

"What?"

Dox cleared his throat. "I was waiting for you to finish telling Liam about the Veil."

A blatant lie, his face flushed up and he wouldn't meet my eyes. Interesting. But I went along with it.

"Okay, where do you think we should start?" I checked the traffic as I pulled off Shawnee Road onto the main drag. Tracking Calliope, I focused on her, let her threads pull me in her direction.

Dox clapped his hands together, like the sound of two giant meaty symbols clashing. "You know about using your second sight to part the mirrored reflections?"

Liam nodded. "I figured that out pretty early on."

Yup, that had been the first time I'd tried to leave him behind. It hadn't worked so well.

"Well, the thing with the Veil is, a human has to use a physical entry point in order to cross over. And just because they use that point, doesn't mean they will actually be able to cross."

Liam started to lean forward and the engine sputtered. He moved as far back as he could and the truck continued on.

"What do you mean? Like it won't always work?"

Dox shook his head. "Not for a human, no. The entry points for crossing the Veil always work for a supernatural, but not so much for a human. Actually, not so much for a human ever unless—"

"Unless they're holding onto a supernatural?" Liam offered.

Again, Dox nodded. "Right, and those physical entry points can be anywhere, though it might seem like there are a lot, there aren't more than one or two per state."

It was my turn to do a jaw drop. "One or two per state? Holy shit sticks."

The ogre laughed and leaned back in his chair. "Yeah, that I know of."

"What, you've got a map of entry points?" Now I was asking the questions. As well as Giselle had trained me, and for all my experience, I still had a lot to learn, because, damn, every time I turned around, there was something new. Something dangerous and brutal. I could only imagine how Liam felt being thrown into the deep end of the pool with me when even I floundered. Then again, so far he'd handled it as if it were just another day at the office.

Liam reached forward, his fingers just brushing along my shoulder. "You think Milly has a map of the entry points?"

"Hell, I hope not," I said, though I knew there was a good chance she did. Would explain how she was able to move around, even before she learned to jump the Veil.

"Speaking of her, what the hell happened with you two?" Dox again shifted his weight, long legs obviously cramped even in his big truck. I was saved from having to talk about Milly by a red light pinging on the dashboard. I tapped it with one finger.

"We're running low on diesel. I'll take the next exit." I flicked my blinker on, checked my mirrors and pulled off the interstate. The thing was, Milly was on my shit list, and nothing could change that. There would have to be an absolute miracle for her to no longer be on the wrong end of my sword. Yet even with that, with my resolve to end things with her, it still hurt me. Made me vulnerable to her. More than anything, I was happy to have dodged that particular conversation. Much as I hated her now, Milly had been my closest friend at one time. Had been like my sister. Which I had no doubt was why when she betrayed not only me, but Giselle too, the rage she inspired in me was like nothing I'd ever felt before. Love and hate, so entwined in me when it came to Milly, that it was like a physical pain. One I avoided as much as possible.

Fuelling up didn't take long, and then Liam offered to drive. Dox, laughing, shook his head. "Don't think that's a good idea, man. You need to ride in the back seat, as far from the engine as possible."

With a frown, Liam climbed back in, but he didn't argue. I stretched my back and legs before getting into the truck on the passenger side, feeling my vertebrae pop and my muscles protest the movement. My body was pretty much all healed up, but sitting for so long made me stiff.

Dox started the truck, the engine turning over twice before it coughed to life.

"Now, you were about to tell me what happened with Milly?"

Shit.

"I don't want to talk about it." I slumped in my seat like a sullen child and closed my eyes.

"I didn't ask if you wanted to talk about it. I asked what happened."

Liam made a choking sound in the back seat and I whipped around to see him looking at me all too innocently. I narrowed my eyes at him, but he just smiled.

I shifted in my seat so that I could stare out the windshield. "She tried to kill Alex, Eve, and Liam, and succeeded in killing Giselle."

Dox's hands tightened on the steering wheel. "Giselle's gone?"

I lifted my feet and set them on the dash. "Yeah. Just before I headed to London."

"Shit! Rylee, I didn't know. How is it that Milly's still alive then?" He knew me well enough, apparently.

"She's pregnant," I said, softly.

"Oh."

That one word encompassed it all. I couldn't kill her while she was pregnant or I'd be breaking my oaths. And as much as she might be willing to do that, I wasn't.

"Since we're spilling secrets," I said, spinning in my seat and setting my feet against the middle console. "Why did you get booted out of ogre country? Or is Doran wrong about that?"

The ogre's mouth thinned to a tight blue line. Hmm. Interesting.

"Hello, Dox? I asked you a question." I tapped a foot on the console, but his hands just tightened on the wheel and his mouth thinned even more, if that was possible.

"I told you about Milly."

He hunched his shoulders. "This is different."

"Really, why?"

"Because it is."

Gods, childish much? "Is it going to affect this salvage, the reason you were booted out?" I needed to know at least that much.

He tipped his head a little to one side, and the tip of his tongue flicked out and touched the ring through the middle of his lower lip before he answered. "It shouldn't."

Well, as long as he was right, I couldn't get too pissy. I let him be. I could see that there was going to be no convincing him at this point to say anything more than he already had. Maybe later. Though, if what Doran had said was true, and Dox had been kicked out because of some perceived weakness, we could actually have more difficulty with him along for the ride than if we were going in alone. Liam chilled in the back seat, his hand resting on the console next to mine. Not touching me, just being there.

"What did Doran tell you?"

I didn't want to keep anything from Liam, but telling him that Doran thought I was going to fall in love with someone else was not high on my list of priorities, even if it was weighing on my mind as heavily as the salvage.

"He thinks that there might be a demon and a sacrifice involved."

Liam groaned. "Haven't we already done this once?"

"Yes, so we should be fucking amazing at it this time, don't you think?"

Dox barked out a startled laugh. "You're kidding, right?"

I shook my head. "Nope. But then, Doran could be wrong."

Liam rubbed his hands together, and then leaned back in his seat again. "Anything else?"

Almost like he knew I was holding back. So I spilled about everything else, about how Doran could read me a little, about some of what he thought he saw for me.

About trying to kiss me. Liam's jaw tensed up with that. "And?"

I frowned at him. "And what? I didn't kiss him. He's saving it so he can royally piss you off at some point."

Dox snickered. "Yeah, that sounds like Doran."

Liam didn't ask anymore questions after that, thank the gods, and since I wasn't much of a talker and Dox didn't seem inclined to encourage a conversation, there was pretty much radio silence. And in the most literal sense too, since the radio wouldn't work with the three of us in the truck.

At least there were no rampant wolf farts. A twinge settled around my heart at the thought of Alex. I missed him, missed his constant companionship; even Liam couldn't really compete with that, though I'd never tell him. Alex, there had been something special about him from the beginning, even if I'd been loathe to admit it.

Hell, I missed Pamela, even though in some ways it would be easier to do this salvage without the whole freaking three-ring circus. I missed them. And I was worried as hell about Eve.

Fuck it, Doran was right, my life was a big ass mess of trials. I wanted to cross my fingers that he would be wrong about them never ending.

Every few hours Dox and I swapped out driving so that we didn't have to stop. Though Calliope's threads hummed along nicely, I was worried. A demon sacrifice, if Doran was right, might mean we had a little time. If it was just the Roc, we had zero time. And if there was something in between that had taken the Roc over *and* was trying to raise a demon, we were royally screwed. For some reason, I was betting on the last scenario. It was just a matter of who was controlling the Roc, and who was trying to make a sacrifice to a demon and why.

Easy. Right.

I dozed off and on, and when I was awake, I watched Liam in the reflection of the windows.

I could see he was bothered by what I'd told him about Doran. Or maybe he sensed that I'd held back from him. Hell, maybe I should tell him. Then again, if I did and he had a meltdown, I would be the one dealing with it. And for all I knew, Doran was just dicking around with me. Which wouldn't totally surprise me. And the last thing I needed was Liam in meltdown mode in the middle of a salvage that likely involved a demon.

No, this was one secret I was keeping to myself.

A full twenty-four hours we drove—and with no major catastrophes. Of course, I was expecting something. After the car chases in Europe, I couldn't help but keep checking behind, waiting for someone to throw a spell at us from a passing vehicle. The fact that nothing happened made me, at best, suspicious.

Dox pulled off the interstate at the border range of the Cascades. "This is where ogre territory starts. From here on in, there are a few rules you both need to follow."

He turned the engine off and turned in his seat to face us. This was a lecture I hadn't been expecting.

"Don't challenge anyone. No matter how much you want to. Challenges can be taken up by a whole Gang. Meaning if you challenge one, you are challenging all of them."

"Fabulous," I muttered.

He glared at me. "Don't lip off. Respect is earned here. Though I doubt you'd get it even if you wiped out an entire Gang. In an ogre's eyes, you two are worse than humans. Supernaturals who can blend in with the rest of the world are not tolerated around here."

Liam shifted in his seat. "I thought we were just going to go in, quiet-like, grab the foal, and leave without the ogres knowing we were even here?"

Yeah, that's what the two men had discussed for the last hundred or so miles. Guerilla tactics that may or may not work. Likely wouldn't, in my humblest of opinions.

Dox shrugged. "Ideally, yes. But they have sentries and the minute they know we're here, they're going to be on top of us."

"Will they try to kill us outright?" I fiddled with the sleeve of my leather jacket, my mind racing ahead to all the possibilities.

His face was grim. "Yes."

"Then what does it matter what the niceties of your society are if we are going to have to fight our way through?" I snapped, irritated that he would stop us to tell us meaningless shit. Although Calliope was still alive, I could feel the pressure of time running out weighing down on me. Like a sixth sense, I knew we had to get to her soon or it would be too late.

It was then, staring at Dox, that I realized he was scared, and he was covering it by telling us whatever he could. A curl of pity bit at me, but I pushed it down. Dox was here to help us and pitying him would get us nowhere.

He stared at me. "Because IF you can earn their respect, they'll help us. And if we really are dealing with a Roc and a demon sacrifice, we are going to need their help. All that we can get."

"That's a mighty big if," Liam said, his tone dry.

Dox slammed his hand on the steering wheel. "If a Roc took the foal, we are going to need their help. Besides, the Roc will live on the highest peak around here, if my memory serves me right about the beasts, which would mean it is on Mt. Hood."

It was my turn to get snarky. "If it's that damn simple, then let's just go to Mt. Hood. What's with all this posturing shit?"

Dox glared at me. "At the base of Mt. Hood is where the different Gangs meet to fight and . . . mate . . . on every full moon."

I didn't have to ask him if it was a full moon. I knew it without even looking it up. How? Because that's just the way my life went.

Dox took a deep breath, maybe seeing me get the implications of what we were dealing with. "Which means we will have to go through all of them to get even close to Mt. Hood. And a full moon, when else would be a good time for a sacrifice?"

I let out a groan. I'd kinda been hoping I was wrong. This was fantastic, just what we needed. I Tracked Calliope, to be sure she was still with us. The fact that she was still alive told me the Roc was certainly not working on its own ideas. A steady hum of uncertainty had started up in the foal, making my skin crawl with her growing fear. Whatever was happening, it likely wasn't all that good. On an impulse, I Tracked the Roc as a species, felt the threads of them tangle around Calliope, and then Tracked ogres as a species, ignoring Dox beside me. The threads of the three types of supernaturals intersected with a precision that made me want to puke.

Liam held up his hand. "Wait, how can a Roc go unseen if it's so damn big? I know Blaz has his own magic, is the Roc the same?"

Dox spoke before I could. "Likely whoever is running the show has folded the Veil, like at Doran's house. The humans just won't see it. Nice and simple."

Time to get this conversation back on track. "Dox, you're telling me there's no back door? No way in that you could find for us?"

He scrubbed his hands over his head, rubbing vigorously. "I might be able to get some help. Maybe. But the triplets are a long shot. As in betting on them will either be a windfall or will wipe us out."

Liam's eyes met mine, and I nodded. There was no other choice. I knew when we were outnumbered and out-manned; I knew I was no freaking superwoman who would swoop in and save the day. "Dox, whatever help you can find for us, do it. It isn't just the foal's life on the line, but Eve's too. And if there really is a demon involved, maybe more than that." Not to mention all three of our lives. But that was our choice, to be here and put our lives on the line for the sake of two children who needed us.

He gave a sharp nod, started the truck, pulled an illegal U-turn, and got back on the interstate. "Portland it is, then."

With each mile marker we passed, the tension in the truck grew until I choked on it. I rolled the window down, breathing in the deep sharp bite of the west coast winter. The air was humid, not unlike London, and rain spattered down. I lifted my face to it.

"Roll the window up," Dox snapped.

"Chill out," I snapped back, leaving the window down.

"Roll it the fuck up! If we're anywhere close, an ogre can smell the difference between human and supernatural. They don't have to see us to know that we are trespassing on their territory."

I rolled the window up. "You could have just said that, no need to get your extra large panties in a twist."

He glared at me and I glared back. Dox didn't scare me. The idea of *other* ogres gave me pause, though.

There was a hell of a lot I didn't know about that species, despite having Dox as a friend, despite having read everything I could find about them (which wasn't much) after meeting Dox for the first time. Despite everything that Giselle had taught me.

So we drove with the windows up and recycled air that very quickly smelled like corn chips and sweat socks. Liam's nose wrinkled up and his mouth clamped shut. Hell, how much worse was it for him with his extra sensitive nose?

Mid afternoon, and we were in the city proper. Clean and picturesque, overcast and dreary, Portland had a relaxed feel to it. Maybe it was the west coast, maybe it was the weather keeping everyone mellow, maybe everyone was taking an afternoon drag, but whatever it was, I could feel it under my skin as we drove.

Dox's eyes softened and his breathing, which I hadn't realized had been hitched and shallow, evened out. Apparently, it wasn't just me feeling the vibe the area was giving off. Liam though, I checked him out in the mirror If anything, he was on high alert. No relaxing there.

"Hey, you smoking something over there that we can't see?" I punched Dox lightly in the arm. He shook his head, his eyes never leaving the road.

"It's the smell of home." As if that said it all. Maybe it did; I couldn't wait to get back to the farmhouse, to my own bed and my own space. But I surely didn't look stoned when I was jonesing for my own bed. But if it was the smell of home, why was I picking up on it?

"It's a ruse." Dox glanced over at me. "Something to keep other supernaturals calm and mellow before—"

"Before they get slaughtered?"

He nodded and I took a deep breath. Clever, very clever.

Dox parked the truck at a pay parking lot, slid out of his side and looked around, like a seven-foot tall trying-to-be-subtle FBI agent. I slid out, checked my weapons, and Liam followed, checking his two blades and straightening his clothes. Around us were red brick buildings, each one no lower than three stories. Stamped concrete below our feet collected miniature rivers in the grooves with the steady rain that fell from the overcast sky. At least it wasn't snow.

"I'd like to go somewhere warm after this," I muttered.

"Mexico?" Liam's eyebrows quirked upward and I nodded.

"Yeah, Mexico, where I can just slowly roast in the heat."

Dox glared at us. "Shut up, you two. And don't speak unless you're spoken to."

I opened my mouth and he clamped a big hand over it. "I mean it, Rylee. Your mouth will get us killed without so much as a 'fuck you' slipping out of it. And if things go sideways, you will get the hell out of here. Understood?"

There weren't too many people I would let get away with man-handling me. Dox was one of them, Liam the other. And that about did up my tally of man-handlers.

Jaw tight, I gave him a stiff nod. Damn, I had no idea that Dox could be such a hardass. Even if it was kinda warranted. But if he thought I would leave him behind, for any reason, he didn't know me as well as he thought. I didn't leave my friends behind, not ever.

With long strides, Dox crossed the wide open courtyard that cut between the buildings. I scrambled to keep up, trying to take everything in, our feet slapping in the accumulated water on the concrete.

There were no humans around that I could see; maybe everyone really was on a doobie break. Or maybe it was just the steady rain. Or maybe it was something I hadn't quite put my finger on yet.

Liam and I settled into a jog, catching up to Dox as he rounded a corner and entered a second wide courtyard, this one with small metal trivets sunk at intervals in the ground. It looked like a setup for a fancy water fountain, but I didn't ask. Nope, I managed to keep my mouth shut. At the center of the courtyard, I could feel the difference in the air. I let my eyes droop to half mast, seeing the slightest of differences. This was not a mirrored reflection like Doran's house, this was an actual entrance to the Veil. In the middle of the gods-be-damned courtyard. The entrance point seemed to be one of the sunken metal trivets, rusted and bent; I would have bet good money that the humans didn't think it worked anymore.

Dox crossed the Veil as he stepped on the metal trivet, his body shifting between the human world and the supernatural. Liam and I followed.

Before we could finish crossing the courtyard, three ogres stepped out from the buildings around us, their skin shimmering in the rain. Each one of them towered over Dox, their faces bejeweled with gold. Bright gemstones pierced not only in their eyebrows, lips and ears, but were set in their cheeks and chins too. Dressed in deep brown leather pants, knee-high boots, and vests, their arms and much of their torsos were bare to the weather, but they didn't seem to mind. I caught a glimmer of steel when they moved.

Weapons, of what kind I couldn't be sure, but they were packing. And they were big boys.

More disturbing than the weapons though—they had violet skin, the skin that had covered the book of the Lost. The book Milly had stolen. A chill swept over me that had nothing to do with the inclement weather. Coincidence? I think not.

"Motherfucking pus monkey, will you look who it is," the largest of the ogres crowed, his hands on his hips, violet eyes dancing with laughter. I took that as a good sign. An ogre who was quick to laugh, that had to be good, right?

Dox though, he tensed. Maybe I was wrong.

My friend shifted his stance and lifted one big blue hand to the others, palm out. "You are hale, Tin?"

Tin gave a laugh. "We don't stand on puke drinking ceremony here, little man. You know that."

The second largest boy stepped up, eyes narrowing as he eyed me up. "You bring dinner with you? A little Tracker with a side of wolf. Not bad. Not the best combination, but I've had worse. Remember those smelly shit waffles that Sas brought home?"

It took everything I had to stand still, to not tell him where he could stuff his dinner and just how to season it, shit waffles or not.

Dox laughed, but I could hear the force in it. "Yeah, those were . . . not good. But don't tell Sas I said that, she'd skin me alive. And no, these are my friends. Rylee and Liam, meet the triplets. Tin, Dev, and Lop."

The second biggest one was Dev; the smallest one, who still stood at least nine feet, was Lop. Their eyes widened as Dox spoke, and it was Lop who blurted it out.

"Listen, dick nose douche biscuit you might be, but even you aren't that stupid, are you? You don't bring 'friends' here."

Everything in me wanted to let them have it, and it took all my willpower to keep my mouth shut, though I had no doubt Liam could hear my teeth grinding. Doran had said to follow my guts, and my guts were screaming at me to give these three a big freaking piece of my mind. The potty-mouth piece.

Lop took a step forward, his eye's widening as he took me, and all my barely contained fury, in. "Ah, look at the little Tracker. I think the white trash taint jockey wants a shot at us."

I sucked in a sharp breath, and then glared at Dox, but it was Liam who stepped forward. Yeah, neither one of us did so well with insults.

"What did you say?" His voice was a bare growl, his lips rippling as they pulled back over teeth that didn't look so human.

A swell of appreciation caught me off guard. In my life, there weren't a lot of instances where someone stood up for me. Usually, it was the other way around.

The triplets started to laugh, slapping their big hands on their thighs, like distant cracks of thunder. "Ooeee, I think the Tracker is banging the dog. What a slutty cock knob she is!"

I managed to get a hand on Liam before he took another step, but his whole body vibrated with anger. I knew what this was about; they were trying to get us riled up, to make us stupid. I'd dealt with supernaturals long enough to know that Dox was going about this the wrong way, even if it was his species.

Again, I looked at Dox, whose eyes were lowered. "You think submission is going to gain their respect? Look at them; we're a joke to them! *You're* a joke to them." I kept my voice as low as I could. "You think that they respect you because you won't defend yourself or your friends?"

Their laughter continued and I knew then that perhaps, as much as these were his people, Dox didn't understand them. This, in some ways, was more my world than his. He'd lived, hiding out and being 'human' for too long.

"I trusted you." I stepped out in front of Dox. "And now you're going to have to trust me."

His head snapped up, his eyes uncertain. But he didn't try to stop me.

That's what I'd thought.

With my boys at my back, I faced the triplets. "You three about done with your idiotic fuckery?"

Roaring with laughter, Dev actually went to one knee, holding his guts with one hand. "Oh, gods. What a pompous bitch nazi she is."

I sensed Liam moving without actually seeing it, and I held up my hand, staying him. This was a game, one I'd played before. Like a schoolyard stand off. I'd never lost one of those, and I wasn't about to start now.

I smiled at them and took a few steps closer. "Which one of you is the youngest?"

Without error, Lop and Dev pointed at Tin. He smiled at me, all big white teeth.

I beckoned him with one finger. "Mind coming a little closer, ass face?"

With three long strides, he was more than a little closer. He loomed over me, all ten-plus feet of him.

"Close enough for you, pie eating—"

I swung hard, the height perfect for an upper cut. My fist connected with his oversized man jewels, and he dropped to his knees, where I grabbed the ring piercing his eyebrows, pulling until blood dripped. "I am not a child, to follow the rules of your children. You are going to be polite to Dox, and you are going to be polite to me, or I will let my wolf rip your tiny little purple balls off and feed them to the Roc. You understand?"

He groaned, but I saw the flicker in his eyes, the twitch in his muscles. With a roar, he jerked backward, but I didn't let go, the rings tearing out above his eyes. He slapped his hands over the open wounds, covering his eyes as he bled.

"WHORING SLUT BLOSSOM!"

His brothers didn't join in the fight, which I was counting on. Instead, Dev rolled on the ground with laughter, while Lop leaned against a building heaving for breath, tears running down his violet-skinned cheeks.

"Tin, you're getting roasted by a WOMAN! A pussy is taking you out!" Dev shouted, his voice reverberating through the courtyard.

Dox moved up beside me. "You cannot do this, Rylee. You will have to kill him!"

I looked up at him. "I know. But I have no choice. They do not respect you, and I don't want you to have to kill one of your friends. So I will do it."

That seemed to get their attention. The two ogres stopped laughing, and Tin rubbed the blood from his forehead.

"What did you say?" Lop straightened.

I pulled a sword from my back and rolled it in my hand, the weight and feel of it a steady comfort. "I'm going to kill him. Will you respect me then?"

They went very still, like statues.

Dev shook his head. "Nah. We'd have to kill you then. And what the hell kind of fun is that?"

I frowned at him. "Are you three always this confusing?"

They shared a glance, then nodded and spoke in unison.

"Yes."

I glanced over my shoulder at Dox. His eyes were wide as he shrugged. "I played with them when I was a child; they were my only friends. They are the only ones I could bring you to that I didn't think would try to kill you outright."

"Bitch tore out my rings," Tin grumbled, swiping the blood from his forehead.

"Then don't talk to me like that. Only my friends get to call me names."

Maybe we wouldn't have gotten any further, except for one thing.

A new group of ogres showed up. And they were not laughing.

# 9

There were ten of them, and they had the deepest ebony black skin I had ever seen, and I'd tangled with demons. Their clothing echoed their skin, and it was hard to tell where cloth began and skin ended. Even their eyes were black, the depthless dark of a predator made to kill. The only splash of color, if it could be called that, was their weapons. They carried an array of weapons, but mostly spiked clubs that carried flecks of blood and flesh on them from whatever slaughter they'd come from. There was no time for thought, though, after the initial realization that the courtyard had just filled up with ogres.

They spared us and the laughing triplets no words, just launched an eerily silent, brutal attack.

Seven went for the triplets, and three came for us. Dox hesitated.

I didn't. I ran forward, ducked under the swing of the closest ogre and drove my swords upward, through his ribs and pierced his heart. As he fell, I spun toward the ogre going after Dox.

Liam's snarls ripped the air, and I thought at first he'd shifted again. But no, he stood, dodging blows, using his now seemingly puny blades against the ogre.

But he was doing damage, hamstringing the ogre, dropping him, and then slicing his throat. Fighters, the ogres might be, but they hadn't expected us to fight back, or to know how to fight.

The third ogre had Dox by the throat and had his back to me, which made killing him swift and easy. I slid my blade through his black hide from the back, again piercing the heart and dropping him instantly. Dox shook him off and scooped up the club the black-skinned ogre had held. A rage I'd never seen before clouded his eyes.

Screaming a wordless battle cry, he ran toward his onetime friends and the melee across the courtyard.

Apparently, we'd had the weaker ogres come for us, because the seven that were left were not dying so easily. The triplets had their backs against each other, their roars raised above the clash of the black-skinned ogres' clubs against the finer swords and axes that the triplets carried.

Three more of the black-skinned ogres peeled off and faced us. Close up, I could see the battle scars on their bodies, glimmers of faint silver against their skin. These were the battle-hardened warriors. Whoever we had faced first, I'd bet it was their introduction into raiding. Or whatever the hell this was.

Fan-freaking-tastic. A chill of fear swept me and I forced it down. Liam moved up beside me.

"Don't let them separate us," He growled.

Easier said than done. The ogre closest to Liam had a club with no spikes, just a solid smooth wood made for bashing, and he swung it hard, catching Liam in the stomach and sending him flying into a door on the building closest to us.

Which was rather bad because Liam didn't slide to the ground like I'd expected.

He disappeared.

Damn it! There had to be a doorway through there, and the courtyard was like the castle, a gods-be-damned gateway for travelling through the Veil.

But all that passed my mind in a flash, and then I was dodging two ogres and had no time to worry about Liam.

Liam hit the wall hard, the sounds of the fight ringing in his ears, but as he slid downward the world twisted, and then he was face down on a rocky beach, waves crashing up around him, startling him out of his momentary stupor.

"What the hell?" He pushed himself to his feet. The shoreline stretched for miles on either side of him, the smell of rotting fish and salt water filling his nose.

A tittering laugh spun him around. There, just behind him lay a stunningly beautiful woman, her blonde hair studded with pearls and curling around her heart-shaped face, with luminescent blue eyes that stared up at him. Her soft curves were bared to the open sky, but there was no shame in her. He blinked a couple of times and she reached for him.

"Stay with me, wolf." There was a command in her voice, a spell that stirred his wolf and the strength to deny her more than anything else could have.

He snarled, reached out, and grabbed her by the throat, lifting her high. She let out a scream, high-pitched and warbling, the lower half of her body coming clear of where she'd hidden it. From the waist down she was all fish, a pearlescent collision of scales, a rainbow of colors that danced in the lights.

"How do I get back?"

Fury lit her pretty features, twisting them into something ugly and monstrous. "The darkness will rise and he will swallow you, wolf. I see it, even now. You will die. And your death will be meaningless."

"TELL ME OR I'LL SNAP YOUR NECK."

She trembled in his hands, but he didn't care. With a thrust, she pointed at a rock, somewhat more square than the others, one that almost resembled a doorway.

With no ceremony, he dropped her to the jagged rocks and ignored her grunt of pain. Leaping past her, he didn't hesitate, but hit the doorway at full speed, expecting it to give way to him.

Thank the gods it did.


Liam was gone all of three minutes, but it was enough to land me in a seriously bad spot. The triplets had dispatched two of the interlopers, screaming obscenities at them the whole time. In another place, I would have been laughing at the ridiculous, imaginative cursing they came up with.

The triplets still faced two of the black-skinned ogres, and Dox and I faced three. But we'd been separated, and while Dox was holding his own, he didn't have the experience with a full-on fight to the death.

Bar brawls he was used to, but throwing drunks out of the Landing Pad was a hell of a lot different than trying to actually kill someone. This did not bode well for his long-term health. Hell, it didn't bode well for his short-term health.

I, on the other hand, had plenty of experience with this kind of fighting. Didn't mean I was faring any better against the big bastards.

A blunt club smashed into the ground, missing me by a single hairsbreadth. I rolled to my feet, then spun, arms outstretched at the full reach of my blade. I caught the ogre in the thigh, but while blood spilled, it was not a killing slice. Or even a particularly crippling one. But I couldn't focus on just one of them, I had to dance between the two, dodging blows without being able to get much in by the way of strikes of my own.

Fast, these ogres for all their size were damn quick: both with their swings and their feet. A booted foot swung at me, sweeping my legs out from under me. I hit the ground hard and rolled before a club could finish the job.

A snarling growl brought their heads around, but for all their speed, it was too late. Liam hit the one on the left from behind, driving both blades through the ogre's neck, nearly severing his head from his shoulders. While the second ogre was distracted, I drove both my swords through his guts, jerking my blades up and sideways in an attempt to bisect his body.

The black-skinned ogre slowly turned his head toward me. "Well done, Tracker." He slumped forward to his knees as I yanked my blades free.

I didn't stop to thank Liam for the help or acknowledge the ogre's words, just pointed at Dox. Liam leapt from the back of the ogre he'd nearly decapitated to hamstring the ogre facing Dox. As the black-skinned ogre fell with a scream, I cut it short with a hard strike from my own blade. His head rolled from his shoulders, the sightless eyes staring up at the rain clouds hovering above us.

"Now what?" Liam panted.

"Now we make some friends." I ran toward the battle, saw Tin go down to one knee, stunned from a blow to his head. As the ogre opposite him lifted his club to finish the job, I swept my sword upward, taking his arm.

The black-skinned ogre stood as the blood flowed, stunned long enough for me to drive the point of my second blade through his neck. Liam and Dox pinned the last ogre between them and the triplets. The triplets worked over the ogre with shouts of glee blasting the final black-skinned ogre, literally pounding him into a pulp, the spray of flesh and blood like some sort of macabre splatter paint art on the courtyard tiles. That wasn't what shocked me, though. Dox joined in, sprays of blood flicking up along his bare arms and face. He didn't seem to mind; no, he seemed to be enjoying himself.

I backed up, unable to stop the way my stomach rolled. Even for me, that was a bit much. Overkill suddenly held new meaning. I needed to stop their spree or I was going to lose my lunch.

"You boys done?" I calmly wiped my blades off on the few scraps of un-bloodied cloth left on the bodies. The triplets paused in mid-swing, turned, and stared at me and Liam. With grins splitting their faces, they rushed us, scooping up Dox in the process. I let Tin grab me in a crushing hug, seeing it for the camaraderie it was. Liam dodged their advances, lips curling in a snarl.

Lop gave him a salute. "Damn, that was some fuckery, wasn't it? We'd have been toasted without you three. Mind-blastingly brilliant, that was!"

Tin put me down and gave me a salute. "Respect, in our world, is earned. Tracker, you might be, but you fight well enough to have that much from us."

Dox let out a big sigh and clapped his hand on Dev's shoulder. Something in him had loosened, the fight bringing out the ogre in him. I wondered if he'd ever killed anyone before. I doubted it.

I sheathed my swords. "We need your help, if you'll give it."

They shared a glance. "Does it involve fighting?"

I nodded. "Sneaking past a number of Gangs and stealing a unicorn foal back from a Roc. Probably some high speed chases, knowing my luck. We need you to help us avoid as much detection as possible."

Dox's eyes bugged out, and even Liam lifted an eyebrow at me. They thought me reckless, but I knew when a gamble was weighted in my favor. These three might come off as goons, but if I remembered my recent studies correctly, now that they respected us, there would be no going back.

Dev, who turned out to be the oldest, put one hand on his knee. "And if you're wrong?"

I shrugged. "We'll find you someone, or something, to fight. Sound fair?"

He held his hand out and I set mine in it, shaking it as firmly as I could, considering the size difference. "We need to go now—"

Lop interrupted me with a swing of his ridiculously large hands. "Tonight, under cover of darkness is best. If your unicorn truly has been taken by the Roc, it roosts at night and getting past it will be easier."

Before I could answer, things took an unexpected turn.

A set of high-heeled footsteps turned us all to the side.

What had to be the most striking woman I'd ever seen swayed toward us. In heels, she was well over six feet, close to Dox's height. Her curves flowed from the gentle swell of her hips up to the rather large swell of her breasts. Sheathed in a cream-colored low cut, sleeveless dress, there was a lot of skin showing. Pale violet skin that peaked in a rosy color across her cheeks and the tops of her ample breasts seemed to have every male's attention. Even Liam's. Not that I could blame him. She really was stunning, right down to her violet eyes, which were shadowed with silver dusting that only accentuated the color. Crap, I suddenly felt how very tomboyish and unfeminine I was. This felt like standing next to Milly when she was all dolled up. I let out a resigned breath; at least I was used to it.

Her hair was done in tiny dreadlocks beaded up with jewels and stones that clinked lightly with each step she took toward us.

"You three boys, are you done with the fighting for today? And more importantly, are you ready to move on with the more interesting activities I have planned?" Her voice was husky and sensual and it curled around the six of us. There was magic in her voice that skittled off me, but I could sense it nonetheless.

The three triplets bobbed their heads, the crotch of Tin's pants swiftly tenting. That, along with the way they looked at her—I was guessing they weren't related, despite their similar skin color. Her eyes drifted over us, pausing on Dox. "And you brought me a new friend. Who is he?"

Dox cleared his throat. "Hello, Sas. It's been a long time."

Her eyes widened and she put a hand to her throat in an elegant gesture that I never would have applied to an ogre. Then again, I'd never met a female ogre. To say she surprised the shit out of me was an understatement.

"Dox." She breathed his name, and the triplets let out a collective groan. Dox smiled at her, but it was sad and wistful and full of a past I was pretty sure we didn't have time to dig into.

"You two, break it up. We have a job to do, remember? *Dox.*" I breathed his name out like Sas had. His body shook and he shot a glare my way.

"Rylee, we have to wait until dark, you heard them." He waved a hand at the triplets who were openly grinning now, their eyes darting from Dox to Sas and then to each other. An image of the five of them in bed together flashed through my mind, and I shook my head to clear it. Dox didn't seem the type, then again . . . Liam spoke in a low whisper that I thought only I could hear.

"Fighting and fucking, that's what you said, right?"

Dox at least had the grace to look chagrined. Apparently, he heard Liam too. "I can't, Sas . . . ."

She sashayed to him and ran a hand over his well-muscled blue shoulder. "Dox, tell me you're going to stay awhile. Please." Her eyes brimmed with unshed tears. Shit, I would have had a hard time saying no to her. There was a compulsion in her words, and her voice tugged at me. That wasn't magic; that was whatever chemistry she had going on. Liam put a hand on my lower back as if he knew.

Dox shook his head, disappointment etched into his face. "I can't. I have to stay with my friends."

Now *I* felt like a gods-be-damned ogre. What he said was the truth, but if the triplets were going to make us wait anyway, there was no reason to make Dox suffer. And suffer was the right word, he looked freaking miserable standing there, denying Sas.

With a laugh, Dev darted forward and scooped Sas up, taking her away from Dox, her long, bare legs dangling over his arms right under Dox's nose. But he never looked away from her face, nor did she look away from his. Shit on a sharp stick. Why did things always have to get complicated?

"We meet back here in three hours time. You should be fine, no other ogres frequent around here, and if they do, just punch them in the balls," Lop said, giving me a wink.

Dox stared after them, a longing in him that was plain as the three colors swirling in my eyes.

I was going to regret this. Damn it. "Go with them. You can make sure they keep to their word, and then we'll meet you back here." I pushed him after the brothers, and though he paused, he gave me a smile. Hell, Sas gave me a smile that made me blush with all it promised.

They welcomed him, arms slung over his shoulders, pulling him along with them. But more importantly, Sas welcomed him. She grabbed his face and kissed him long and hard and deep.

I gave a shiver, the pheromones they were throwing off suddenly making me horny. Not something I was terribly wanting in the middle of a salvage. Liam pressed himself up against my back as the ogres disappeared through one of the metal trivets that led to the gods only knew where.

Liam slid his arms around me and nipped the side of my neck, his body hard against mine. Fighting and fucking, the books weren't kidding. Whatever the ogres had going on, it seemed to be contagious.

"Let's go get something to eat—unless you want to follow their example?" Liam said, his voice softening even as he gripped me tighter.

I spared a glance for the bodies at our feet. Eat? No, not likely. Sex? Yeah, that's what I wanted, the ache in my body a steady thrum.

"Yeah. Let's get something to eat." I stepped away from him and over a puddle of blood and dark grey matter I chose not to identify even though my own brain did a quick comparison.

We slid back through the Veil over the metal trivet we'd come in by, and I crouched beside it to get a better look. Anything to distract me from what had just happened. The trivet was indeed not functioning, which was apparent by the sudden spout of water around us from all the other miniature spouts. Clever, very clever. No doubt the triplets were assigned this area to keep the humans from it, maybe even direct them back if they accidently stepped through. No, I knew that wouldn't be what happened. If a human stepped through, either they'd be killed or sold into some sort of slavery. At least, that is what the books on ogres I'd found had called it. The description, though, had been less like slavery and more like bondage.

I shook it all off and headed toward the truck. There were a few humans wandering about now; the rain had slacked off and apparently that was enough to draw them out into the weather.

Back at the truck, we cleaned up, getting the worst of the blood and gore off—meaning it wasn't obvious unless you looked *really* close. Liam brushed a strand of my hair back and tucked it behind my ear, his eyes lingering on my mouth as if he were hoping I'd change my mind. I shook my head ever so slowly. I wasn't an ogre, and now that whatever pheromones had been floating around had eased off, I could think more clearly. I couldn't go from fighting to sex in the space of a few heartbeats. "Do you smell coffee?"

His eyes widened. "You're asking *me* if I smell coffee?"

Around the corner was indeed a small coffee shop, and within ten minutes I had a hot raspberry tea cupped in my hands. Liam had two sandwiches and a large coffee.

"You need to eat," he said between sandwiches.

I glared at him and sipped my tea. "You don't find this weird?"

He shrugged and took a bite out of his sandwich, answering around it. "You and weird are tight like a fat kid in spandex. I'm getting used to it."

I burst out laughing, stunned at the unexpected joke. "Yeah, I guess you're right. But even for me, going for tea after a fight like we just had is a bit much."

He popped the last of the first sandwich into his mouth and leaned back. "I'm not the one to talk about normal, not anymore. Besides, there was another option." His lips tipped upward and his golden eyes began to dilate. Heat flared between us and the lingering effects of whatever pheromones Sas had been throwing off reared up. He slid his hand under the table and up my thigh, massaging as he went.

I shook my head, took a deep breath, and pushed his hand back. Nope, not going there. At least, not today. "Ease up, after the salvage."

The coffee shop was busy, humming with people, and I'm going to blame our stupidity on that. If you'd asked me, I would have told you that with that many humans around, another supernatural wouldn't have shown up. Certainly not a supernatural we both hated. Not one that I had told on more than one occasion that I would be removing her head from her shoulders ASAP.

Milly slid into a chair at the table next to us, a drink in her hand. Frozen, that's what I was, and Liam seemed about as stunned as me, his eyes widening and jaw dropping. Her brown locks flowed down over her shoulders, the bump on her belly the obvious show of her budding motherhood. Green eyes regarded me with no malice, but with a soft sorrow that ate at me; damn, she knew my weaknesses. Liam's hands clutched the table, shaking it with the force of his fury. Not good, this was not good at all. Three seconds. That's how long I was betting she had before he strangled her in front of all these humans.

"Liam, believe it or not, I am happy that Rylee brought you back. What I did, I did because I had no choice. But if I must, I will hold you down with a spell. Please don't make me do that. It will scare the humans, and if you two are truly on a salvage, the last thing you need is human interference by way of a police tail. Or worse, your old boss showing up. I've heard that Agent Valley is hoping to keep tabs on you, perhaps trying to get you to work for him again." Milly took a sip of her drink, and I just sat there and stared at her. Surely I'd drawn a smash to my head in the fight and this was some semi-conscious waking dream.

But no, the tremor in the table, the uncertainty in my gut, the smell of Milly's rose perfume. Too real, this was happening whether I liked it or not. Liam held himself together, but the wolf was strong, and I could feel the rise of it along my skin like a forest fire gathering speed. We had to get out of here. I made a move to stand and Milly lifted her hand, palm out.

"Please, I know that you owe me nothing, but give me a moment to explain. Things have changed for me."

"What are you doing here?" I managed to get out, lowering myself back into my seat. There had to be a good reason she was here, putting herself and her baby directly in harm's way. With her, there was always a reason; the whole problem was just figuring out if the reason she gave would be the truth or another lie.

"I am trying to keep you safe. That has been my goal all along. Though you would be hard-pressed to see that, I suppose." A tear slipped from her eye and trailed down her cheek, and I fought the twist of pity in my guts, seeing her cry. The pity was followed quickly by a spurt of anger I didn't bother to repress.

"Enough of the fake waterworks."

She nodded and wiped her tears away, her voice soft. "I have made a mess of things."

"You can fucking well say that again." I leaned back in my chair, to get a better look at her, but also to give me room to move. If she made one flinch toward Liam, I was going to tackle her. "Do you feel bad at all about killing Giselle, about almost killing Eve and Alex? About taking Liam captive and essentially trying to kill him by letting his wolf take over?"

"For all those things and more, yes, I grieve every waking moment. But I can change none of it; my soul was sold long ago, Rylee. Long before we ever met. There has been very little in my life that was because I decided it. Ethan was one of my few choices, and I loved him fiercely for that." She lifted her eyes to mine, shimmering with intensity, as one hand dropped to cup her belly, where she carried Ethan's child. I could see her desire to make me believe her one more time. But that wasn't the worst of it.

I wanted to. I wanted so badly to have her back in my life, to believe that all she had done wasn't really her. Yet I knew that for what it was—a childish wish for a time long gone.

"Why would I believe you now? After everything you've done?"

"Because in my own way, as much as I could, I have been trying to thwart him and he has found out. It is why I asked you to protect my child. I am only good to him as long I carry my baby, for he seeks to kill my child, to use my baby's blood to help him free himself." Her hand slid around her belly again, cupping it protectively.

Liam slid his chair backward, his breathing evening out, and a surge of pride whipped through me. Gods, he *was* a man to be proud of. The fact that he'd held himself together, when she sat within inches of him, was beyond what anyone else could have handled. "Who are you talking about?"

If I'd thought I'd understood Milly and her treachery, if I'd thought I could pinpoint where she'd gone bad, where Giselle and I had fallen down, I couldn't have been more wrong. Of all the things I expected her to say, it was not his name. The world spun out from under me as the name she spoke rocked it.

Not Faris, as I'd thought she'd spit out. Not even Berget, as I was thinking perhaps it could be.

"Orion."

# 10

"**Y**ou do not remember meeting him, do you?" She turned in her seat, and crossed her legs.

"I've never met Orion; I'd think I'd damn well remember that." I glared at her, how stupid did she think I was?

"The day you fell down the stairs . . . ."

"What of it?" I vaguely recalled what she spoke of. I'd fallen down the stairs not too long after Giselle had taken me on as a ward, and when I'd come to, I'd been in the hospital, Giselle at my bedside with a new wayward soul in tow—Milly.

"You never fell down the stairs. Orion had me erase the memory of how you met me—and of meeting him, of meeting a semblance of him anyway. He can't take form here yet, he is still trapped, thank the gods. But yours and Giselle's memories—both—he had me take." The tears flowed freely down her face. "He will kill me no matter what I do now, so I feel no obligation to keep his secrets anymore. And you need to know what you're up against. I can help you, if you'll let me. The plans he has woven are thick; he has help in more places than even I realized. But I swear I will do all I can to help you stop him."

I shared a look with Liam, tried to discern his thoughts. But his eyes were unreadable, hooded and yet, still burning with intensity.

"So because you aligned yourself to a demon, and now find yourself on the outs with him, we are supposed to feel sorry for you?" Liam's question was ground out between his teeth.

"No, I never aligned with him. My father sold me to him when I was but a young girl, not long before I met Rylee and Giselle."

I was having a hard time swallowing this new side of her, as much as a part of me wanted to believe she had never turned on us—or at least that there had been more reason than her own selfish whims—there had been too many lies. Too much death. At any point, she could have told me, and I would have fought to the death to free her. But she hadn't.

I stood, indecision rippling through me, forcing the words out. "We have to go."

"Wait, take this." Milly held out a small, brown canvas bag. I took it, carefully, and peered in. A shimmering red and black stone the size of a golf ball lay in the bottom of the bag. Spikes erupted out of every piece of it, like a porcupine on steroids, some straight, some twisted like corkscrews. The main stems were black, the tips red, as if dipped in blood.

"What do I want with this?"

Her lips trembled. "It's a demon stone; Orion uses it to compel me. Destroy it, if you can."

Her eyes never left my face, and I gave her a slow nod. That much I could do for her and not feel as if she were manipulating me.

I backed away from her for two steps before turning to leave. Liam went first, every line of his body taut with pent up anger. The humans moved out of his way, sliding away from him, their eyes following him as one would a stalking beast. Smart humans.

"They will use the foal as a sacrifice to raise Orion. That is their plan. You can stop them. The full moon is the catalyst. Tonight, you have until tonight."

Milly's words stilled my feet as nothing else could.

She went on. "You have time yet, but not much. I tell you this because as long as he is trapped within the deep Veils, he can only harm me. But if he is brought through physically to the point of crossing fully into our world, he will be able to harm my child. To spill my baby's blood and seal his own life here."

"You can't believe her, Rylee." Liam grabbed my arm and dragged me out of the coffee shop, the whispers and stares of the humans following us. I let him drag me. I wasn't sure I could have left of my own volition, not with her words ringing in my ears. The thing was, I still *wanted* to believe her. Her green eyes met mine, pled with me as Liam shoved the swinging door open and pulled me through after him. What she was saying aligned with what Doran had already told me. Only now she gave me the details. Orion was the demon, not some nameless demon like the Hoarfrost, but Orion.

The demon included in the prophecies that had me fighting him to the death over the potential end of the world.

Even more than before, we had to move our asses. If Milly was right, Calliope had very little time. If she was right, a demon that I was destined to meet on a battleground somewhere at a future date was about to be pulled through the Veils and into our world. Just peachy.

We all but ran back to the courtyard. We were early, but there was nowhere else to wait for Dox and the triplets. Nowhere else to go. Damn it all to hell and back! I paced beside the truck, my mind racing.

Hours, it would be hours before Dox and the triplets were back, depending on their sexy romp with Sas, no doubt, and whether or not they were having a good time.

Liam grabbed my arms and stared into my eyes. The man knew me too well, read my mind before I'd really even formed the thoughts myself. "We can't go without them, Rylee. It would be suicide; we barely managed the ogres that came after the triplets and us. And that was with help."

I stared up into his gold eyes. "If Milly is right, then we're dooming the world to a demon prophesied to take it over. There isn't enough time. We can't wait for them to finish their sex antics." I didn't jerk out of his arms, didn't shove him away. I laid my fingers on his forearms. "You know I'm right, or you wouldn't be trying to convince me otherwise."

He let go of me. "You don't know that. We don't know if she was telling the truth or not."

I bowed my head, feeling the weight of everything I'd learned in London, of the prophecies and the secrets. Maybe this was what they had been pointing to, that I had to stop Orion from using the foal to come through the Veils. Shit balls. I Tracked Calliope, just as a spike of fear sliced through her and into me. Intense and teeth rattling, I clenched my hands tight, digging my fingernails into his forearms. Whether or not Milly was right, and my gut said she was telling the truth for once, it was time to finish this salvage.

"I'm going. Are you coming with me?" I lifted my head to see Liam shake his head, his eyes full of worry. A flicker of what he could do danced through his eyes. We both knew he could pin me down, hold me to prevent me from moving, and I wouldn't try and kill him. He could stop me if he really wanted to.

"This is a bad idea."

"You got a better one?" I pulled the truck keys out of my pocket and headed toward Dox's baby.

"We wait for Dox and the triplets. That's a better idea." He still got into the truck, slid into the backseat with only the muttering to show he wasn't behind this idea 100 percent.

Calliope's fear spiked again, and I backed the truck out of the parking lot, following the threads of the foal's life. Leaving without Dox and the triplets wasn't really a choice. Calliope was in trouble, and a demon summoning was no small thing to ignore when you knew when the deadline was. Mere hours were all we had.

Fuck, why did it have to be *this* that Milly told the truth about?

"Maybe she believes it, Rylee. Maybe this is a plan that Orion has put into place and he's using her and she doesn't know it." Liam's voice rolled over me, his words settling in my gut. He might be right, but Calliope needed us and that superseded anything else.

"You handled that very well, seeing her." I peered in the rearview mirror at him, traced the lines of his body with my eyes.

He snorted. "I couldn't kill her in the middle of a coffee shop, surrounded by humans. Even I know that much. Even my wolf knows that much."

That was where he was wrong, but I wasn't going to correct him. He could have killed her, and while it would have put us on the run, the humans would have chalked it up to a psycho going on a spree. Hell, I could have run her through and if I'd timed it right, no one would have seen her body slumping until after we were gone. We could have called Agent Valley and had him clean up our mess.

So why hadn't I? Why hadn't either of us taken that chance? I told myself it was because of the baby; I couldn't hurt an unborn child. But in my heart, I knew that wasn't the only reason.

Liam scooted forward and put his chin on the back of my seat.

"What's the plan, Tracker? And yes, I'm going to keep after you about this. You do have to have one this time. We can't go in blindly, this is dangerous enough as it is."

I took the next right hand turn, felt Calliope's threads settle a little, the fear easing off before thrumming back through me at high speed. "Same as always, which is a type of plan."

"Crash the party and hope we get out alive?"

I eyed him up in the rearview mirror as he curled back into his seat and tucked both hands behind his head, his eyes thoughtful.

"There is no way to know how bad it's going to be. Even Dox didn't know, so there is really no way to plan this."

After that, he dropped it. Though, I could see the worry etched in his face. I was just glad my back was to him and he couldn't see the worry in mine.

Damn her. How the hell was he supposed to keep her safe if she continued to walk into situations where her life was perpetually on the line? Leaving the ogres behind had been a bad idea, but if there was even a small chance that Milly had been telling the truth, then they had to act. He knew that, though it soured his gut with acid.

His training as an FBI agent kicked in, and he let that take over for now. They had to follow the lead that they'd been given, see it though. It would either vindicate Milly or be the final nail in her coffin. Not that she needed any more nails, but he could see that Rylee still wanted to believe that her ex-best friend was under duress. That it wasn't really Milly's fault that she'd caused so much damage.

Lounging in the back seat, the wolf in him struggled to rise to the surface, still raging with the proximity of Milly. He closed his eyes, thought about Rylee, about holding her tight, smelling the soft, unique scent that was hers alone. Wild and passionate, surprisingly vulnerable, even at times uncertain, which he was quite sure she didn't show many people. The images and memories soothed the beast in him, eased the out-of-control fury that had been building.

This was closer to the truth of why he let Rylee win this fight so easily. If it hadn't been for Milly, he would have pinned Rylee down, kept her there to wait for Dox and the others. But with Milly so close, he needed to be as far away as possible.

For all the wolf he had become, he knew it wasn't time yet to finish the witch off.

*There is a reason for everything, even for her.*

He ground his teeth against the words his own mind gave him. Like an echo of someone else's voice, the words sounded suspiciously like the Guardians they'd met in the past. He shivered. The last thing he needed was another part of himself to be sliced into a third portion, even though he knew it was there. Lurking. Easier to ignore that part than the wolf who paced inside him like a caged beast.

The truck rumbled along a deeply rutted back road, bouncing through mud puddles and dirtying up Dox's 'baby'.

Rylee's eyes were tight around the edges and he could smell the anxiety rolling off her, the worry for the foal they sought. Fear from the encounter with Milly. Something else too, though, a hint of a new scent, one that reminded him of . . . damn he couldn't pinpoint it. He wanted to soothe her, but knew from past experience that she wouldn't appreciate it or accept it right now. Not even from him. Better to focus on the salvage.

"How close are we?"

She tipped her head to the side, a long swath of her auburn hair brushing across her shoulder. The truck slowed as the back end slid around a corner, thick with mud.

"About as close as we're going to get with the truck."

The trail ended against the shoreline of a lake as we rounded what turned out to be the final corner. There was a bit of an opening, suitable for turning around, but that was it.

Cranking the wheel, I turned the truck, and then backed it up so the bumper was against the tree line so that at the very least, we would have a quick getaway. Just in case.

I snorted; hell, who was I kidding? There was no doubt that a quick getaway was going to be a necessity. I opened the door and slid out, my feet landing in a big puddle I couldn't avoid.

"Freaking awesome." I stepped out of it and slammed the door behind me, the sound echoing around us. I could feel the heat of Liam's glare, didn't need to look over my shoulder to know his eyebrows would be drawn sharply over his eyes.

"You want to ring the dinner bell while you're at it?" His voice was low, but it still carried across to me. Without turning around, I flipped him off. He was right, I was wrong; we both knew it.

Tracking Calliope, I turned my face upward, toward the mountain hovering in the distance. Terror suffused her and leaked through her threads into me. Sweat broke out along my spine, soaking through my t-shirt in a matter of seconds.

"Let's go."

Liam brushed past me. "I'll lead, you navigate."

I ran my hands over my weapons quickly, thought about going back to the truck for my crossbow. No, if we had to climb the whole mountain, I needed to pack light, and if Liam shifted he wouldn't be any help with a stack of weapons. Sword, whip, and smaller blades were all I could carry, and hopefully all I would need.

The snap of a twig brought my head around. Bushes and trees surrounded us on three sides. Ahead of me, Liam had stopped walking and was eyeing up the same bush I was, a bush that seemed to melt and move.

A grey skinned hand large enough to palm two basketballs pushed the foliage away, and through the bush stepped the biggest damn ogre I had ever seen. Twelve feet, maybe taller, his face twisted in a snarl that turned his human-like features into something out of a horror movie. Covered in a light chainmail, he held a sword that had been obviously sized up for him. Fuck, the thing was at least five feet long, maybe even six. His muscles rippled like water flowing over rocks as he lifted his sword, using it to point at me.

"You think to trespass on these lands?"

Calliope's fear spiked again, which made me reckless. At least, that's what I'm going to blame for what I said next.

"I don't see any signs, nothing that says 'Stay the fuck away.' You should put some up if you don't want anyone here but your big grey ass." I lifted an eyebrow at him, cocked my hip and put a hand on it. Really, there was nothing else to do. He wasn't going to let us pass without a fight, so no need to be submissive to him. Liam let out a soft groan as three more grey-skinned ogres slipped in around us. Well, this was not good. Maybe I should have been polite. Too late now.

A light rain began to fall and the air went still. The ogre didn't say anything, just cocked his head to one side, before whipping his sword into the air and letting out a roar that I *felt* as the reverberations hit my chest. Not that I let it last long. There were times to fight and there were times to run.

This was a time for the latter.

Spinning on my heel, I ran for Liam, who waited the split second it took me to reach him, and then we were sprinting full tilt along a narrow trail that wound along the base of the mountain.

Liam stayed behind me and I didn't dare look behind. I knew we couldn't keep this up, knew that they would run us, or at least me, into the ground.

"Tell me you have an idea." Liam leapt up beside me as something hammered into the ground behind us.

"Working on it."

"Work faster."

My brain felt scrambled with the adrenaline and I fought to remember all I knew. From what Dox had said there were components of all the ogre tribes around here. From what I knew—and was obvious with the violet and black skinned species—very few of them got along. I let Calliope's threads go and Tracked ogres as a species, pushing the ones behind us away to focus on what was in front of us.

Shit, *right* in front of us! But there was nothing there that I could see . . . I grabbed Liam and ducked sideways as a red-skinned ogre literally appeared out of nowhere. He swung a mace over our heads, connecting with the grey-skinned ogre that had been closest on our heels.

The mace buried into the grey's chest, but I didn't pause long enough to see what happened next. We were on a side trail and I spread out my Tracking, taking into account all the ogres around us.

"Ah, fuck," I whispered, knowing Liam would hear me.

We were completely surrounded.

# 11

The thing was, I was pretty sure I could lead us around them; the trick would be to stay downwind so they couldn't smell us. I put a finger to my lips and Liam nodded. Behind us the fight raged, drawing the ogres around us closer, and tightening the noose around us. For the moment, they'd forgotten about the intruders, too intent on fighting one another. Score for us.

I dropped to the ground and shimmied forward, the muddy ground cold and slimy. The muck slipped through my jacket zipper, like a pervy old man's wandering hands. Damn it all, this was disgusting. The bush covered us, hiding us from above, and the mud should have helped with our scent. Then again—

A foot the size of my upper body landed in the muck beside me, squishing up and through the bare, jet-black toes. I dared to look up.

Thank the gods the ogre didn't look down, just took another step toward the fighting, leaving us behind. Liam squeezed my leg and I continued forward, Tracking ogres, dodging them all.

From behind us, the sounds of the fight escalated as more ogres were drawn to the blood. Like sharks, but instead of a feeding frenzy, they were in a fighting frenzy. When they were a half-mile behind us, and there were no more ahead of us, I stood, mud sliding down the front of my body.

Liam wasn't faring any better, his clothes stained a dark brown slop.

No words, I just reached for Calliope's threads. Fear, brilliant and untamable, sung through her and into me. I didn't let go of the ogre's threads. As soon as they quit fighting, they'd remember us.

I worked my way back to the trail, checked my weapons, and then set out at a jog. Liam tucked in close beside me, our strides eating up the ground.

Around us, the forest dimmed. Too early for the sun to be setting . . . I looked up and stopped running.

The Roc skimmed silently above us, his shadow the cause of the loss of light. Grey-green, mottled leathery skin, claws on the tips of his wings, big nasty claws on his back feet. His head was long and narrow, teeth jutting out of the partially opened jaws.

"Good gods, he's as big as Blaz," I whispered. Liam didn't answer except to push me forward. He was right, this was not the time to be pointing and staring when there was little doubt we'd be dealing with the big fucker soon enough.

From behind us, the ogres' fighting went silent as the Roc passed over them. Settling back into a jog, we continued to put distance between us and the ogres. Ahead of us, I could sense nothing but the unicorn foal, and thank the gods not a single damn ogre. About damn time we had a bone thrown our way. Lady Luck might be fickle for the rest of the world, but I was pretty sure she had it out for me and my friends.

The incline took a sharp upward turn, but neither of us slowed. Calliope was up ahead, the Roc scoured the skies around us, and there was a colorful mess of blood-thirsty ogres behind us. Yeah, there was going to be no slowing down for us anytime soon.

A sudden, jarring shot of pain ripped through Calliope and into me, dropping me to my knees. Liam's hands caught me on the way down.

"The foal?"

I nodded, struggled to breathe, struggled to convince my body it wasn't my pain but another's. A few seconds passed and I had it under control, the pain a steady distant throb. She was still alive, but whatever happened to her was bad enough that the terror slipped into despair. Calliope was giving up. The sky darkened as a bank of clouds skittered in front of the sun. A reminder that we had very little time to make this salvage happen.

"We aren't going to make it to her in time, are we?" Liam's question caught me off guard, the words setting off a trail of anger down my spine.

"Don't. Just don't."

I pushed him away from me and started back up the trail, forcing myself to keep a steady pace despite the incline. The rain made the slope slippery, and the higher we climbed, the colder it got until the rain wasn't rain anymore but a snotty slippery slush.

An hour passed, and then another, and it seemed that we weren't getting any closer. My legs shook with each step, and even Liam was breathing hard. Two hours, jogging straight up a mountainside, was not something I did on a regular basis.

Worse though, Calliope was slipping, the despair stealing away the fight in her to survive.

I refused to believe that Liam was right. That we wouldn't make it in time.

*Hang on, Calli. Just hang on.*

There was a pause, like someone taking a breath on the other end of the phone.

And then a bright shining thread of hope swirled between us. No words, no thoughts, just an emotion so warm and full of life that it took everything I had not to give a fist pump. Ah, fuck it.

I jammed my fist into the air, then put my head down and powered up the next fifty feet.

"She's alive . . . and she knows we're coming."

"That's great. But we have a problem." Liam caught up to me and spun me around. Maybe two hundred feet behind us, the ogres had caught up. How the hell had they snuck up on us? I'd been Tracking them!

The red-skinned ogre gave me a wave of his fingers and a wink I could see even from that distance.

It took me a second to put two and two together. Of course, certain ogres had magic and if the Lighteaters could mess with my abilities, masking their presence, then likely the ogres could too. And the triplets had known right away what I was and what I could do.

Apparently, my secrets were out.

With a single finger, I waved back.

Laughter rumbled through their group and up to us. We were in trouble. They were too close, and . . . .

There was no sound as the Roc curled around the mountain. The ogres froze, stilling their huge bodies. Between a Roc and a horde of ogres, which were we more likely to survive?

"Trust me." My eyes met Liam's for a brief second, as I plucked a small blade from my boot, then spun and threw it toward the Roc as it drew close, the blade not doing any harm as it caught the beast in the belly.

But it got its attention. Oh, shit did it ever.

The Roc arced toward us, mouth open, wide eyes trained on us without blinking. There was no sound though, no growl, no thunderous roar. Not even a whoosh of wings. If I hadn't been looking at the big bastard, I wouldn't have known it was there.

"Dodge the teeth, but let it catch us!" I yelped, as we scrambled out of the way, just barely dodging the open mouth.

"Good idea, Rylee!" His sarcasm was not lost on me. Liam grabbed me, pulled me out of the way of one claw. But we couldn't dodge the other. Which was exactly what I was hoping for. Kinda.

The grey-green talons closed around us like a bear trap snapping shut, crushing us against one another, and clamping on us in a breath-stealing squeeze. With a sudden, ear-shattering screech, the Roc soared back above the mountain. From below, the ogres still didn't move, but I could see the smiles on their faces. They thought we were toast. The Roc's wings moved silently in the falling snow, its body shivering. Three wing beats and we had climbed almost to the top of the mountain.

"Rylee, please tell me this is a part of your plan. That you have a plan." Liam squirmed against the Roc's claws that held us tight.

I smiled over at him as the top of the mountain drew closer and the Roc began to descend to a depression between two plateaus near the snow-covered peak. The air was thin, cold, and not suited to the Roc's nature.

"Actually, this time I do. I was tired of walking."

His jaw dropped. "Are you serious?"

The Roc gave us a squeeze and then it was landing. With a flick of its talons, it sent us tumbling over the thick crust of hot snow . . . wait, what the hell?

I didn't have time to wonder at the hot mush below us. We had a Roc to deal with. Before I could get to my feet, Liam scrambled to my side and wrapped his arms around my body, holding me to the ground.

"The ogres didn't move and it didn't see them." Our bodies sunk into the hot mud and I stared, silent and unmoving, at the Roc who tipped its head sideways, not unlike Eve when she was considering something. Two steps toward us, head cocking again, eyes blinking, the triple eyelids fluttering closed one after another and then opening back up one at a time. Creepy fucker.

It let out a screech, three feet from our heads. My eardrums rattled, and it felt like the left one might have popped, but both Liam and I held still. Held our breath. Sunk deeper into the uncomfortable hot mud.

Damn, this was like some sort of *Jurassic Park* remake. The big leathery bird held its head there, waiting for us to give ourselves away.

The Roc stepped back, giving up on it meal. Or so I thought.

It strode to the far side of the overheated area and settled down into the mud. But no, it didn't close its eyes. It stared in our direction, eyes wide and again unblinking. Several minutes passed, and my ears slowly stopped ringing.

"Liam." I kept my voice pitched low and soft, and the Roc didn't twitch.

"Yes?"

"Not how I imagined my day going."

"Really? I expected something along these lines. I'm actually surprised it's mud and not shit we're up to our necks in."

I shouldn't have found that funny, not with how dire our situation was. Yet there I was, sides shaking, fighting the laughter that bubbled up.

Liam's arms tightened on me. "Track Calliope."

I did as he said, and the contact with her threads sobered me like a dash of cold water. She was still hopeful, but the pain coursing through her made her weak, the fear that had slipped away from her was building once more. But close now, she was right below us, inside the mountain and so damn close.

Well shit, how the hell were we going to get out of this? Sucked down in the mud, I knew that getting out would be hard and would slow us enough that the Roc would have no problem picking us off.

"There's a drop down into a lower level, and the opening is too tight for the Roc," Liam said. "I think we can make it."

He was right. An opening the size of a small car was close enough that potentially we could make it through before the Roc snapped us up.

"Not unless we slow him down."

Which we could if we gave him something nasty to chew on. A plan, yes a plan, formed quickly. Shit, it wasn't perfect, but it was all I had.

"Can you reach either of my swords?"

Under the mud, Liam worked his hand up to one of my swords. "Yes."

I reached back through the thick mud and grabbed the other handle. "We pull them as we stand, and when he gets his mouth close to us—"

"Rylee, you're crazy, you know that?"

"Yeah, I do. But it'll work." Gods, I hoped that I was right, that it would indeed work.

Liam let out a slow breath. "I hope you're right."

Gods help me if I ever lost Liam; there would never be another like him, no matter what Doran said.

"On the count of three." I tightened my grip on my sword. "One, two, three."

In tandem, we lurched upward, the mud not only slowing us down, but throwing us off balance. The Roc shot forward, mouth open wide, eyes staring wide.

Our timing, though, was perfect even if our balance was off. Liam's blade shot upward for the top jaw as mine sliced down and through the bone and cartilage, the spelled blades driving through with ease. Teeth shattered, blood gushed and the Roc backpedaled, mud spraying all over us. We scrambled, fighting against the mud to get to the opening and the drop.

But I wasn't looking forward, my eyes trained on the flailing, bleeding Roc, and when Liam missed the step down, I tumbled after him. Stairs cut into the mountain rose up to smash into me as I slid down them, the mud coating us acting like a fucking slippery slide.

The stairs curled and I got a glimpse of something bright red and bubbling, a swirl of a brown cloak and a flash of Calliope's bright white coat.

We hit the ground and Liam was on his feet first. "Rylee, you aren't going to believe this. Hell, I can't believe it."

I rolled to my feet, sword still in hand, and turned to see what he was talking about.

He was right, I didn't believe it. Not for one second.

# 12

**D**aniels, my nemesis from London, stood slack-jawed in front of an open pit that looked to go straight into the heart of the mountain. Or, more accurately, the gods-be-damned big ass, half awake volcano. A deep rotten egg, gag-inducing, tongue-coating scent of sulfur lay heavy in the air. Being deep in the mud up top must have kept the smell from us. Because there was no way we could miss it where we stood.

"Couldn't you have picked a place that didn't smell like goblin shit? Seriously." I sidled toward Calliope, huddled in the corner. Not that I didn't want to run Daniels through, but my main objective was the foal, bringing her home to her parents and freeing Eve. Priorities, and Daniels was low on the list right now.

She lifted her hands, her voice deepening as she intoned something I'd heard before. "It is the heart of the mountains that we will prick, and the land will know Orion's fury for being condemned to the seventh Veil. He shall cleanse the land with fire for his coming."

Wait . . . that was what Agent Valley had asked us about, before we'd left London. I was an idiot. Why hadn't I listened? Too bloody ready to run away, to hide from the prophecies . . . and now I was paying the price, as would Calliope if I didn't get her out of here.

Daniels smiled at us, her eyes wild with the power she'd been given. We had to take her out. Possession might seem like a good idea at first, a demon giving their vessel fantastic abilities, but it wouldn't be long before Daniels found out that she'd gotten the raw end of the deal.

Liam lunged for her first, and with a flick of her hand, she wove her magic around him and lifted him into the air. I hit her hard, tackling her to the ground, but she didn't release Liam. She kept talking as if we were having a pleasant conversation.

I moved to cover her hands with mine, take away her magic, and let Liam go.

"Rylee don't!" He yelled and I looked up. Daniels had shifted him over the middle of the pit. If I used my Immunity to block her magic . . . .

"FUCK!" I scrambled off Daniels, and she stood back up, brushing off her brown cloak.

"Rylee, you are the last person I expected to see here. I take it Milly did not slow you down at the castle? Orion said that she was weakening, but I'd hoped to use her a little longer."

Fuck, shit, damn it all to hell and back. Of course it was Milly. Yet, if she had laid the trap and Giselle was right, then Milly had tried to help us too. Which meant that maybe, just maybe, she'd been telling the truth at the coffee shop. But that was for another time, when we weren't dealing with a psycho druid, a pit of lava, and a demon. Like some sort of twisted riddle, I had to get us all out of here. Right now, the only thing I could think about was keeping the ex-druid talking.

"Daniels, how did you get away from the Beast?"

She paused, her left eye twitching as she smiled at me. "I killed him. My master gave me the strength and now I cannot be stopped."

Liam shook his head. "Impossible."

"I don't think you should take that tone with me, wolf. You will be far easier for my master to kill than the Beast was." Her voice was off, and it took me a moment to realize what was different about her.

"What happened to your accent?" I stepped sideways so I could get a better look at her face.

Her whole body gave a shiver and Liam dropped a few inches. My heart lurched upward. "Daniels, I'll give you what you want, just don't drop him."

She turned to face me and when she did, she seemed to inadvertently bring Liam with her. While he wasn't out of danger, he was closer to the edge of the pit then he had been.

"I want your head on a pike on London Bridge, I want you to suffer as I have suffered, to see your innards twisted around a stick and removed from your body inch by inch while you scream for mercy that will never come," she whispered, her lips not moving in tandem with her words. Like a poorly dubbed old school Kung Fu movie. Freaky-ass demon possession.

And then she wasn't really Daniels anymore, or at least her voice wasn't.

"Tracker." Male, and a lower octave that she should have been able to hit, the voice rumbled out of her mouth. "Do you remember me?"

I blinked at her, and a cold sweat popped out all over my body. A memory buried deep flickered to life.

The barest whisper of a snake, Milly, and my first understanding of what I was. And then it was gone as if it had never been. I shook my head. "No. But I know who you are you nasty motherfucking piece of shit. You're the demon I'm going to wipe off the face of the world."

"Ah, I see your foul, unimaginative mouth hasn't improved since last we spoke," the voice said, and Daniels stepped toward me, and then snapped her fingers without turning around. Liam dropped like a stone, down below the lip of the pit.

"NO!" I launched myself at Daniels, and when she flicked a hand at me, her magic slid off. Only it wasn't magic the way Daniels had. It was a heavy thump of power that grasped me, and the snowflake on my chest burned, pushing the power aside.

A snarl twisted her features as the demon's taint slid away from me. What the hell had just happened? Didn't matter, I would figure it out later.

He roared a wordless bellow as I body-slammed Daniels to the ground for a second time. The back of her head connected with the hard rock and I thought she would be out cold.

No such luck.

She rolled and pinned me below her with a strength that was far beyond her own. And it wasn't Daniels' eyes that stared down at me. No, these eyes were not the muddy brown I recalled. A swirling dark red fog covered the brown irises up, swallowed what was left of Daniels. I'd never seen it, but I knew it from

Giselle's teachings what I was looking at. Daniels had been well and truly possessed. There was no coming back from it, no magical ceremony that would save her from Orion. He had taken her in one fell swoop. Which, considering she had been the one tangling with him, she deserved, in my eyes.

Once a demon had you, that was it. Say good night to everything you ever knew and loved.

"You, I let you live once. Because I didn't think you could be the one to stand between me and this world. There were others and I wiped them out one by one. Yet here you are; though I must say, your attempt is, at best, pitiful." His strength was beyond anything I could fight against, and he held me easily. He leaned in closer, eyes wide. "You don't even know what you truly are, do you? Even I know where I come from, you don't even have that."

"Go fuck a troll, you ass hat. You aren't going to win."

I tried to flip him off me, bucking my hips, straining against his hands with everything I had. It wasn't enough. He was too strong. I couldn't reach my weapons, and Liam . . . gods, let him have been able to reach the edge of the pit.

Orion lowered his face to mine, his voice frosting over me, stilling my efforts. "You will belong to me; I will have to thank Milly. She tried to do me a disservice, sending the Hoarfrost demon to build your immunity to a demon's taint, but then she so kindly sends you here to me. Truly, she is a sly one."

His words hit me and the past seemed to swallow me up. The black Coven of witches and the Hoarfrost demon. Milly had engineered it all? So that I would be immune to a demon that I would one day have to kill . . . .

"Now you will witness firsthand my rebirth into this world. And then I will eat your soul."

Okay, panic wasn't even close to what spun up through me. Blind with the fear that he could actually do what he said he could, I flailed, all my training going out the window. Demons were bad enough, but a soul-eater . . . motherfucking pus buckets. I'd read about them, in the black-skinned book. They were at the top of the demon food chain, for good reason.

This was who Milly was bound to.

This was who I was supposed to stop.

A demon—who when he was only just possessing a body—held me down without breaking a sweat. If he came through the Veils, physically came through, all his powers would be intact. I had to stop him now. This was the only chance I had.

He threw his head back, laughing, the sound bouncing off the walls. "Oh, please do struggle, I love to play rough." He jerked me up and then slammed my upper body back into the ground.

Three times he used me like an oversized fly swatter. I curled my head to my chest, to keep my skull from being cracked open wide, but it was the best I could do. Even so, the warm spread of blood trickled down the back of my neck, as he twisted me to the side, catching me off guard, smashing me into a protruding rock.

A soft nicker floated across to me. I turned my head to see Calliope struggling to her feet, one front leg hanging at a bad angle, snapped at the top of her black sock. Her violet eyes gazed at me, her would-be rescuer. Hope flared between her and I, the belief that I would save her as real and solid as the mountain below us.

Fuck, if I couldn't get him off me, I wasn't going to be saving anyone.

Orion turned his head to follow my gaze. "Ah, the innocent. They are made to suffer. They are made to be taken, and broken, and used."

"Not as long as we're around." Liam's hand wrapped around Orion's neck and yanked him off me.

Orion's howl was cut short as Liam snapped his neck, the crunch of bone the most heartwarming sound I'd ever heard. With a casual thrust of his arm, Liam tossed the body away from him, and bent over me.

"You okay?"

I reached up, my hand hovering over an ugly burn on his forearms, the skin black and weeping. "I'm fine, but—"

He grabbed my hand and helped me to my feet. "It's all good. I've had worse frying bacon."

Calliope let out a sharp, blasting neigh, what could only be the equivalent of a scream.

Orion wasn't done yet. Head flopped to the side, wobbling with each step, he stumbled toward the filly, mumbling under his breath. A spell cloaked in the darkness of the demon's power, I could feel it gathering around us. The lava bubbled upward, the sulfurous air quickly choking out what oxygen there was.

No time for insults, much as I wanted to hurl one of the triplets' epithets at Orion. I pulled a sword free, ran and leapt in the air. As I came down, I used my weight to leverage the bite of the blade, slicing through Orion's stolen body from his left shoulder, through his torso, and out through the lower right side of his ribs.

He gasped, red swirling eyes turning to me, filled with hatred.

"Yeah, I feel the same about you, bitch." I kicked his body with my foot, the two halves sliding apart to the ground.

To be sure, I bent, grabbed a still twitching leg and hauled it to the edge of the pit. With a heave, I threw the lower half in, the lava swallowing up the legs in two gulping burps of bubbles.

Liam followed my lead and held up the upper half of the body. Though Orion still gazed at us, he seemed to have lost any ability to actually control the body.

"Any last words?" I smiled at him, feeling pretty damn good. Prophecies fulfilled, we'd killed Orion. I could rest easy; the foal was alive, Eve would be fine.

Life was looking up. Please, gods, let it be.

"This isn't over." The words were slurred, hard to hear, and strangely didn't surprise me. Not from a demon.

"Pitiful last words," Liam said as he threw what was left of Daniels and Orion into the pit. I blinked as the body slid below, eaten by the lava in seconds.

From the pocket inside my jacket, I pulled out the small brown bag Milly had given me. I opened it and poured the spiked demon stone into my hand.

"Lava should do the trick, don't you think?" I held it up, the spikes pressing into the flesh of my palm. I rolled it to get a better look at it, wondered if I would ever know if Milly really had been enthralled.

Liam bumped my hand and the demon stone fell, landing with a hiss and a gulp as thick lava swallowed it up.

We stared down, the heat curling up around us, drying the sticky mud on our clothes. Thirty seconds passed and Liam stepped back, but I continued to stare, my throat tightening up.

"Does that seem higher than before?" I pointed at the lava as it freaking well surged upward. We fell back, the blast of heat singeing my eyelashes and eyebrows.

"Okay, time to go." I ran for Calliope. There was no way to set her leg; she'd have to be carried. "Liam!"

"I'll do it." The voice was not Liam's. I looked up at the lip of the overhang, a grey-skinned ogre staring down at us. "You don't really have a choice, Tracker. You're going to have to trust me."

From behind him came a voice I did recognize. Dox.

"Rylee, just let him help!"

Liam scooped up the foal. "I'll carry her as far as I can." She rested her chin on his shoulder, trust shining through the threads I still held onto. Keeping pace with Liam, we ran for the stairs, bolting up them as the lava spilled over the lip of the pit, eating up the ground where we'd stood only moments before.

The grey-skinned ogre didn't ask, just took Calliope from Liam's arms, and she didn't fight either of them. Fatigue washed through her and I finally let her threads go. I didn't need to feel that; I was tired enough as it was without her adding to it.

The grey-skinned ogre spoke to Liam. "We have to move fast, and you may have to carry the Tracker."

Across from us stood ogres in every color possible. Like a bag of Skittles, see the fucking rainbow that would like to taste you after roasting you on a spit. This couldn't be good, yet they weren't trying to kill us.

"The Roc—" I started to ask, and the grey boy cut me off.

"Time for answers later. We have to move our asses if we're going to all get out of here alive."

Dox ran to my side, the distinct imprints of teeth all over his neck and shoulders. At least he'd had some fun. "Rylee, you . . . ."

I shoved him to get him going. "We couldn't wait."

We took off, running blind down the mountain in the dark, night having fallen fully as we'd fought Orion. The ground around us shook, and a blasting spurt of lava erupted out the side of the mountain, three hundred feet to the left of us.

The ogres covered the ground in leaps in bounds, literally jumping and letting gravity taking them farther down the mountain with each stride, snow flying up around their feet as they landed. An explosion behind us spurred me on. Out of the frying pan we were, and into the big-ass fire.

A crackling sizzle reached my ears, but I didn't turn around.

"It's hot on our heels, get your fat, monkey-sucking asses moving!" Dev shouted, and the ogres seemed to find a new gear. Liam didn't scoop me up, but Tin did, snagging me around the waist and throwing me on his back. I clutched around his neck with my arms, and stood on the thick edge of his belt.

Then I looked behind us, sucking in a sharp, horrified breath. The entire top of the mountain was crumbling inward as the lava burst up and out. Brilliant red and orange geysers of liquid death shot into the starless sky followed by massive billows of black smoke illuminated by the lava that spilled down the mountain toward us. With each passing second the lava drew closer, eating up everything in its path.

"We aren't going to make it," I yelled, hoping that their mages had some way to help us.

Two of them turned around long enough to toss a spell, that to my eyes, did nothing.

"They pushed the gases in the other direction," Tin said. My understanding of volcanoes wasn't at its peak, but I did recall something about a flow of gas and rock that outpaced even the lava. I looked back, and all I saw was the red flow of death. I suppose that was better than the alternative of choking to death on fumes and *then* being consumed by the lava.

Grey boy glanced over his shoulder. "Head for the lake."

As one, the ogres turned, angling toward the lake that surrounded the base of the mountain. Though it had taken us hours to climb Mt. Hood, riding ogreback on the downhill took mere minutes. We were out of the snow now, but the ground was sloppy and wet, thick with ash, and a red ogre to the right of us lost his footing, tumbled and fell.

The lava caught him, swallowed him in one gulping wave, leaving behind his hand reaching up for a second, the fingers blackening before the lava even touched them.

I swallowed hard, heart pounding, my adrenaline racing and there wasn't a damn thing I, or anyone else, could do.

The sharp incline leveled out and the gang of ogres thundered into the forest. Like a living thing, the lava flowed ever onward, devouring everything in its path. This was what Orion did, with a few words? With a gesture and a single spell when his host's body had a broken neck? Son of a fucking bitch, he was as bad as all the prophesies made him out to be.

Maybe worse.

Thank the gods he was done.

Tin leapt over a downed log, and my feet slid off his belt, leaving me dangling from his back. All thoughts of Orion fled as I fought to hang onto the bounding ogre, the vision of what had happened to the red ogre who'd gone down seared in my mind. That would be a seriously bad way to end this salvage.

"Tracker, if you fall, I can't stop," Tin puffed out.

"Got it," I barked out. Shit, I was sliding; there was nothing I could hang onto, his slick bare skin giving me no traction whatsoever.

There was nothing for it. I either fell from his back in a heap, or I leapt and had a chance at keeping my feet under me. As I slid down his back, I pushed to the side and hit the ground running.

In seconds, the lava was at my heels, kissing the backs of my boots, heat rolling up and around me, stealing the air I needed. Liam dropped back to my side, grabbed my hand and jerked me forward as a gulp of lava rolled ahead of the rest of it.

We burst through the bush into the parking lot where Dox's truck sat waiting for us. But the trail ran parallel to the edge of the flow of the lava; the truck was going to be toasted. The lake it was.

With the searing heat behind us, the multi-hued Gang of ogres dove into the lake, swimming out into the open water. I caught sight of Calliope being floated between Dox and the grey boy.

And then I dove in, the icy water sluicing over my head. I floated for a minute under the water, looking back the way we'd come. The lava hit the shoreline, flowing into the lake, lighting it up from inside.

A pair of red swirling eyes hardened in the lava, as the water cooled the deadly flow.

*We are not done yet, Tracker. I will have your soul yet. Yours, and the souls of all you love.*

I kicked myself to the surface, anger searing my synapsis. "And that's your mistake, Orion. You can threaten me, but threaten those I love and you will regret it beyond the grave."

# 13

The ogres were in high spirits, having no problem with the winter-chilled, glacier-fed lake. I, on the other hand, was freezing. My eyes drooped with each breath I took, fatigue dragging me down.

While the ogres splashed and played, exultant from having outrun the lava, I swam to Dox, each movement of my arms and legs causing shivers of cold-induced pain to ripple through me. Liam kept pace with me, seemingly as unaffected as the ogres by the cold. Before I could speak, Dox slung an arm around my waist and gave me a hard squeeze.

"Thank you, Rylee."

I looked up at him. Even through my wet clothes and the water, I could feel his body heat, which I was intensely grateful for. "Thanks for what?"

"I would never have come back without you needing to be here for a salvage, and I would have missed out on this. On the fight, and seeing the triplets again. On Sas. For the first time, I finally belong, I'm finally home. I don't know if you can understand what that means to me." He grinned down at me, a new light in his eyes. I understood what it was to want to belong, to finally find that place. I glanced at Liam over my shoulder. Yeah, I really did understand. I gave Dox a nod.

"I'm happy for you. And glad you came too. Our asses would have been fried up there without your help."

Teeth chattering as a wash of cold water thick with ash swirled between us, I pointed at the shoreline. "But we have to get me and Calli out of this lake, or it won't matter that we dodged the hot sauce."

He nodded, gave a holler, and the triplets swam over to us, helped to get us across to the far side. Ash floated down around us, coating the lake's surface. It stuck to my face and neck, and as we stepped out of the water it clung to every piece of us.

As much as I wanted to complain, I didn't. We'd survived something that should have taken us out. Would have died without the help we'd received. Which still made no sense, but I wasn't going to remind them that they were on the hunt for us.

The triplets got a fire going within minutes and I crouched beside it, peeling out of my jacket. Calliope lay beside me, her legs tucked under her and as close to the fire as she could get. The firelight flickered and danced against her white coat. I ran a hand over her back, and she turned to look at me, gold nubbin catching the light.

*Thank you, for saving me.*

I smiled and gave her a tired nod. "Just try to avoid Rocs in the future."

She bobbed her head. *I will do my best.*

Crouched beside her, I stared out at the lake, all of the ogres still hanging out in the water except for Dox and the triplets.

"What happened?" I turned my face up to Dox, who stood over me.

"You mean after you left without us?" He growled.

Lop laughed, slapping his hands on his thighs. "That was fucking wicked awesome, woman. If you were an ogre, I'd be banging the hell out of you." His brothers were nodding in agreement.

Liam slowly stood, every line of his body tense. Lop held up his hands. "Easy wolf, I said IF. She's too fucking puny for my taste. But that took balls, to head into hostile territory without help. Ogres like a good, strong woman. None of this pansy ass, 'I broke my nail' shit."

Liam relaxed, then snorted. "No, it takes a stubbornness that one day is going to get her hurt. But if I ever get tired of her, I'll let you know."

My jaw dropped and the triplets fell over themselves laughing. Even Calliope let out a soft nicker.

"It wasn't that funny," I grumbled, but I bit the inside of my cheek. Not for one second did I think Liam would ever get tired of me. Gods, I hoped not.

Dox dropped to a crouch beside me. "You killed the Roc, that's why they were willing to help."

Dev crawled toward the fire, stretched out on his belly. "Yup, you did what no ogre has been able to. You got rid of the big bitch of a bird. The ogres are in your debt."

"What they say is true."

I turned to see the rest of the ogres emerging from the lake, water glistening on their many-colored hides. They were surreal, the lava still erupting on the mountain behind them, the dark night above, and the reflection of the lake. The scene was damn near poetic.

Grey boy crouched beside me and held out his hand. "I am Sla, and I speak for all the ogres, all the Gangs. You are welcome here, Tracker. And we will stand with you when the time comes."

I swallowed hard, and set my hand in his. "Just for killing the Roc?"

He smiled down at me. "Killing the Roc was the sign that you are the one who will lead us into battle."

Oh, no. Not this shit again. "Nope, sorry, that isn't going to happen; we threw him into the pit." I tossed a twig into the fire, to illustrate my words.

Sla shook his head. "It is not so easy to kill a demon. If it was, there would be none left. You took away the body he possessed, nothing more."

"How do you know all this? Are demons a hobby for you?" I lifted an eyebrow at him. Dox groaned softly, but Sla didn't seem to mind my attitude.

He flopped to the ground and stretched out lengthwise as if he, and all the other ogres, hadn't tried to kill us just a few hours past.

"We have prophecies too, though you will not find them in any ogre-skinned book." His eyes flicked up to mine and I gave him a nod. No point in denying it. He shrugged. "If an ogre is stupid enough to be skinned alive, they deserve it."

The ogres around us gave a resounding rumble of agreement.

"More to the point, you are the sign that the final battle is coming. *When the Roc dies and the lava flows, the battle is nigh.*" He eyed me up. "I'd hoped you'd be a bit more intimidating, though. The triplets speak true, you are rather puny to be a hero."

I really didn't like the direction of this conversation. "Orion isn't coming back. There is not going to be a gods-be-damned battle. And I am no one's hero."

Dox put a hand on my shoulder. "You have their loyalty, whether you want it or not."

I shook his hand off and stood. I didn't know what to say, how to stop them from believing these prophecies. Or to get them to see that it was over, that Orion was done. So I walked away from the group to the edge of the firelight, where Liam caught up to me. "Hey. We're alive, they aren't trying to kill us, and we have Calliope. Don't throw a fit because they want to believe in something that scares you."

I could have slapped him. For telling me the truth and for pointing out that I was afraid. I didn't do fear well, never had.

"You aren't the one being set up as some gods-be-damned savior of the world. I'm nobody, just a Tracker. That's it. There is nothing more to me. I don't have any special powers; I don't have any magic. Hell, if we'd been a little longer crossing the Veil at the castle, I would have died. I am not cut out to be in any prophecy. If it comes down to me and Orion, he will win!"

Note to self: when anger is flowing, try to recall that you might be a lot louder than you realize. Like as in yelling at the top of your lungs.

All the ogres stared at us in the sudden silence after my outburst. I closed my eyes, shame flooding me.

Liam stepped back, his face shuttered from any emotion. "I'm going to go and find a vehicle. Try to stay out of trouble while I'm gone."

"Liam, wait." I started after him but in an instant, he disappeared into the bush.

Once more, I'd screwed things up.

"Good fucking job, Rylee," I muttered to myself. "Good fucking job."

I made my way back to the fire and flopped down beside Calliope. I wished Alex was there to break the tension. Or Pamela to point out something good and beautiful. I Tracked Alex first, pinpointed him in a heartbeat. Almost directly east of us, his threads were strong and healthy, but he was afraid of something. Not totally unusual with Alex; he could sometimes get spooked by his own shadow.

Then I Tracked Pamela.

While she was in the same place, she was bruised and scared. I sat up straighter and Tracked Eve. No, this couldn't be happening, not when I was all the way on the other side of the continent. Eve's threads, I could barely feel them, weak and fading fast.

Eve was dying. I shot to my feet.

"Dox, go help Liam—we've got to go. Now."

The ogres around us rustled, Sla stood slowly. "What is it?"

"One of my wards is dying. I have to get to her."

I reached out and put a hand on Calliope's neck.

Warm and dry, her coat was silken under my fingertips. "Calli, do you have any way at all that we can reach your tribe, let them know that you're okay?"

She shook her head. *No. I would have done so on my own if there was some way.*

I put my hands on my head and clung to Eve's threads. So far away, I was so gods-be-damned far away. Calli's father had said they would wait for us. It had only been three days; surely they wouldn't have hurt Eve? Fuck!

If only there was a way I could jump the Veil . . . my eyes snapped open and I stared into the flames. Faris had said I could learn. Maybe. I paced in front of the fire, my mind racing as I struggled to remember exactly what Faris had done. The triplets spoke with their heads bowed together, and Sla made a motion with his right hand that sent the rest of the ogres melting into the darkness.

"Where is it you must go?" Sla asked. "Perhaps one of our magic wielders could help you."

"You got a place to cross the Veil close by?" Hope flared. If there was a place we could cross the Veil that would take us at least closer to North Dakota, we might have a chance.

Sla nodded slowly. "Yes, we have such a place. Though I do not know if it will lead to where you need to go. Our entrance leads to a castle."

Hell yeah, that was what I wanted to hear. "How close is it?" I gathered up my jacket, slid it on over my damp clothes.

The grey ogre stood slowly. "An hour from here, a little more if we go slowly."

I did a quick check of my weapons. "And if we hurry?"

Dev bent and scooped Calliope into his arms. "Come on, enough dicking about. Let's go."

"Wait, Dox can carry her; you aren't all coming, are you?" Please tell me I hadn't acquired a Gang of ogres.

Dox and Liam stepped out of the bush as I was trying to figure out how many ogres were coming with us. Apparently, Sla and the triplets had appointed themselves my newest bodyguards. Liam took charge, slipping once more into Agent mode. "Rylee, stay tight with me; Dev, you and Tin trade off if you need a break from carrying Calliope." The two ogres gave him a salute. "Lop, you bring up the rear. Sla and Dox, take the lead."

Surprising the shit out of me, everyone did what they were told. Sla and Dox set a fast pace, crashing a path out in front of us. Jaw tight, I held Eve's threads and struggled not to let her pain affect me. Her life leached from her, and I knew she had hours at best. Whatever damage had been done to her, it was bad enough that her natural healing abilities wouldn't be fast enough. She needed someone to heal her.

No one ambushed us and we made it to the entranceway through the Veil in less than half an hour. A massive cedar tree that had to be at least twenty feet around was our destination. Split in the middle, cored out by fire, the black opening beckoned. With my second sight, the entrance was clear as day and more welcome than anything I'd ever seen.

"Rylee, you ready?" Liam touched my shoulder. I nodded.

Sweat drenched even in the cold night air, exhausted from the day's events, I struggled to hold onto Alex's and Pamela's threads alongside Eve's.

And then Pamela's threads shimmered like a candle being blown on. Not dead, but across the Veil, the gods only knew where.

"FUCK!"

Their voices clamored over me while I fought the nausea that rose in my gut. "Just go, get through the Veil."

They did as I said and we all stepped through the Veil, the tingle of it sliding over my skin. The cedar tree opened into an inner courtyard that I hadn't seen.

And Pamela's threads were suddenly clear as a bell.

"PAMELA!"

There was a scuttle of feet, and then, "Rylee, I'm here!" And then her threads disappeared again. This time though, they were gone, like as in across a body of water gone.

Motherfucking vampire, I was going to kill Faris. He was the only one that would have the balls to snatch Pamela. But why did he want her? Or was it just another way to control me?

Eve's life dimmed again and my feet stilled. There really was no choice; Eve had to come first.

"Hang on, Pamela. I'll come for you," I whispered, turning away from where I'd heard her call out. We bolted through the castle to the exit we needed. I knew where we had to go, which doorway would take us to the mineshaft in the badlands just outside of Bismarck.

"We'll need light, grab some of those torches." I pointed to the walls as I ran. No time, there was no time to waste.

*Hang on, Eve, just hang on.*

We had to cross paths with the bloodshed of the red caps. Their bodies were putrefying, maggots crawling over them, their eyes pecked out by the carrion eaters.

"What the hell happened here?" Dox breathed out, gagging on the thick air.

"Pamela and Liam," I said, tearing my eyes from the scene.

I sensed more than saw the approval in the other ogres. But none of that mattered, not at that moment.

We ran through the empty stone hallways without a problem; no one had been expecting us this time around. The exit we needed was open and we piled through into the dusty old mine shaft that was buried in the badlands of North Dakota. The ogres lit the torches, and I paused to get my bearings.

Sla spoke softly. "This is the home of Seps. I can smell her, but it is faint, from many years ago."

"Great, you can visit another time," I snapped. With the light held high, Liam led the way, and I let him. Eve's threads were unraveling, weaker by the minute. Once I got to her, how was I going to help her? I had no ability to heal. Milly did, Terese did . . . .

"Here, the climbing gear is still set up." Liam handed the rope to Sla. "You go up first, make sure the area is clear."

Sla nodded, taking direction from Liam far easier than I would have thought. Then again, Liam wasn't asking.

The grey ogre climbed the rope quickly and, within minutes, was at the top. "All clear, wolf, send Rylee up first."

I grabbed the rope and Sla hauled me up. If I'd thought his ascent was fast, it was nothing compared to mine.

Thirty seconds, tops, and I climbed out of the mine shaft. Stumbling, I gained my feet and lifted my head. Across from me was a white vehicle that, with a gut-wrenching lurch, I recognized.

It was one of Milly's vehicles. An SUV that she'd gotten after her last beau dumped her. I jerked a sword from my back and Tracked the witch. Remarkably, I couldn't feel her at all, which meant she was across the ocean somewhere. The last thing I needed was for Milly to show back up again, proclaiming she was here to help. Scratch that; I'd suffer through it if she would heal Eve.

Liam was the next one up and he drew me toward the car. "This is how Milly brought me across to London. I was pretty sure her car would still be here."

He jerked the door open and felt above the driver's side visor. A set of keys fell down into his hand, which he then tossed to me.

"You drive, me and Calliope can ride in the back."

It was then that I realized Liam was running things because I wasn't holding it together. The thought of losing Eve, or Pamela, or both, had turned me inside out.

I clenched the keys in my right hand. No, I wouldn't fall apart, that wasn't doing Eve or Pamela any good.

"Liam, give Dox directions to the farmhouse." They put their heads together; Liam was worried. About me.

*Pull it the fuck together, Rylee.*

One of the triplets set Calliope into the back as I slid into the driver's seat. Liam got in behind her. "Let's go."

Eve slipped further and I threw the car into reverse, peeling out backward, and then slamming it into drive at the same time I pushed the pedal to the floor.

"Rylee, we'll get there."

I knew he was trying to soothe me, to keep me calm.

"You can't feel her inside your head. We're losing her." And that was the crux of it; Eve was slipping too fast—unless Terese was there, waiting for us, there was no way we'd save the Harpy.

Eve was going to die and it was going to be on my head. This was my fault for sending children into battle, for asking children to protect each other.

The SUV powered over the ruts and bumps in the road, and then we were on the interstate. I pushed the SUV as hard as I could, weaving in and out of traffic with a cold precision that I clung too.

We were on the road to the farmhouse when it happened.

Eve's life blinked out. There was no pain, no fear; she was just gone.

This couldn't be happening. Not again. I sucked in a sharp breath and clenched my teeth tight.

*Eve, how could Eve be gone?*

"Rylee." Liam reached forward, cupping the back of my neck with his hand. He knew, even though he wasn't in my head, he knew.

Spinning the wheel hard, I cranked the SUV onto the driveway, jerking the emergency brake up, which brought the back end drifting to a stop. I leapt out and ran for the barn where I could still sense her. What was left of her.

A howl erupted out of the barn, Alex's mournful cry burrowing into my heart. I wasn't the only one losing someone they cared about. Alex's howls broke through the thin grasp of control I still had; his pain on top of my own was too much. Tears streaked my face as I ran. She was so young, too young to be gone already.

I burst through the barn doors and Alex spun, a snarl on his lips, the fur standing up all over him, teeth snapping at me. "No more hurts Evie!"

Then he saw me, really saw me, and his snarl faded into a set of trembling lips. "Rylee, Evie . . . ."

Behind him, Eve lay in a slump, her tawny feathers covered in blood, her wings twisted at angles that shouldn't have been. I fell to my knees, reached out and touched her back. Still warm, but I knew she was gone.

Eve was gone.

# 14

Head bowed, I didn't hear Liam bring Calliope in. The filly stumbled up against me, her broken leg healing, but still not strong enough to support her well.

*You grieve for your Evening Star as if she were your own.*

I reached up and touched the filly's nose, my voice cracking on the words. "She is a part of my family."

Calliope said nothing else, just leaned forward, and touched Eve with her muzzle.

*My father believes that she will help the other Harpies remember the bonds they once had with us.*

"Why then would he let them do this?" I swiped my tears away, angry that I'd let them out, angrier that the Tamoskin Crush would break their word.

*This is not my crush's doing. This is something else. But I think I can help.*

I frowned up at her, but it was Liam who caught my eye.

"Peter S. Beagle." He mouthed to me. And I frowned harder. Then I caught it, but damn, how could I have been so stupid?

Calliope leaned forward, pressing her nubbin of a horn into Eve's side. A soft shimmer of golden light spread from the young unicorn to the Harpy, travelling over Eve's feathers, lighting each one up before fading into her body.

*That is all I can do. She will still need to be healed.*

"All you can do?" I whispered, and then jumped as Eve let out a groan and took a deep breath. Calliope had brought her back to life. Her threads were suddenly there again, and I could grab them. She was alive. But not for long if we didn't get her healed.

"Liam, stay with Eve!"

I leapt to my feet and ran to the house. Terese, we had to get Terese here.

The back door was locked and I kicked it open, the glass panel shattering. Alex was on my heels howling. "Evie, Evie, Evie!"

"Alex, shut up and watch for the glass!"

"Okie dokie."

I grabbed the phone, my hands shaking. We weren't going to lose her. Terese would get here in time. The leader of the local coven picked up on the first ring. I didn't give her a chance to speak.

"I need you at the farmhouse to heal someone who is going to die without you."

"Rylee?"

"Yes, now hurry your witchy ass up."

Alex bounced at my side whispering, "Hurry, hurry, hurry."

"I'm coming, it'll take me at least a half hour."

It would have to do. I slammed the phone down, grabbed some towels from the bathroom, and then ran back out the door. "Alex, get some blankets!"

"Going!"

Back in the barn, Liam had set Eve's head up on a bale of hay. "She's in and out, but hanging on. The worst injury is there." He pointed under her left wing at the gaping wound. Blood and bone, torn muscle and the flutter of something moving inside that I suspected was her heart. Whoever did this was going to be wishing their mother never whored herself out to their father. Because I was going to fucking slaughter them. Slowly, and with great amounts of creativity and pain.

I folded the towels and pressed them against the open wound. Eve let out a groan, her eyelids fluttering. "I tried to stop them, there were too many of them."

"Shhh. Just hold still. Terese is coming and she'll patch you up," I said, hoping that Terese would get here in time.

Alex came barreling in, two blankets streaming out behind him like capes. Liam took them and laid them across Eve. Calliope curled up next to Eve, laying her head against the Harpy's side, mortal enemies no more. Alex shuffled next to me and then wrapped his arms around Eve.

"Evie hang on."

Liam cleared his throat, and I looked up to see the moisture in his eyes. "She'll make it. I'll go wait for Terese."

Seeing Eve lay out like that . . . he hadn't realized how much he had grown to care about Rylee's 'crew', as he called them, until that moment. When he'd thought they'd lost Eve.

Not since he'd had to bury his parents had grief swamped him like that. The bracing cold air outside the barn helped clear his head. What could have taken Eve out? What had the strength to kill a Harpy without leaving any evidence behind?

Had the unicorns gotten fed up with waiting? Somehow, even knowing as little as he did, he doubted it. Something else then. Milly? No, this wasn't her style, too messy.

He paced the barnyard, then paused, lifted his head to the air, and took a deep breath. The scents were jumbled. Alex and Rylee came through loud and clear, a whisper of Eve, Calliope, and then another scent. One he recognized all too well.

Faris, the motherfucker; he'd been here.

There would be no respite this time; he'd seen it in Rylee's eyes. It was one thing to hurt her, one thing to take a child she didn't know, but to hurt one of her own?

Liam had a feeling that Faris was about to meet a side of Rylee he'd not yet encountered. A side that Liam had seen glimmers of over the years, but that she'd never fully unleashed.

The squeak of tires on the hard packed snow brought his head up. Terese pulled into the farmyard in a small red truck. He waved at her and she ran toward him.

"Who is it, who's hurt?"

He didn't answer, just led her to the barn. Gods, let her have made it in time.

Terese stepped into the barn followed by Liam. A fierce look settled on his face, reminding me of his

Agent days when he thought he'd caught me in a lie. There was only one thing I could think of that would leave him looking like he was ready to interrogate someone at the end of a hot poker.

He'd figured out who'd done this, or at least, he thought he did. I didn't ask him, though; right now, there were more pressing matters. I'd kill who I needed to kill soon enough.

"Terese." I pointed at Eve.

The witch stopped. "Are you serious? You called me out in the dead of night to help a *Harpy?*"

I fought not to reach over and smack her for her assumption Eve wasn't worthy of healing. Pissing Terese off wouldn't help anyone. "They took Pamela, the young witch I told you about. We need to help Eve and then we can figure out who has Pam."

That seemed to get through to her. "They took . . . ." Her eyes widened and she dropped to her knees next to Calliope. Startled, she stared at the filly for a full ten seconds.

"Terese, we are running out of time." Eve was slipping again, and I didn't want to take anymore time than we had to.

"Right." She leaned forward and put her hands on Eve, words breathed out past her lips as she wound the spell over Eve's body.

The Harpy let out a low, pain-filled moan, her body jerking as it knit back together.

"Hang on, Eve, I know it's bad. But it'll ease," I said, but I kept my hands to myself. No need to have my Immunity interfere with the healing.

Eve shifted, clacked her beak, and Alex started to jump up and down. "Evie!"

Evie, indeed. Her threads were running strong, if fatigued. She rolled to her feet, and I pointed at Calliope.

"Watch out, your savior is rather tiny."

Eve ducked her head down. "Little foal, you brought me back. I am forever in your debt."

Calliope bobbed her head once. But stayed where she was.

Terese bent to her. "Since I'm already here." She laid her hands on the foal, and the broken leg knit in a matter of seconds.

The filly scrambled to her feet, startling us all as she reared back, front legs flashing in the air. I Tracked her, felt the joy running through her.

Two Salvages now, one for Calliope and one for Eve. One more to go. One that I couldn't feel.

A fucking blind salvage. Why, oh why did Doran have to be right about this?

Terese stood, dark circles under her eyes. "I hope you have no more injuries because I am done. I do not have the power you are used to seeing in Milly. Most witches are lucky to perform one spell a day, never mind curatives of this level." She waved her hand at Eve. The Harpy bowed her head. "Thank you, Terese. I am, it seems, in your debt as well."

Calliope stomped her foot into the straw, then flicked her head to the doorway. Standing there was her father, the leader of the Tamoskin Crush. The filly ran to her father, butting her head against his shoulder.

*Tracker, you have brought her home. You have our undying loyalty.*

At that moment, I didn't give a shit about his loyalty. "Where were you when Eve was attacked?" I snarled, pissed off that they would just allow this to happen, to just stand back and watch Eve get gutted.

*They came on suddenly, and we ran them off, but it was too late. We grieved the Harpy's loss. How is it she is yet alive?* He tipped his head to one side, then flicked his nose toward Eve.

"Your daughter saved her."

*Calliope saved . . . the Evening Star?*

I nodded, the anger flowing out of me. "Yeah. She's going to be something when she grows up. They both are."

He bobbed his head once. *A new generation, a new understanding. So it begins; Tracker, you are the catalyst we have waited for.*

With no more words, he backed away from the door. Calliope reared up, tossing her head, her thin-spiked mane waving, and struck her front feet into the air.

"Stay away from Rocs!" I called after her as she bolted, bucking and leaping after her father into the night.

I turned to Eve. "There is no time to waste, Eve, who did this?"

"There were two groups; they hit us at the same time." She ruffled her wings and settled away from the blood that had pooled in the middle of the barn. "First was Faris. But we didn't think he was going to be trouble. He asked only that we take a message for you, and he took Pamela into the house to write it down."

I Tracked Faris as Eve spoke, while my anger rose into a white heat that would put the lava we'd dodged to shame. He was on the other side of the Veil, which wasn't terribly surprising. But Pamela wasn't with him. With her, there was still a large, blank nothing. Not even that shimmering sensation of knowing she was alive, but not being able to pinpoint her, that came with someone being across the Veil. With her, there was nothing. She wasn't with him. She was across some large body of water.

Eve continued. "The second group was like vampires, but not. I know that doesn't make sense but—"

Liam lifted his hand. "Shadows, the servants of the vampire. They have abilities, but not quite at the level of their masters if they are like the ones we tangled with in Venice."

"They came with weapons, in the dark. I did not hear them, and they did this while I slept." She hung her head. "I was caught unawares. I am sorry, Rylee."

"This is not your fault, Eve." I put a hand to her side, just grateful she was alive.

The barn door creaked open and Dox stepped in. Alex waved at him, his claw-tipped paw flopping bonelessly.

"Hiya, Dox!"

"Hi, Alex." He stepped into the barn. "The others are checking the perimeter. Is Eve . . . ?"

"I am well." Eve fluffed her wings once, settling deeper into the hay.

Everyone looked to me, even Liam. I was going to have to make the call.

And again, I was going to have to leave Eve behind. Logically, I knew that the chances of another attack on her were slim to none. But I didn't like it. And there wasn't time for any other preparations.

"Terese, you stay here, keep an eye on Eve and call in reinforcements if you have to."

She spluttered, all her dulcet tones lost in her disbelief. "You can't possibly think you can save Pamela from a group of vampires, do you?"

"I have something they want. Something I can bargain with." I quickly went over the weapons I had on me, and then lifted my eyes to hers. "Can you say the same?"

"Rylee, this is what they want, what Faris wants," Liam growled.

"Faris isn't the one who has her," I said, striding toward the barn door.

"Alex comes too." The werewolf shoved himself up against my side. I dropped my hand to his thick black fur.

"Yes, you're coming this time."

Terese threw her hands into the air. "You think *he* can help you better than I can?"

I stared down at Alex, and then flicked my eyes up to Terese. "He has saved my life more than once. He's my wolf as much as Liam is. Maybe more."

Liam grunted, but he couldn't really argue. Alex listened to me, let me lead no matter what. That quality was good and bad. Right now, it was a good thing.

Terese put her hands on her slim hips, but I turned my back on her before she could say anything else.

"Dox, you, Sla, and the triplets set up around the barn. Hold down the fort."

Dox nodded, his face grim. He'd finally realized the realities of my life, what I dealt with everyday. Between that and making his first kill, I could see a part of him was lost. He was no longer just a gentle ogre; he'd found a dark side to himself. Whatever his past had held, he'd overcome it on this trip, and he would be stronger for it. His words only confirmed what I thought.

"Kill the fuckers, Rylee. Kill them and be done with it."

I nodded. 'That's the plan."

Liam led the way out of the barn, toward the farmhouse and the dry cellar around the back. I followed him down the steps and turned the light on. At least my weapons stash was still here.

Liam grabbed a couple more blades and my back up crossbow. I went to one knee and opened up the army green lockbox that held all the pre-made spells Milly had prepped for me, and the one spell Terese had prepped for me. A holding spell, one that would bind Milly and make it so she couldn't use her magic, as well as be unable to move. My hand hovered over it. No, that wasn't the right one. Not yet, anyway.

I carefully lifted out three pre-made spells, firebombs that worked like napalm and would stick to everything they touched. I slid them into their hard carrying cases that would keep them from breaking and, if they broke, would snuff the fire. Then there was the obsidian blade, a four-inch fragile blade that would break the first time I used it. I slid it into a sheath and hung it from my neck, under my shirt. What good it could do, I had no idea, but Doran said to take it. So take it I would.

"Rylee, can you tell where Pamela is at all?" Liam slung the crossbow's strap over his shoulder.

I headed back up the stairs and stared into the dark night sky. "I don't know. Across water."

"Then how the hell are we going to find her?"

I gave him a half smile. "I've got an idea."

# 15

Her idea was not what he'd expected, not at all. Liam stood in the center of the castle breathing deeply through his nose. He could smell Pamela, but not well, just faintly.

Alex, on the other hand, had his nose crammed to the ground and was working through the castle with an intensity and focus the submissive werewolf didn't often show.

Rylee trailed Alex, a few feet behind, her eyes searching the castle as they went. When Eve had been slipping, he wasn't sure if Rylee was going to pull through. There had been too much loss for her, too much pain and grief.

Yet, here she was, her shit together and on another hunt. There was a reason others let her lead. Though he'd had to cover for her for a bit, she'd gotten herself under control again.

"Liam, anything?" She called over her shoulder.

He took a deep breath, caught a faint whisper of Pamela and vampires. "Still there, Alex is doing well."

Alex's tail wagged twice with the praise, and he lifted a paw with a single thumbs up, and then he was back to scenting the trail.

They wove through the castle, pausing at intersections for several minutes to be sure they were on the right track. Liam was almost certain that the vampires were Berget's. Hell, there were only two factions of vampires, and Rylee said that Faris wasn't with Pamela . . . though that didn't mean he wasn't going to cause trouble.

Liam jogged to her side, and lowered his voice. No need to announce his thoughts to anyone who might be lurking in the castle. "Can you Track Faris, didn't you say he was on this side of the Veil?"

Her tri-colored eyes flicked up to his, her brows furrowing as she Tracked the vampire.

"Yes, he's on this side of the Veil, close too. Fuck, that is the last thing we need," she muttered as she loosened up a sword from her back.

Liam stepped back and shifted the crossbow so that it was angled and ready to be used. He would only make a full shift to wolf if he had to.

Focusing on his sense of smell, he did his best to block the other scents and zeroed in on Faris. The vampire was nowhere close, and he hadn't been this way. All Liam could pick up was Pamela and Berget's scents.

"You know who took her," he said softly, not wanting to hurt Rylee, but knowing that they had to discuss tactics. That was the only way they were going to get in and get out with them all in one piece.

Rylee's back stiffened, but she didn't turn around. "Yes."

"Then we have to talk about this. She will use Pamela as a bargaining chip to get you to do what she wants."

She exploded, spinning on her heel to face him, eyes bright with anger. "What the fuck, you think I don't know that? There is nothing I can do about it right now. I will do what I have to do to get Pamela back."

His body chilled, his blood running cold.

That was what he was afraid of.

The castle seemed endless and it didn't take me long to wish we'd brought something to mark the stone with. Alex followed Pamela's scent for close to half an hour before he froze at the head of an intersection. His whole body stiffened and a long low snarl rippled out of him; even the hair along his spine bristled up.

I yanked my second sword out. Whatever it was that Alex was picking up on was about to have a very bad day.

Liam moved up to my side, crossbow lifted and ready to shoot.

"Alex, what is it?" I kept my voice as low as possible.

Both of the boys answered at the same time.

"Faris."

The vampire stepped out from around the corner of the intersection, as if he were waiting to be announced, his hands lifted to the air. "It seems that you did not get my message, since the messenger has been snatched." His bright blue eyes were hooded, lazy, and I could feel him try to bespell me. Something he'd not done for some time.

I stared at the hollow of his throat and lifted my swords so they lined up with his neck. "I don't have time for your games. So get the fuck out of my way."

He gave us a mocking bow, sweeping his arm forward. "Be my guest, take on your precious little sister on your own. See how far it gets you. Wait, you've done that once already, haven't you? Remind me again how that went?"

I clenched my swords and lifted my eyes to his, fury keeping me safe from the lure of his eyes. Now they were just eyes, nothing special.

Liam took a step, placing himself in front of me. "What was the message for Rylee?"

Faris laughed, a chuckle really, but he seemed truly amused. "Simple. I want to make a deal with her. I want her to Track for me. I do believe we've already agreed that Berget taking control of the vampire nation would be a very bad idea."

"I'm not helping you," I snapped, moving so that Liam was to the side of me. Alex moved with me, and though he was no longer snarling, his teeth were bared and the fur along his spine hadn't lowered.

"Fuckity fucker," the werewolf grumbled, snapping his teeth once for emphasis.

Faris looked from Alex to me, blinking several times. "And she shall teach the submissive to stand. I wasn't sure it was going to be you, Rylee. I truly wasn't."

This was not the time to get into prophecies. Pamela needed us. I put my back to the wall and slid along it. "Alex, which way did Pam go?"

He took a couple long drags from the floor and then he started forward.

"Liam, let's go."

Liam backed toward me, never taking his eyes off Faris. "You don't want to kill him?"

"I do, I just don't have the time right now."

Faris clapped three times, condescension in his every movement. "You will regret this."

I flipped him off. "Regret not killing you? You've got that right, you monkey-sucking taint jockey."

His blue eyes narrowed. "You shouldn't hang around ogres, it will be bad for their health."

We slid around the corner and he was out of sight, though most definitely not out of mind.

"Jack warned you they would fight over you, that's what he said, isn't it?" Liam and I continued to walk backward, our eyes trained on where Faris would come from if he were to attack us.

"Yes, he said that's why he got sick, because he wouldn't work for them." Jack had no one in his life to use as leverage, so they'd used his health against him. At least, that's what he'd told me. This was what I got for caring about other people, and this was why I hated the soft emotions. They caused nothing but grief.

We walked like that for another thirty feet before I bumped into Alex.

"Pamie through there," he said, a whine escaping him, whatever tough guy exterior he'd had slipping back behind his submissive nature.

I turned to see a thin door, maybe a foot across at the most, with a large, ornate doorknob in the shape of a skull. I looked closer. The skull had a perfect set of miniature fangs. Nice touch.

Without waiting, I opened the door and Tracked Pamela. The faintest whisper of her threads responded to me. "This is it."

Liam put a hand out, blocking me. "I'll go first, you next."

Alex pointed at himself. "Then Alex?"

Liam gave him a nod. "Yes, you come through last, guard the rear."

There was no point in waiting, we stepped through the doorway, the Veil twisting and wrapping around us before spitting us out on the other side. We stepped across the threshold into a beautiful room, done all in white, creams, and gold. There was a bigger than king-sized bed, covered with pillows and pale pink rose petals.

Alex grabbed my legs and whimpered. "Bad, bad, bad."

I looked to Liam as his face drained of color. I wasn't sure I wanted to know what the hell they were picking up on. I stared around the room, tried using my second sight, but there was nothing to see, nothing hidden from me.

Pamela was close, really close, maybe a few hundred feet down and to the right. I turned slowly, pinpointing her with ease. But before I could take a step in her direction, Liam barred my way with his arm.

"This is worse than bad, Rylee." He shook his head as if to clear it. For Alex to be spooked was something of an every day occurrence. But for Liam to be so spooked? That did not bode well.

"What is it?"

He swallowed hard and looked around the room. "It shouldn't be this clean, not for what I'm smelling."

Shit on a stick, where the hell had we ended up? I walked to the bed, though Liam sounded as if he were choking with each step I took. I trailed my hand on the cream blanket, picked up a rose petal. Soft and squishy . . . I lifted it higher, my gorge rising into my throat.

They weren't rose petals, they were pieces of skin peeled and shaped to resemble rose petals. I threw it down onto the bed. It didn't matter where we were, or what had gone on, we needed to get Pamela and get the hell out of there.

I strode toward the oversized double doors that led out of the room, twisted the handle, and stepped into the hallway.

While I couldn't be sure, if I was a betting kind of gal, I'd say we were back in Venice, below the city.

Back in the nest of vampires. Damn it all to hell and back, this was the worst kind of déjà vu.

A scream, high-pitched and violent, echoed down the hallway and Alex bolted past me. "Pamie!"

I leapt after him, Liam right behind me. There was no thought as to what we were running into, there couldn't be, not with her screams echoing in our ears. Alex galloped down the carpeted hallway, putting distance between us.

"Keep up with him!" I shouted at Liam, as a vampire's servant stepped in front of us. How did I know it was a servant and not a vampire? The bastard was missing an arm. I'd fought him once before and obviously needed to finish him off. I brought my sword up in an arc that removed his other arm. He fell to his knees and sucked in a lungful of air to shout or scream. It didn't matter.

On the back swing, I took his head.

I didn't stop to wipe my blades, just ran. Alex was gone from sight, but we were close now. Curving around a corner, we ran down a single flight of stairs, skidding to a stop as we hit the ballroom that we'd escaped only weeks ago.

Motherfucking pus buckets, I did not want to be here. In a matter of heartbeats, I took the scene in.

Like an arena, there were vampires in a semi-circle around the main event, their faces intent on the spectacle before them. In the center, Pamela stood with her legs apart, hands stretched out in front of her, and a snarl on her lips as she poured out her magic. She was cut and bruised, her hair was a mess, but she was at least alive and still standing. And Berget, she stood there, cocky and sure of herself, one hand on her hip, a golden gown clinging to her curves while she almost nonchalantly batted Pamela's magic away.

My sister acted as if she was truly just at a gala event and not in a fight. Alex stood between them, his back to Pamela, his face a wicked visage of teeth and fury that for once, didn't seem out of place on him.

Before I could do anything though, a crossbow bolt flew from behind me, catching Berget in the middle of her chest. Blood blossomed over the shimmering golden material, but Berget barely flinched. Liam cursed under his breath.

I yanked the three firebombs out and threw them toward the onlookers. The fire burst open, clinging to anything and everything. Screams erupted out of the melee, and most of Berget's shadows fled.

Berget turned her face toward us as she flicked her hand toward Pamela. The young witch dropped to her knees, panting for air, her head lowered.

"Sister." Berget took a few steps toward me, a smile on her lips that I didn't trust for one second. "I'm so glad you could come. I need to speak to you about a deal." She flicked her fingers and Pamela went flying toward her, caught by Berget with a single hand. My sister clutched Pamela to her chest, so that Pamela faced us. Son of a bitch, how the hell was I going to get Pamela away from her?

Berget, Child Empress, drew them both back closer to the throne. Her smile, tight with anger, only made her look less like the Berget I'd seen in my unconscious state. She looked like she was about to throw a temper tantrum.

I glared at her, steeling myself for what I was going to have to do. With a slow, precise movement, I lifted my swords, my intent clear. I might not be able to say it, but I would do it. I had to.

*She's not Berget; just remember that.*

Easier said than done. Berget's blue eyes widened and she put a hand to Pamela's throat, squeezing just enough to get Pamela to react.

Berget tipped her head again to the side. "You would kill me?"

"Let her go," I said, walking toward them.

She tipped her head from side to side, not shaking it, but touching it to her shoulders, back and forth. Her eyes clouded and the blue faded to a shimmering green. The color of the late Empress's eyes. Doran hadn't been kidding about where Berget's powers had come from. When she spoke, her voice had a lilting accent to it, one that was most definitely not her own.

"I will kill her one day, but not today if you agree to help me. You are a Tracker, and the prophecies state that you must help me find the last of the Blood."

Of course, maybe if things had been just between me and Berget, maybe I could have convinced her. Or at least I would have had a better chance than with what happened next.

Faris strolled into the ballroom, taking us full circle. Hell, the only difference was this time Alex was with us. I glanced down at him. He'd moved back to stand with me and Liam, but he hadn't gone back to being submissive; he still had his teeth bared and he continually grumbled under his breath.

"Bad, bad, yuppy doody, bad."

Berget's hold on Pamela tightened. "Well, isn't this lovely, we're all back together again."

Faris held up one hand, as if he was going to beseech her. "I wouldn't say that. You have not a single vampire here with you. Only servants. That is a rather large change."

Her eyes narrowed and her hand tightened on Pamela's throat. Damn it all, what was he trying to do, get Pamela killed?

But his words made me take a quick look around. Hell fire, he was right. None of those who stood with her were vampires, but servants. The differences were subtle, darker skin, their movements were slower, and their eyes had zero hypnotic effect. Things I'd learned *after* my last encounter with them.

Servants. Only mildly easier to kill than a true vampire. That explained the effectiveness of the firebombs.

"Berget." I lifted my sword, pointing it at her head. "Let her go. You asked me to save you, but I can't save you if you keep putting those I love at death's door."

With a laugh, she pushed Pamela to her knees. "I never asked you to save me. And what would you save me from? A life of power? A life where I ruled the world of the supernatural and the humans?"

I stepped closer, my sword tip never wavering. "Yes. I would save you from those things." Gods be damned, I would fight for those I loved time and again, no matter how much they hurt me.

A flaw that would likely get me killed, but for the first time, I truly embraced it. She was my sister, and I would fight for her until I could fight no more.

*Where there is life, there is hope.* I hated clichés. Even when they were true.

Her hand tightened on Pamela until her face went bright red. "I will kill her if you take a step closer."

Pamela lashed out, yanking the bowie knife from her back and slashing Berget across the face. An arc of blood spurted out across Pamela's shirt, splattering her in a brilliant red splash. But Berget didn't flinch, just reached out and snatched the knife from Pamela, acting as if it hadn't happened. As her face healed up, I realized that for her, in a way, it hadn't happened. It was an inconsequential moment in her life.

We were so screwed.

Tense, I stared my little sister down. "I will kill you if you end her life. No matter what is between us, Sister."

Another truth, the dark side of the same coin; I would kill her if she killed Pamela.

"Then we are at a standoff. One where no one wins, everyone dies, and the world goes on as it was." Berget tossed her hair. "Completely unacceptable."

"I agree."

We all turned to the newcomer who stepped into the room to the far left of us.

Milly, dressed all in black with a long dark green cloak that brushed the ground.

What. The. Fuck.

She lifted her hands and a bolt of lightning slammed between Pamela and Berget, sending Pamela skidding across the floor to Milly's feet. Milly bent and pulled the girl upright.

"Rylee, I see you're up to your neck again," she said, never looking my way.

I managed to get my shock under control. "Same old, same old."

Berget stood at the back of the room, glaring at me, fury etched into her face. "You think you can end this with your witches? I will show you power."

She flung her hands toward Milly and Pamela, and while Pamela flinched, she snapped her hands up to brace against the flow of death coming at them, sweat sliding down her face. I'd never seen her so determined, so damn fierce. Her lips were pressed to a thin line and her brows were drawn deep over her eyes with the intensity of her concentration. While she defended, Milly attacked. The spell she unleashed wasn't a death spell, but one of light, the brilliant splash of magic slamming between the three women blasted my eyes and I had to look away. With a triumphant yell, Milly forced Berget back, step by step.

"You cannot win, vampire. Not against both of us."

As a team, Pamela and Milly were beyond formidable. They were downright fucking scary. And I could see already in Milly the calculations, of what she could accomplish if she brought Pamela under her tutelage. The way her eyes darted to the younger witch as they fought side by side. Shit, that could not happen.

Minutes passed and finally the standoff broke in a rather anti-climatic way. Berget bolted, flinging her hand back toward Milly and Pamela one last time before disappearing through an archway and into the darkness of the tunnels.

The crackle of flames behind us was the only sound as the firebombs continued to eat at the walls.

I lowered my sword, but realized too late that we were far from done. The sound of the flames was drowned out by a new sound. One that was, in it's own way, far more deadly. Especially considering the simple fact that we were far underground. Far from any semblance of rescue.

I stepped back, understanding what was coming a split second before it happened. Water, thick and dirty, erupted out of the tunnels and swept toward us in a wave that threatened to swallow us whole.

*Damn it all to hell and back, here we go again.*

## 16

There was no time for thinking, no time for anything but running.

"Move." I shouted as I bolted toward Milly, grabbed Pamela's hand, and headed for the stairs, the water already up over my ankles and deepening with each breath I took. Our only saving grace was the narrow tunnels keeping the water from flooding us out within seconds. A glance back showed me Milly was gone. Probably jumped the Veil, leaving us to our own devices. Nice, really nice.

Liam and Alex were right with us, quickly passing us to lead the way. Pamela stumbled halfway up the stairs, and I pulled her to her feet as the footing below us began to crumble, a wave of water slopping up and over us both as we sank. Hands yanked us up and out of the water.

"No dawdling now," Faris said calmly, as he pulled Pamela out and Liam pulled me from the ink black, angry water. Faris helping us was the least of my concerns, though. My vision was obscured by water and the flickering lights as they were doused, one by one. Again, I grabbed Pamela's hand, but this time I jerked her away from Faris. Whatever his game was, we didn't have time for it. He laughed, shaking his head as if I'd delivered a punch line to a particularly funny anecdote. I would never understand vampires, not if I lived to be a hundred. Which, by the way things were going, was not looking like a particularly good possibility.

A groan shuddered through the underground palace, and the walls around us leaned closer, water spurting through cracks that widened before my eyes. Oh we were in trouble. We had to move faster or we weren't going to make it to our exit across the Veil.

I shoved Pamela toward Liam. "Take her."

He scooped her up into his arms and booted open the door.

He paused before crossing the Veil, glanced over his shoulder at me. I shoved him forward as the lights went out, leaving us in a dim shadow, the only light coming to us from through the doorway. "I'm right behind you."

Only I wasn't. Liam stepped through, Pamela clinging to his neck, her eyes dull with fatigue and fear. That was my last glimpse of them. I took a step to follow them, Alex right with me. The sound of the roof cracking overhead didn't give me enough warning. Plaster and chunks of cement fell and with it, and the water over our heads sluiced in with a thunderous rush.

Faris snaked his arms around my waist and jerked me back as the roof fell, and the black water flooded the room and filled my mouth with the taste of death and rotten things. A clawed set of hands gripped my legs as Alex grabbed me, and all I could think was that at least Pamela and Liam had made it.

And at least I wouldn't die on my own.

Rylee was wrong. She wasn't right behind him. The water flooded through the door from the Veil into the castle, and swept him off his feet. Pamela tumbled out of his arms, hitting the rock ground hard.

Liam spun on the floor and lunged toward the open door. "Pamela, help me!"

Only she didn't do what he thought she would. He wanted to go back, to yank Rylee out of the water.

Pamela, a groan escaping her, lifted her hand and the water stilled long enough for him to see that there was nothing in the dark water.

Rylee was gone. He stood there, staring into the room where she'd been only a brief moment before, his hands gripping the door jams.

"Liam, I can't hold it much longer. Hurry," Pamela whispered, the broken tones of her voice catching him off guard.

She wasn't there; Rylee wasn't there. No denying it, either she had made it out, or she'd been swept away from him. His heart twisted into a knot as he said, "Shut the door."

"But you don't have her." Pamela limped to his side, and slid her small hand into his. "Liam? Is she dead?"

He reached across with his free hand and forced the door shut, the lock clicking into place. The door shuddered, and then began to fade.

"What's happening?" Pamela reached out and put her hands on the door as it disappeared beneath her fingers.

He wasn't sure, but he could guess. "A fail-safe. A protection against things coming here and destroying the castle through the doorways."

His mind was a complete and utter blank as he struggled to comprehend what the hell had just happened. Rylee was gone, Alex was gone, and he and Pamela had no way to find her.

Pamela threw her arms around his waist and let out a gulping sob. "She can't be dead, she can't be. She saved me, Liam, why couldn't I save her?"

With a reluctance he couldn't deny, he lowered his arms to carefully hug the sobbing witch. "We don't know that she's dead."

She clung to him, her body shaking. "She's the . . . only family . . . I have."

It took everything he had to say the words that came out of his mouth. "You have me, too. And Eve. You aren't alone, Pam."

Her sobbing eased and she looked up at him. "You don't hate me?"

Surprising himself, he shook his head. "No."

She gave him a tentative smile, and the wolf in him seemed to shake his head with resignation, accepting that this witch, at least, was worth not killing. She was a part of this strange family, not on the outskirts as he had wanted to keep her.

A whiff of rose perfume snapped his head up and he shoved Pamela behind him. Before he took another breath he let his wolf rage to the top, his skin and bones shifting until he stood on all fours, his teeth bared to the witch who strode into the room. "This is all very touching, truly a sweet moment, but if you're done with the Disney scene, I suggest we go get your mate." Milly lifted an eyebrow, looking confident, but he could smell her and the uncertainty that spilled off her.

Pamela stepped up beside him and buried her hand in the fur along his back. "Why would we trust you? You killed people Rylee loved; you tried to kill Alex and Eve. You tried to kill me." With each word she spoke she tightened her hand on his fur until it pulled. But he didn't dare look back at her. Besides, Pamela wasn't afraid. No, Milly was afraid, the sour scent of fear rolling off her.

Pamela, on the other hand, was pissed, her anger a sharp, spiky spice that the wolf in him heartily approved of.

He snarled and took a step toward Milly. She narrowed her eyes and held up a hand. "Don't make me do it, O'Shea. I will spell you and you can be my pet again. This time permanently."

Pamela flung her hands in the air, her arms quivering and her accent strong. "I'll stop you. You can't hurt him, not with me here."

Liam angled his body so that he stood between them, but still faced Milly. Her green eyes flicked from him to Pamela and back again. "Quite the pair. But how do you expect to find Rylee? Hmm? You can't Track like she can, you can't scent her in all that water."

Pamela didn't lower her hands. "We'll go get Jack. He can Track her."

Milly snorted. "And if you go to Jack through the doorway, by then, Faris will have enthralled her and made her one of his creatures. I don't think anyone here wants that, do we?"

Pamela stiffened, but Liam held still. He knew what Milly was doing, trying to weasel her way back into Rylee's life. The shit part was Milly was right. If there was a time limit to how long they had, then there was very little choice as to whether or not they could take her help.

The green-eyed witch folded her hands over her more than ample bosom. "I can take Pamela with me, we can jump the Veil and have Jack here in a matter of minutes. Your way will take far longer."

Damn, why did she have to make logical, sound sense? There was no point in delaying the decision. Much as he might want to.

He made eye contact with Pamela and bobbed his head. Just once. She lowered her hands. "Are you sure? We could get Jack on our own."

While they knew which doorway would take them back to Jack, they then would have to make the trek to his home, and hope the old Tracker was up for a journey back to the physical crossing point. He shook his head.

Pamela's lips pressed together and she nodded. "I'll go with you. But we go now, and come right back. No sneaky stuff or I'll blast you and your brat."

Milly's eyelids fluttered, but she nodded and held out her hand. "Let's go, then, little girl."

Liam watched as Pamela took Milly's hand, and they jumped the Veil, disappearing in front of his eyes. Minutes passed, minutes where he began to doubt whether or not he'd made the right choice.

Ten minutes and he paced the small hallway, his claws clicking on the stone. Where the hell were they? Would Pamela be able to take Milly out if she had to?

Son of a bitch, what had he been thinking letting her go with Milly? A whine escaped him and he knew that Pamela wasn't the only one worried about losing those who had become like family to them all. There was nowhere else that they all belonged.

Ten minutes faded into twenty and he stood in the hallway, his head hung low with shame, fear, and guilt crushing down on him. He should have pulled Rylee through the doorway too; they should have stepped across the Veil together. And now he'd let Pamela go to—

The scuff of a footstep and the thump of a cane spun him around at the same time the smell of liniment and herbs caught his nose. Jack stepped toward him, Milly, and Pamela, and—ah shit, they'd brought Will.

Pamela had her arms full of clothes. "I thought you might want to shift back."

He shifted as she spoke and she spun away, tossing the clothes behind her toward him.

Jack thumped his cane on the floor. "So, she got snatched by the bloody fang face, did she? Not surprised about that, not for one gods-be-damned minute. That'll teach her for not listening to those who know better."

Liam dressed fast, yanking the clothes on. "What took you so long?"

Pamela peeked back at him, saw he was dressed, and let out a breath. "Jack was being difficult; Will remembered Milly and attacked her, and then Will wanted to come, but Milly didn't want him here. It was really all quite a mess."

Milly's eyes glittered with anger. "It seems that young Will has an advocate."

Jack snapped his cane out and smacked Milly up the backside of her head. "Enough with this shit. Let's find Rylee."

Milly's mouth dropped open, her eyes widening as her hand went to the back of her head. "You nasty, filthy little—"

"Enough." With one word, Liam silenced them. "Jack, can you Track her?"

He bobbed his head. "That's what I was trying to tell them before they dragged me here."

"Tell us what?" Will put his hands on his hips, eyes narrowing.

"Rylee ain't that fucking far away. Whoever took her has her back home." Jack leaned on his cane, and took a deep rattling breath.

Liam frowned, his brain slow to catch on. "They have her back in North Dakota?"

Jack shook his head and tapped his cane on the floor. "No, they have her somewhere in London."

Faris yanked me and Alex, with him as he jumped the Veil, a gut-lurching twist that left Alex puking filthy grey water the minute we stood on solid ground. The werewolf's sides heaved until I could see ribs, even through his thick fur. I stumbled, gasped for air, and spun to see that we were indeed out of the catacombs that had almost been our death.

We stood in a sumptuous room layered with carpets, draperies, and paintings. I didn't know where he'd brought us, but I was betting that it was nowhere near North Dakota.

"I suppose we should get right to it then." Faris slid up behind me, pinned my arms to my side and licked my neck. "Even if I would prefer you didn't smell like that rotten water, this will have to do. I want you bound to me before the night is over, Tracker, one way or another."

I dropped my weight forward, and kicked back, catching him in the ankle and unbalancing his fangy-ass so he stumbled away from me. "Really, you want to play this game again?" A part of me knew I should be afraid of him. Hell, I had been terrified when I'd first met him. But I held the ace up my sleeve now.

He needed me, and I didn't give a shit about him.

"Ah." He dusted his hands together, regaining his balance without looking like I'd knocked him off-kilter at all. "Shall we talk about the oath you took? The one that said you will do—what was it now, yes, I remember—all in your power to kill the Child Empress?" His icy blue eyes snared mine and I forced myself to look away.

"You're a lying piece of shit, you do know that, don't you? If I'd known who she was, I never would have taken that oath."

"Please, are you telling me you can't come up with anything better than that?" He quirked one blond eyebrow. Standing there, all in black, soaking wet and totally bedraggled, he still managed to look better than most men on their wedding day. I had no such thing going for me. On the other hand, I had every-thing I *did* need to end this.

I yanked a sword from my back and uncoiled my whip with my other hand. "No, nothing better than that today. Unless you want a taste of this." I lifted my sword hand and pointed the blade at his mouth.

"You're not even going to thank me for saving you, are you?"

"Alex says thanks," Alex whispered at my side. He coughed twice and then stood there, shaking, fur dripping onto the carpet. I hoped it left a stain.

Faris gave me a thin smile. "Your wolf has better manners than you do."

When he moved, I wasn't ready for it. No, that wasn't true, I was ready, I just couldn't match his speed. His shoulder slammed into my chest, and he sent me sailing across the room, tumbling through the air until I hit the wall with a resounding thud I felt all the way down to my boots.

I slid to the floor and pushed myself up to my feet while I fought to catch the wind that had been knocked out of me. My brain didn't compute what I was seeing, not right away. Alex sat facing me; Faris crouched behind him. In the thick ruff of Alex's fur around his neck, Faris's hand was buried deep. The vampire shook Alex hard, twice. "Rylee, I do hate to take this to the extreme, but you are— like always— being difficult. If you won't let me draw blood and attempt to bind you to me, then we must do this another way. Since I have met you, I have tried to be patient. I have tried to help you. But there is no time left to play the nice vampire."

Alex scrabbled to get away from him, claws flailing and muzzle snapping, but Faris held him easily.

I didn't tell him to let Alex go, didn't ask him what he wanted. I knew. We both did. And there was only one way to make sure that Alex made it out of this alive. The werewolf let out a barking whine as he fought, gasping for air.

"Alex, be still." I didn't want this, but I didn't know that there was any other way. There was no one coming to rescue us, no way they could find us here, wherever here was. Alex settled down, staring at me with nothing but trust in his big golden eyes. There was no way I could betray him, not even for this.

I would have to do what Faris wanted.

Faris smiled at me, wide enough that I could see his fangs clearly. "You understand? Let me be very clear so that there is no possibility of buyer's remorse here. Binding you to me is tricky at best, and temporary. But what I've learned is that you, unlike Milly, wholly stand behind your word. You do not have it in you to break an oath. And you follow your misleading heart, even when you know better. So." —he tipped his head to one side and smiled again at me— "you will Track the Blood for me so that I will become the Emperor, and you will hold to your oath to kill the Child Empress. And you will swear to both of those things on the redemption of every soul you've ever loved. And if you break your oath, I will kill everything, and everyone, you hold dear."

He tightened his grip on Alex. "To continue this clarity, if you do not swear to these things, I will start with him and kill him now."

My stomach flopped and my heart sank to the bottom of my guts.

Faris had finally won; he'd left me no choice. I lowered my sword, bitterness flowing through me. How in the world had I thought at any point he'd been there to help me? He was a douchebag who'd had hundreds of years to perfect his motherfuckery. "I'll kill you for this one day. You know that, don't you?"

Laughing, the vampire bared his teeth at me. "You can try; I would like to break you to my will. And one more thing, you will also swear that your oaths must be completed when I demand. Now swear it."

"On killing you? Gladly. I swear on pain of—"

"Do not play with me, Rylee. I am not in the mood." He shook Alex, who dangled from his hands like a rag doll, his eyes foggy with lack of air.

"Loosen up on him. I will swear to your stupid oath." I watched as Alex took a deep breath, Faris's hands easing up ever so slightly.

"What is the Blood we are going after? I need that much, to know if I can do it or not." Not really the truth, but I needed to stall, and I hoped that with a little more information, maybe I could get us out of here in one piece. Even if it was a long shot, I had to try.

Faris' eyebrows shot up. "You didn't read any more of the book of the Fanged?"

I shook my head and he let out an exasperated sigh. "The Blood are the first three vampires, the ones who begat our race, the origin of our lives."

"Are they dead?"

He barked a laugh and a glimmer of humor sparkled in his eyes. "Well, no more than I am. But they have been interred in a prison to keep them from the world. We have to find their prison so I can drink their blood and seal my life as the new Emperor. Now quit stalling, speak your oath."

Every gods-be-damned word I spoke burned through to the core of me, acid eating me out from the inside. "I swear to you on the redemption of every soul I've ever loved that I will Track the Blood for you, that I will—" Gods, it stuck in my mouth. I swallowed hard. "That I will hold to my oath to kill the Child Empress, done within the time frame you dictate."

"Well done, Rylee." He threw Alex toward me, and the werewolf's two-hundred-pound frame crashed into mine, taking us to the floor in a tangle of limbs.

"Alex sorry," he whispered, lips turning down at the edges, as he scrambled off me.

"Not your fault, buddy." I stood slowly, dusted my clothes off. Alex pressed himself into my leg, and I dropped a hand to the back of his neck. My fingers came away sticky with blood. Anger, hot and sweet, raged through me. Faris would be dead the second I had the chance.

Faris moved to a side table and poured what I knew wasn't a glass of red wine, though it surely looked like it in the crystal glass. "Now, let us discuss how this will work, our little business arrangement."

I had to get close to him if I was going to kill him. That was the only way I could nullify my oaths and avoid this whole situation. Killing him was not going to be easy with his speed, but maybe he wouldn't expect an assault so quickly. I took a step toward him, keeping my breathing slow and even.

"Remove all your weapons. I'm not so easily fooled. I know you, Rylee." He lifted his eyes to mine as he took a deep drink from his cup. "I do realize you will take any chance you get to try and kill me, so from now on, you drop your weapons when you are close to me unless otherwise directed."

"Fuck you. That wasn't part of the oath." To prove my point, I raised my sword and pulled my second sword from my back. "My oath was to find the Blood you seek, and kill the Child Empress. Nothing in there about not slicing your head in half."

He let out a sigh and his shoulders slumped. "I realize this is the only way to do things with you, but I'd really prefer to be civil. After all, I've done my best to keep you, and your little pack, alive. But, be that as it may, we can do this the hard way. And you will learn to do what I say, when I say it, like the well-trained bitch you will become for me."

With a flash of movement, he was gone. "The bastard jumped the Veil. Where the hell does he think he's going?" I muttered, as I lowered my swords.

"Alex wants to go." He limped toward me and tugged on the end of my shirt. "Really wants to go."

"Yeah, I agree." I walked to where the long black curtains hung closed and jerked them open. A blank, grey cement wall stared back at me. Of course, there wouldn't be an actual window. What was I thinking? I snorted to myself. Faris would go to extremes to keep himself safe. The old tales of sunlight killing vampires was more than true, but most of them were so savvy they would never allow themselves to be caught off guard by daylight.

"Let's get the hell out of here," I muttered, as I strode toward the only other exit, a simple black door with a tarnished silver knob that turned smoothly in my hand. At least it was unlocked.

I opened it and found myself staring at a cement-fucking-wall. I swallowed hard, the realization settling over me as heavy as the four walls and roof I had no doubt were also cement.

Faris had put me in a box of his making, one that didn't require doors, or windows or a way out, because the bastard could jump the Veil and leave whenever he damn well pleased.

Alex poked at the wall with the tip of his claw. "Hmm. Tough shit."

I stepped back from the wall, unable to take my eyes from it. That was one way of putting it.

# 17

Searching the room proved Faris was savvy, indeed. There was no alternate exit, nothing I could use to break out. The walls were thick enough that wherever we were, there was no way I was getting through them. But it was Alex who coined it best.

"Coffin."

I turned and looked at him, his lips trembling as he said it again.

"Alex is in a coffin."

Fuck it all, he was right, we were in a giant coffin. Which meant we were, most likely, underground. My stomach flopped and sweat popped out on my forehead. I wouldn't have said I was claustrophobic before, but I'd never been somewhere where there wasn't even a possibility of escape. I dug my hands into my hair, as the air around us shifted and I spun to see Faris slip through the Veil, a squirming sack in his hands.

His blue eyes were cold, and they bored into mine. "I do not think you believe me or my threats. In that, I have done you a disservice. I won't kill you; we both know that, so I need to make this very clear. You will do as I say, when I say, or your people will begin to die off. I'd use Alex as an example, except I think your friends might notice if he goes missing. But this one, no one except you will notice his loss."

From the bag came a muffled, "Yous be taking yours hands off the lassie."

Charlie!

I made a move toward them and Faris lifted the bag high, twisted the Veil, and I could see through the opening into a bubbling, spitting pit of lava.

"Faris, don't do this." I held my hands open to him, dropping my sword to the heavy carpet at my feet. There was no choice here. "I get it, you're the boss; you don't need to prove the point." A whiff of sulfur curled through the Veil, and a vision of the red ogre going under the rushing lava rose to the front of my mind.

Faris tipped his head to one side. "Since you activated this particular volcano, I think this is fitting." He paused and shifted his stance so he stood sideways to me, his hand that held Charlie dipping ever so slightly. "Do you understand me now? I own you, Rylee. You will do what I say, when I say it. There will be no questions; there will be nothing you do unless I will it until your two oaths are completed. At anytime I can snatch one of your loved ones and destroy them. Up until now I have been . . . gracious."

Bile rose in my throat and I forced it back down, counting in my head the thousands of ways I would chop Faris up and feed him to the fishes, how I would make him regret this day.

He, of course, was oblivious. "And you will breathe a word of this to no one. This will be our little secret. Not even your wolf will know of this."

"Yous thinks I won't be telling on your ass?" Charlie mouthed off from in the bag.

"Shut it, Charlie," I snapped, my eyes pleading with Faris. "He won't say anything."

Faris shrugged. "Well, I can't be sure, and you need to never forget this."

"I'll give you something else," I sputtered, thinking only to get Charlie out of this in one piece. To make sure another person I cared for didn't die on my behalf.

The vampire's eyebrows rose slowly. "And what would you offer me for his life?"

The bag squirmed and shifted. "Don't yous do it, Rylee. Not a thing do yous give this bastard."

I licked my lips. "What do you want?" Fuck, fuck, fuck. How did we get to this point and, more importantly, how the hell was I going to get out of here with all three of us intact?

Faris smiled, his lips lifting so I could see his teeth easily. "Well, there is something your wolf has that I would like very much."

I glanced down at Alex.

Faris chuckled. "Not that wolf. The one you are fucking."

The term 'blood running cold' finally made sense to me. There seemed to be no heat left in me as Faris's eyes drifted up and down my body. I shivered involuntarily.

Charlie screamed. "Don't yous dare. Nothing yous can say will shut me up, vampire. I be screaming yous deception from the rooftops. Rylee, don't yous fuck him!"

With a casual flick of his wrist, Faris tossed Charlie through the Veil toward the lava. Before I could even move, Faris snapped his fingers, and I could no longer see through to the lava. Just the other side of the room. Shaking, I fought to comprehend what had truly just happened. What Faris had done. That Charlie was gone.

"Do you understand, Rylee? Up until now, I have been kind. I am running out of time. I do not think kindness will work with you. Even for your body, I couldn't have your brownie friend blabbing."

Charlie was gone, killed because Faris wanted to make a point. That he could destroy those I loved while barely lifting a finger.

From cold to hot, my blood raged with fury, but I could do *nothing*.

Faris walked toward me and at my side, Alex bristled, stepping in front of me.

"No hurts Rylee," he growled through bared teeth.

I put myself between them, pushing Alex away with my knee, more than cognizant of just what Faris could do. On our own, we couldn't face him. So I was left with bargaining.

"I need to make sure things are settled before I do your Tracking." I crossed my arms over my chest, struggled to keep my voice even when I wanted to rage at him, slice his head open like a rotten melon, and rip his dead heart from his chest, feed it to Blaz, and laugh when the dragon shit out pieces of the undead blood sucker.

Yeah, I was a little pissed.

"One week is all you get. One week and I will come for you, you and the wolf." He pointed at Alex.

Alex snapped his teeth, chattering them together before he spoke. "Piece of shit fang head."

I lifted a hand to him. "Why Alex?"

"Because he's the weakest link of your pack, but he will make for a great motivator." Faris winked at me, twisted the Veil, and stepped through leaving us alone once more.

"How the fuck are we supposed to get out of here?" I yelled, my voice bouncing back to me in the small space.

How the fuck indeed.

There was a major flaw in their plan as far as Liam could see.

"You can't go after her without me," he snarled, tension rising in the air like a fog he could almost see and could surely scent.

Milly put her hands on her hips. "It's not my fault you can't jump the Veil. I don't understand why, but you can't."

Pamela glanced at him, but he shook his head slightly. The less Milly understood, the better.

Jack poked at Liam with his cane. "You'll just have to wait here, wolf. We'll bring her back to you."

That was just it, he didn't want to wait, but he also knew he was inadvertently stalling them from rescuing her. Stopping them from doing his job. Damn it all.

"I can stay with you." Pamela moved to his side, concern rolling off her. He shook it off, all of the crap going through his mind.

"Just go." He turned his back so he wouldn't have to see them leave without him. Wouldn't have to see Will, and worse, Milly, rescue Rylee.

They left, jumping the Veil back to London, and he paced, his mind churning with all the things he should have done. All the things he had done and shouldn't have. Like going after Alex. There was nothing wrong with the submissive wolf; he'd been a better friend to Rylee than almost anyone else. When no one else was there, Alex had been her—albeit squishy—rock.

Things would be different when they came back. He would make things right with Rylee and Alex. First, they had to come back, and he had to believe they *would* come back.

That for once Milly wouldn't fuck them over and would do the right thing.

That he could trust the witch.

He let out a groan. Of all the people he had to put his faith in, Milly was dead last on the list.

Yet here he was, betting the life of his mate on her.

Sliding his hands over his face, he tried to focus on the good. Rylee would come back, things would be okay.

They had to be.


I paced the small room, a.k.a. padded cell, Faris had left us in. An hour, maybe more had passed since he'd left, and I still didn't know how to get out.

With little thought, I yanked my sword out and swung it toward the chaise lounge, cracking through the bones of the chair as if they were matchsticks.

"Wrecking stuff?" Alex poked at a vase that stood on top of a side table.

"Yup, wreck it all." I took another swing, this time toward the paneling that covered the cement walls. Somewhere, there had to be another way out.

Alex let out a howl of excitement and ran in circles three times before laying into things. With his claws, and my sword, we demolished the room. The clatter of porcelain and wood clattering to the floor was a grim satisfaction I clung to. Maybe I couldn't kill Faris, but I could destroy the fucking gilded cage he put us in.

Fifteen minutes later, we stood in the middle of the room, and I inspected the damage. Destroying the old paintings, expensive material, and furniture had been a drop in the bucket as far as soothing my rage. The room looked like an explosion had ripped through it. Bits of feather clung to Alex's grinning mouth as he smiled up at me.

"Fun, yupppy doody. Alex likes breaking shit."

I dropped to a crouch beside him, sliding to my ass on the hardwood floor. He lay down beside me and put his head on my thigh.

"Rylee sad." His long tongue lolled out as he panted.

"Not sad, just—" I didn't even know how to put it into words. Frustrated, angry, stymied. All those and so much more; guilt over Charlie's senseless death, fear for the deal I'd been forced into with Faris. I closed my eyes and leaned my head back against a chunk of broken furniture. Charlie had been a good friend, one who deserved so much more than a death at the hands of that gods-be-damned two-faced vampire. But, like always, there really wasn't time to grieve. Later, always later, right now I had to figure out a way to get the hell out of here. A week, I wasn't sure I could last a week in here.

We sat there long enough that Alex fell asleep. Twitching and mumbling, he let out a fart that made me gag.

"Damn it all, what have you been eating?" I muttered, waving my hands in front of my face. He just snorted and rolled over, oblivious to the trouble we were in. That we were at the mercy of a vampire who was no longer trying to play nice. That we were well and truly trapped until said vampire decided to let us go, if he ever chose to.

Ignorance is bliss, and all that shit, I guess.

A twist in the air, a feeling of pressure, and the Veil split in front of us. I expected Faris, and was shocked as shit at who stepped into the room.

I could have almost expected Pamela, Jack, or Will. But not Milly.

Pamela ran to me and threw her arms around my waist, a sob escaping her. "You're okay."

I put one hand on her back as I made eye contact with my ex-best friend. "Yeah, I'm okay."

Her green eyes met mine, but I couldn't read them and that made me nervous. "We need to go, before Faris comes back."

I pushed myself to my feet and nudged Alex with my foot. "Come on, buddy, the rescue party is here."

With a snort, he scrambled to all fours, blinking sleepily. "Pamie!" He leapt toward the young witch, bowling her over in his excitement, until he saw Milly.

His big golden eyes narrowed and his lips peeled back over his teeth. "Milly bad witch."

Milly's jaw tightened. "Behave yourself, Alex."

Pamela moved between them. "You behave *yourself*. You're the one who can't be trusted."

Okay, enough of this. "Pull it in, people, we've got to go."

Milly wasted no time in opening the Veil. On the other side was a pacing Liam, and my heart gave a lurch. Yup, definitely in love with him, if there had been any doubt, it was erased when I saw the look on his face.

For once, I got to be the first one out of the 'fire' and Liam grabbed me, pulled me tight to his chest. The public display of affection was not something we did, but I tucked my head against the crook of his neck, breathing him in for a moment before pulling back so I could look into his face.

"Thanks for the rescue."

Milly snorted behind us. "You're welcome."

"How did you find us?" Did she know where Faris's underground secret hole was? Could she somehow be working for him still?

Milly pointed to Jack. "He pinpointed you, and then I opened up the Veil and took a look through. Not an exact science, but it worked."

Jack snorted. "We got a few buckets of dirt before the dumbass witch opened it up right."

She glared at him but said nothing else.

I turned to face her, not sure exactly what to say. "I don't trust you, are we clear?"

"Yes."

"And you have no more chances with me." I stared at her, all the things she'd done racing through my head. Giselle, Alex, Eve, Pamela. Setting the booby trap at that castle to block us from leaving London. Crap, that seemed like so long ago and yet it had been less than a week. Her rescue of us with Berget, her warning about the unicorn foal and Orion, her second rescue of me and Alex.

Fuck, what was I supposed to do with her?

I took Milly back with us. Yeah, I know, damn stupid, right? But my gut was telling me that this time I had to bring her back. And when we got home, I knew why.

There was a note, nailed to the door of the farmhouse, fluttering in the December wind howling across the badlands straight through the farmyard.

*All those who oppose Orion will be destroyed.*
*Be warned, your allies will die in droves, stupid*
*Tracker. This is just the beginning.*

Nailed with it was Terese's head, still dripping blood, her face slack with surprise.

Milly gasped and Pamela covered her mouth with her hand, but I just stared at it, chills rippling through me. I had a bad feeling about this.

"Milly, contact your coven. We need to know if they're all dead."

She ran around to the front of the house. Orion's people, whoever the hell they were, were on a warpath, and they would systematically wipe out any opposition, even if Orion *was* dead. That much was clear.

"Pamela, Alex, go check on Eve." I pointed to the barn and they ran, Alex skidding and jumping in the fresh fallen snow, Pamela chiding him to settle down; she at least understood the seriousness of what was happening.

Liam moved up beside me. "Any ideas?"

I shook my head. "They called me stupid; the Trolls seem to like that title for me. Can you smell anything to confirm those shits are the ones who did this? And where the hell is Dox and the others?" They should have met us when we showed up. But maybe they were out scouting the perimeter, or maybe they were still engaged with some of the intruders?

"No, whoever did this cleaned it up." He turned in a slow circle. "Some sort of magic scoured it all, but other than that, nothing clear is coming through. I'd agree with you on your moniker, only the Trolls seem to call you stupid on a regular basis. What happened with Faris? Do you think this has anything to do with him?"

"No, this has nothing to do with the vampires, not this time." Of that much, I was sure. Too soon after Berget's loss to have her re-group, and Faris wouldn't risk this kind of mess when he already had me tied to him.

I couldn't tell Liam I'd be leaving in seven days with Faris. That I didn't have a choice but to go with the vampire, to do his bidding, or see all of those I loved killed.

I couldn't even tell Liam Charlie was dead. I clenched my teeth together, held my breath to get myself under control. I was not good at keeping secrets; it was too much like lying to me.

*You have to, to keep them all safe.* Yeah, that was the issue.

Faris, I was going to strip him to the bones and throw what was left of him to the Trolls and then I would kill them all for siding with Orion.

A wailing scream erupted out of the house and I backed away, moved closer to the barn.

Liam stepped in front of me, facing the house. "The coven, all of them, are dead, aren't they?"

I stared at his back, a wave of premonition washing over me, Doran's words floating through me, Milly's screams striking a chord in my soul, understanding filling me to the point of nausea. Ethan was dead, the coven and her lover were dead, and her screams spoke to me of what was to come.

*You will love another.*

The only way that would ever happen is if . . . I continued to back away, unwilling to let the thought form. I wouldn't let it happen. No . . . .

Liam turned, his eyes meeting mine. "What is it?"

"Things are spinning out of control." My words were soft, as the chaos shattered around us. Pamela all but fell out of the barn, retching, puking until she fell to her hands and knees. Alex was right behind her, howling to the air, his head thrown back, and I knew whatever peace we'd had, however momentary, was done.

Almost in a daze I walked to the barn and opened the big doors.

Dox, Sla, and the triplets hung from the rafters. Or at least, I assumed it was them by the colors left on their hands and feet, the only skin left on them.

Skinned, they'd been skinned alive and left to die hanging by hooks in the backs.

I stood there, stared at what was left of one of my closest friends, of allies that had dared stand with me, who threw their lot in with mine.

Dox's laughter, his brownies and ogre beer, the piercings and his big grin that had wavered. The courage he'd found in facing his past and the longing I'd seen in him when he'd looked at Sas.

Mother of the gods, this wasn't happening, I had to be dreaming. A nightmare of the worst kind; I would wake from with sweat pouring off my body, all of my friends still intact.

Fear, stark and ugly, snaked through me. There was only one soul missing from this mess, and it hit me hard.

"EVE!" I Tracked her and she was at a distance, unharmed but freaked the hell out.

I spun and looked to the sky in the direction I could feel her threads.

"Rylee, look." Liam pointed at the distant horizon, but I couldn't see what his eyes had picked up. I grabbed Pamela, dragged her to her feet, and ran around the side of the barn to try and see what Liam pointed at.

Minutes passed before the glittering scales caught the fading light.

*I am here, Tracker, because you are not going to survive without me. And we can't have that, can we?*

Blaz's words, his presence, soothed some of the fear, though his very presence raised questions.

"Eve, did you see her?"

*I sent her to the unicorns, to rally them.*

I slumped where I stood. "Tell me, this isn't happening. Tell me I'm out of my mind."

Sobbing reached my ears and I turned my head, as Milly fell to her knees, her head bowed. For the first time, I thought maybe she really had loved Ethan. Maybe he'd been her Liam.

All around us it was as if a war had been waged and we were seeing the aftermath, the destruction of lives beyond what we'd ever expected.

Blaz landed with a backwash of his wings, let out a heavy blow of air.

*There are others coming. The demon has begun to gather an army, and you must do the same.*

His head dropped so his eyes were right in front of mine, but I could see by the looks on Liam's and Pamela's faces I wasn't the only one hearing his words.

*You are the one I was born to fly with, into the battle that will decide the fate of the world. You are the world's only hope, Rylee. You are the one that will stop this from happening again. You must draw on everything you've ever learned, and we must fight before it is too late.*

*Will you stand or will you run away?*

Liam put a hand to my back. "There is no real decision, Rylee. You know that."

I did know. I slowly turned, taking in all those who would look to me to fight a battle I knew I would lose. Pamela and her innocence, the powerhouse she was only just emerging. Alex and his loyalty, and the laughter he brought to me. Blaz and the connection between us I couldn't deny, the safety he represented. Milly and the past that hovered between us, her loyalty would always be in question, but we needed her strength. Then there were those that had died already at the hands of Orion.

The Beast.

Dox.

Sla, Tin, Lop, and Dev.

I met Liam's eyes, saw the compassion there, saw the love that had grown to be my world and everything I would fight for. He reached out to me, took my hand. "To the end and back, I will stand with you."

This was my family, and even the black sheep in it were loved, and I would fight for them all to my last breath.

I tightened my hand on Liam's, my voice steady even though I doubted my abilities, doubted they had the right person. It didn't matter anymore. Orion thought I was the one that would face him, and so I would, regardless of my doubts. I would make Orion regret ever crossing me and mine.

I let out a breath and hardened everything within me.

"I will stand."

Blaz nodded and I felt his approval as I spoke.

"And I will wipe these fuckers off the face of the world."

COMING MAY 2017 FROM TALOS PRESS

# TRACKER

A Rylee Adamson Novel
Book 6

**"My name is Rylee and I am a Tracker."**

When children go missing, and the Humans have no leads, I'm the one they call. I am their last hope in bringing home the lost ones. I salvage what they cannot.

Bringing my allies together as war approaches is my number one concern. But that means I have to play nice with a vampire who is blackmailing me. If I don't, I'm screwed and my family is dead.

But I don't play nice. And I have a backup plan. Kinda.

Throw in some new weapons being developed that work around supernaturals, and I have more problems than I can handle on my own.

Good thing I have a kick-ass team.

Even if they are on the other side of the world from me.

$7.99 mass market paperback
978-1-945863-00-4

# AN EXCERPT FROM *TRACKER*

Liam and I headed upstairs, Alex trailing at our heels. We said nothing, the stairs creaking under our feet. Inside my room, I walked to the window that looked onto the street at the front of the house. I pulled the sash up. No movement in all this snow, nothing at all.

I turned away from the window and walked to the bed, sitting on the end of the mattress.

Alex let out a yip and leapt up beside me, burrowing his nose into the thick covers, and rolling onto his back. From there, he juggled several pillows above his head, tongue hanging out the side of his mouth. But even his antics couldn't draw a laugh from me, not today. Too much had happened and my emotions were wrung out.

Liam shut the door behind us, the door clicking closed and giving us some semblance of privacy. "So, what is the vampire's game?"

Atta boy, right to the heart of it. "Fuck me if I know." I walked across the room to peer out the window again, as if I could find the answers in the freshly fallen snow.

Liam slid his arms around me, curling my ass tight against him as he placed his chin on my shoulder. "Already done."

I swatted his hip, but let the smile on my lips linger for a moment. "O'Shea, smarten the fuck up."

He let out a growl, most likely from me using O'Shea instead of Liam. "Fine. But Faris is playing a game, and if you don't know the rules, you are going to get killed."

Hands on the windowsill, I leaned forward. My breath fogged the old glass and I drew a circle in it, and then drew a slash through the circle. "It's always a game with the bloodsuckers. Shit, look at Doran. It's fun for him to yank your strings and he does it every chance he gets."

Again, Liam growled, but said nothing. I took a deep breath, my body held tight by his muscular arms.

"Faris doesn't really want to piss me off." The words slipped out of me, a whisper now. "He needs my help, but I wouldn't help him before, not even when he asked."

Liam's voice was as soft as mine. "Because of Berget." No point in answering, we both knew that was the truth. Liam turned me around to face him. "War is coming, Rylee. Is there any doubt in your mind?"

"No."

"And you need allies." He paused and his words sank in.

My eyes widened and I stared up at him. "You agree with Charlie. You think I should help Faris."

Fuck me sideways, was he serious? Despite what I said downstairs, I never expected Liam to agree. Yet, it made sense. Hell, what Charlie said made sense no matter how much I wanted it to be otherwise. One thing held me back.

"I don't want to kill her, Liam. I don't think I could do it."

Always, it came back to Berget. I'd sworn an oath, the strongest oath I could, that I would kill the Child Empress. Of course, that had been before I'd known who the Child Empress was.

"We'll find a way around it."

"And until then?" I put my head against his chest, his heart thumping underneath my ear. "I can't take anyone with me when Faris shows up. Just because Charlie made it doesn't mean Faris won't kill someone else. He might not have known Charlie's tricks . . ."

"Really?" The dry tone in Liam's voice was not lost on me. I slid out of his arms a few inches so I could look up at him.

"Okay, so he probably knew Charlie's abilities. But again, it's a part of the game. Like chess. You do realize I suck at chess?"

He laughed. "Yeah, you're more of a checkers girl, aren't you?"

I lifted an eyebrow. "You mean smashing my opponents as I leap over them?"

"Something like that."

He held me and my mind worked over the issues. Only one question was left.

"I know what I have to do, Liam. Are you going to let me do it?" I stepped away from him and started to pace, stopping in the center of the room to face him.

His jaw was tight, and eyes steely. "You are always leaving me behind, Rylee. Always. As much I hate it, I—" He shook his head and then gathered himself.

I waited for him to say it. Even though I knew it was coming, I needed to hear it.

"I trust you. If the prophecies hold true, you are going to be at the center of this shit for a long time. No matter what I do, or how close and tight I hold you, the danger and darkness will always come for you. Always. If I don't trust you, I'm going to get us both killed." He reached out and slid his hands up my arms, smoothing the goose bumps that rippled along my skin with his near-prophetic words. "And I will always be here, waiting on you, fighting for you when I can, healing the wounds when I must."

"Even if it means me going with Faris, without you? Only taking Alex?" I whispered, hardly believing he wouldn't fight me on this. Even if it was what we had to do. Fuck, I so hated Faris. Even if he hadn't killed Charlie.

He tugged me against his chest, arms banding around me. "Don't fucking well remind me you'll be with that bastard. And don't let him know you know about Charlie. Whatever game he has, play along. Let him believe he's in control. As for Alex—" We both looked down to the submissive werewolf passed out on the bed, ass in the air, face jammed in the pillows. Liam snorted. "He's more loyal to you than anyone else, and even though he is submissive, it's changing. I sense it in him; he's coming into his own and will protect you with everything he's got. You know that. If I can't be there, Alex is the next best thing."

On cue, the sleeping Alex let out a fart that echoed in the small room. Liam reached behind us and opened the window a crack.

I closed my eyes and pressed my face into his chest, breathing him in alongside the rush of clean snow-kissed air. "I can't even kill Faris now. I have to help him take the throne, and Berget . . ."

Liam kissed the top of my head and whispered into my hair, "You'll find a way, Rylee, that much I'm sure. If anyone can find a way, you will."

He held me and everything sank in.

Liam knew I was going to help Faris, on my own, with only Alex for backup. A way to bring the vampires on as allies in this war with Orion and his henchmen. "The enemy of my enemy is my friend," I said.

Liam hugged me tighter. "Yeah, some shit like that."

I let out a heavy breath and stepped back from him. "Come on, let's see if Pamela's scrounged up food."

Alex's eyes flew open and he scrambled off the bed, making an even bigger mess of the blankets and pillows, one pillow exploding in a shower of feathers. "Alex hungry, yuppy doody!"

He bolted toward the door, scrabbling with the handle, and then clattered down the stairs. Liam grabbed my hand. "Wait. What are you going to do to convince the others? Pamela and Milly won't want you to go, either." His face shifted and his lips twisted up. "Fuck, I to have to deal with Milly on my own."

Now I did suppress a grin. "You'll be fine. Let Pamela run interference."

He shuddered. "When is Faris coming for you?"

"Seven days."

"Shit, that isn't long enough to plan."

I smiled at him, but felt the fatigue pull at me even as I tried to work past it. Not fatigue of the body, but of the heart. Though some had lifted, after seeing Charlie. "Like you said, I'll come up with something. You'll have to trust me when I do."

He brushed the nape of my neck with the tips of his fingers as I walked in front of him. "You are the only one I do trust, Tracker."

I smiled back at him, feeling all fucking warm and fuzzy. Another time, I would have scoffed, but now, I was just damn grateful I had someone who loved me so completely.

We headed down the stairs for the second time that night, and I walked toward the kitchen, expecting everyone to be where I'd left them. In front of the living room, I froze in place. In some ways, I'd been expecting this.

Just maybe not this soon.

The blinds were all drawn, candles lit, and Giselle sat in the middle of the room looking as she had when I first met her. Young, vibrant, free of the madness that took her so quickly. Alex sprawled out at her feet on his back, grinning up at her, his tongue lolling out one side of his mouth.

"You don't seem surprised to see her," Milly said, drawing my eyes to the right side of the room. The witch sat in Giselle's chair, the paisley material clashing against her vibrant red dress.

"No, not really." I stepped into the room. "Giselle, you said you could only come through the Veil a few times, that it cost you."

Giselle nodded. "That's true. But it is easier here, with my spirit guides helping me." Her eyes flicked over each of us. "I will Read you all, because there may not be many more times to do so before I am summoned for the final time to the deep levels of the Veil." She pointed at Pamela. "Come here, little witch."

Pamela didn't look to me for reassurance. She walked forward and stopped in front of Giselle. "All right, then. Will this hurt?"

Giselle smiled up at her, reached out a hand, hovering over Pamela's heart. "No, it won't hurt."

Her hand trembled, and then she pulled back and held her hand palm upward to Pamela. "You have a great deal coming your way. The darkness has not seen you yet, but it will. And when it does, it will make a bid for you that you will struggle to refuse. Hold to what you know is truth, to what Rylee is teaching you." Giselle paused and tipped her head to one side, her eyes fluttering closed. "I see you at the end of it all; when the final battle comes, you will be pivotal. Remember, when darkness comes for you, when light seems gone from your life, you will be one of the flames that beckons to those who have lost hope, showing them hope is indeed not lost."

Pamela nodded once and then stepped back. Giselle shifted and turned to Liam and me. She pointed at Liam. "Much has changed for you, Agent. Will you let me Read you?"

I found it interesting she hadn't asked Pamela, but she asked Liam. He said nothing, only stepped forward, crouching beside her. Giselle cupped her hands around his face without touching him.

"Ah, wolf. You have fought the darkness well, and have fought to stay at her side. She's a tough one to stick close to, isn't she?"

He laughed and Giselle laughed with him. The mirth spread through the room, lightening the solemn mood created by Charlie's visit, until everyone was laughing except me. I shook my head. I wasn't that bad.

Giselle took a deep breath and lifted her hands back to his face, her eyes widening, filling with a sorrow I'd seen more than once on her face, and my gut twisted into a large knot.

"The rest of my words are not for anyone ears but yours, wolf."

I knew a dismissal when I heard one. Pamela and Milly stood and followed me into the kitchen. Alex stayed, but since Giselle didn't send him out, I figured it was okay. And no, I wouldn't try and pry it out of Alex. Likely, he wouldn't understand the complexity of what I was asking anyway.

But what did Giselle have to say to Liam that we couldn't hear?

# ABOUT THE AUTHOR

**Shannon Mayer** is the *USA Today* bestselling author of the Rylee Adamson novels, the Elemental series, and numerous paranormal romance, urban fantasy, mystery, and suspense novels. She lives in the southwestern tip of Canada with her husband, son, and numerous other animals.